ON THE EDGE OF MISERY

BOOK 4

I0757855

THE VAMPIRE NAVY SEAL SERIES

S.B. ALEXANDER

Cover designed by Hang Le
Cover copyright © 2021 by S.B. Alexander

On the Edge of Misery
Book four: The Vampire Navy SEAL Series

First Edition: December 2016

E-book ISBN-13: 978-0-9969351-7-3
Print ISBN-13: 978-1-954888-08-1
Large Print ISBN-13: 978-1-954888-10-4

1

JO

I threw off the blankets then swung my angry gaze to the clock on my bedside table.

"Argh," I growled.

Night after night for the last three months, I couldn't sleep. Every time I tried, all I could see was Webb in a coffin. I was numb to the knowledge that he might be dead. I cried my eyes out for the first month. Then all my tears dried up. If I wasn't trying to sleep, I lived in the control room, waiting to hear his voice come over the radio or biting my nails while my dad's team was glued to their computers in the hopes that they too would hear from Webb.

"You have to try and dream," Dad had said.

I laughed at him. The more pressure he put on me, the less chance I would fall into a deep slumber. My vampire powers had grown significantly since Webb's plane went down over the Alaskan mountains. Before then, I could make objects move, manipulate water, air, and earth, and read human minds, but only if I were touching the people. The vampire community considered my father the most powerful of all vampires. But I now matched all his abilities and then some. I'd recently added the fire element to my growing powers. That ability took a great amount of concentration to conjure up fireballs that I could throw like baseballs. Not to mention, I was capable of reading vampire minds, albeit I still had to have skin contact to do so.

The one ability my father didn't have that I had somehow developed was seeing into the future through my dreams, although that power was dead in its tracks at the moment. My dad, Sam, Dr. Vieira, Tripp, and many others were relying on me to find Webb. Again, I'd laughed at them. Aside from my recurring dream, where I was standing in the middle of a cemetery surrounded by coffins, one of which contained Webb, I hadn't come up with anything. If I had, I would have woken up with no memories of the dream world.

Dad hadn't had any luck, either. For thirty solid days, a search and rescue team hunted the Alaskan mountains for any sign of the plane or Webb, Olivia, Kraft, Sloan, and Kodiak. But they found nothing. Dad had finally called off the search.

Through tears, I'd pleaded with him for hours on end. "You're the commander of the vampire SEAL team. You rule this base. You have to keep looking."

"Jo, the terrain and the weather are slowing us down. I've alerted the military base in Alaska. They'll keep their eyes and ears open. I'm sorry, pumpkin. We have work to do here. We still have to get to the bottom of who stole all your lab data. Remember, Edmund is still out there, working toward building that vampire army. And you are instrumental in his endeavor."

"If Edmund needs my DNA for his plan, then why haven't we heard from him in over three months?" I'd asked Dad.

Dr. Vieira believed that I was the key to Edmund's master plan since I had a unique DNA makeup that no other vampire had. I wasn't so sure I believed that I was the one who could help Edmund build an army of vampires out of humans, at least not perfect ones that could fight against us. So far, Edmund's only experiment that held any substance had been with Blake Turner, the human boy I'd been accused of murdering. But Blake's new genetic makeup had only served to kill him. Still, I didn't want to become a lab experiment.

"If I know Edmund, he's not going to do something on a whim. He's planning. In the meantime, try to see if your dreams tell you anything about Edmund or Webb."

I couldn't dream about Webb. How was I supposed to dream about our enemy? I growled again as I popped out of bed. It was four in the morning, and the apartment was deathly quiet. I tiptoed out of my room and into the hall. I was about to get some water when I noticed that my twin brother, Sam's, bedroom door was ajar. That was odd. He never left it open when he slept. He had this odd sense of fear that someone would attack him in the dead of sleep.

I peeked in to find his bed empty. I wasn't exactly surprised. Like me, Sam had trouble sleeping. Many times, I found him in the training room, venting off steam or in the control room, checking for any news on Webb.

I trudged down the hall and into the kitchen, where I poured myself a glass of blood. After I quenched my thirst, I decided I should try to ease my frustrations. I could stand to shed some anxiety or at least tire myself out so I could sleep. Then maybe I could dream or at least get past the scene of Webb in a coffin.

I changed quickly into a pair of yoga pants, a T-shirt, and tennis shoes then quietly dashed out of the apartment, making sure I didn't wake Dad. The hall leading to the stairwell was eerily quiet. Overhead lights blinked on as I trekked down to the basement. While Webb and other sentinels had their own place to call home on base, Dad wanted to live in an apartment above his office, the control room, and all the other military amenities for the staff. It hadn't bothered me too much, although I would have preferred to have a home where we weren't in the middle of the chaos.

Grunts resounded as I drew close, followed by clanging swords. I smiled as I settled against the doorjamb to the training room. Tripp and Sam were going at it, the air charged with electricity. Surrounded by padded walls, they circled each other with their swords at the ready. Tripp's sandy-blond hair was pulled back into a low ponytail, while Sam's black hair stuck to his forehead. For several months, Sam had sported shoulder-length hair until he decided that short was easier and better. So he had it styled in a cut just above his ears. I loved his new look. It made his green eyes and angular jaw stand out.

Tripp lunged at Sam, the tip of his sword breaking the skin just above Sam's heart. "Pussy."

Sam returned the gesture, thrusting his left hip forward, sword extended, forcing Tripp's blade down.

"You drew blood, asshole," Sam growled.

"Then pay attention," Tripp countered.

The two stood facing each other, waiting for the other to make a move.

Tripp cocked an eyebrow. "You sure you want to do this, Mason? You know you can't win."

"Ha! You don't know shit, sentinel," Sam spat.

They both circled the mat, muscles bunching on their bare chests as though they were two wolves vying for the alpha spot in a pack. I laughed out loud at that thought.

Both of them whipped their heads toward me.

"Something funny, Sis?" Sam asked.

"Yeah. Be careful or Tripp will shift into a wolf. I mean, he has wolf blood in him."

Tripp crossed the padded floor to a bench, where he snagged a towel, then wiped his face. "How many times do I have to tell you? I am mostly vampire. My wolf heritage has only graced me with the added ability to detect scents ten times more than a vampire."

Sam wiped the sweat off his face with a towel before he plucked his shirt off a bag at his feet and threw it over his head. "Good thing," he chided. "I'd hate for you to spring claws while we were sparring."

Once Tripp's face was dry of sweat, he switched out the towel for a T-shirt then covered his chest. "Can't sleep, Jo?"

I joined them, sitting down on the slatted wooden bench as a cloud of stinky sweat burned my nostrils. "All I keep dreaming about is Webb in a coffin. I need to get off the base. I need a new venue or something to take my mind off Webb. Then maybe I could clear my head." Dad kept me under wraps, afraid that if I left base, Edmund would strike. He wouldn't even let me go to school, which was fine with me. In fact, Ms. Costner was still tutoring Sam and me on most days at the base library. Dad had said school was too risky. Considering I'd gotten into trouble and killed Blake Turner in self-defense, I agreed with Dad.

Dad was also concerned about Ben Jackson, Sam's human best friend who supposedly had been subjected to Edmund's vampire serum. We weren't sure if Ben was now a vampire or a monster like Blake Turner had been. Ben had escaped from Dad's men when we encountered him at the fundraising gala a few months back. Even Mr. Jackson had been scouring the city, looking for his son. Dad suspected that Ben was probably working for Edmund.

"Good luck convincing Pops to let you off base," Sam said.

"I'm going to ask. I want to see Darcy." She was my best human friend and had been under our protection for a month while her father worked to pay off his debt to a vampire he'd represented in court. "I haven't seen her since she moved back home, and that was three months ago." We'd spoken on the phone, but that was it. Her father wanted her far removed from the vampire world. I couldn't blame him since Edmund had kidnapped Darcy because of her father's poor decision concerning a vampire client of his.

"You need to stay away from the human." Tripp folded his large body as he sat down next to me. "You're only putting her in harm's way. Edmund can use her to get to you. And she's been through enough with him and us."

He was right, but I didn't want to acknowledge that fact. I wanted a friend. I wanted someone who I could talk to about Webb. I wanted a shoulder to cry on. I could cry on Dad's shoulder or Sam's or even Tripp's, but it wasn't the same. They were men, and while they might understand, a female friend understood better, at least to me. Not only that, I wanted to talk about things other than wars, blood, vampires, genetics, and anything else associated with my new world. I wanted to hear all about Darcy's life. She'd started her senior year. Was she dating? Had she decided on college like her father had wished? Or was she still set on beauty school? I could glean all that information over the phone or in an email or text, but I wanted that person-to-person connection, where we could lie around in her bedroom like we used to and giggle or watch a movie or just talk about nothing.

Tripp placed a hand on my knee, his drug-induced touch immediately sending a warm and lazy feeling through my body. "Jo, I don't mean this in a bad way, but you look like shit. Maybe I can help. I can try to put you to sleep."

Sam and I did a double take.

"Since when do you have that ability?" I asked.

"I haven't put someone under in quite some time. I'm not sure the commander would let me do it anyway. The last time I tried was on a family member who didn't wake up for a year. But I think she drank too much of my blood."

"Are you saying you can put someone in a coma if they drink your blood?" I continued to learn something new every day about vampires.

"In so many words, yeah." Tripp swung his bronze gaze from Sam to me. "My cousin had gotten into a bad fight when she was on the cusp of blossoming into her wolf form. Since she wasn't entirely human and hadn't learned how to shift yet, her mother suggested we try to give her a dose of my vampire blood to see if it would heal her. Otherwise, she would die. The good news was she didn't die and is now a healthy wolf shifter. The bad news was she lost a year of her life. She still has issues with me."

"Does my father know you can do this?" Sam asked.

"Oh, yeah. I had to disclose my abilities when I applied for the vampire SEAL program." Tripp removed his hand from my knee.

When he did, the warmth coursing through me turned cold. "At first, your father didn't believe me. So we experimented with a healthy vampire. He fell asleep not long after he drank my blood and didn't wake up for a week. So in emergencies when other vampires need blood, I'm not the one they come to."

My stomach fluttered at the notion that I might be able to sleep for longer than two hours. "If I sleep for a week, then I could dream. Maybe I could find out if Webb is still alive."

"Maybe," Tripp said with a hint of hesitation in his voice. "Your father has to agree."

I didn't see why he wouldn't. If I could sleep, then I wasn't bugging him about getting off base or whining about Webb, and I could possibly help find the team.

No sooner had I jumped off the bench, ready to go in search of my dad, than the sirens blared, the red lights in the room flashed, and Tripp sprang into action, bolting out of the room.

Sam and I followed. When I first moved on base, I'd panicked at any alarm, especially when Edmund blew up a building on base. But now I'd grown accustomed to the chaos. The three of us ran down the hall, up the stairs, and down more halls until we reached the belly of the control room. This was the place where the heart of the military beat, where information came in and went out, and where my father was wide-eyed with his black hair mussed as though he'd flown out of bed, which I was sure he had.

The TV screens lit up on one wall, while vamps shuffled into place, banging on keyboards. As screens changed, showing parts of the base's perimeter, a figure came into view at the main gate. Then three sentinels drew their guns on the dark figure, who held up his hands.

I knitted my eyebrows as I watched the dark hooded figure get down on his knees. Then he lifted his head and spoke. "I want to speak with Commander Mason. Tell him it's Ben Jackson."

Sam and I exchanged a horrified look as my stomach lurched.

2

WEBB

The scent of death lingered in the air as I blinked to clear my vision. Maybe I was smelling my own flesh dying. I lay on the dirt-infested earth, tied to cobalt restraints that were eating into my skin. I licked my parched lips as the hunger gutted me. Vampire hunger was far worse than human hunger. If I didn't get blood soon, my body would wither away faster than any human's.

Keys jangled, then a whoosh of cold air blew in followed by my captor, Bruno Almeida, the only vampire in our existence who was on the Most Wanted list with the human authorities as well as the vampire government for various crimes of drugs, prostitution, and blood smuggling.

He smirked as he stood over me, holding his nose. "You're looking deathly, London, and you smell like a corpse." Sarcasm dripped from his fangs, which were front and center.

"Fuck off," I snarled, my own fangs grazing my lips. Actually, my fangs hadn't retracted since I'd woken up in this dungeon two days ago, or maybe it had been a week or more. I couldn't tell. I'd been dizzy and in and out of consciousness. For how long? I wasn't sure. I couldn't even tell if it was day or night since I was surrounded by rock, somewhere deep in the earth. "Where's my team?" I sat up and adjusted myself as best as I could with my hands behind my back. The scent of my flesh simmered in the air.

He picked at a long nail on his pinky finger. "They're tucked away."

"What does that mean?" I held in my rage, when all I wanted to do was erase the satisfied smirk he had plastered on his unshaven jaw.

He tucked a hand into his black cargo pants. "It means I'm in charge."

I sneered at the white-haired vampire. "Tell me now," I shouted. I swore he was a dead man if I got out of this alive. No way in hell I was bringing Bruno in for questioning or turning him over to the vampire government. He deserved to be buried a thousand feet down into the earth, or better yet, burned. Yeah, the latter appealed to me more. That way, he couldn't return because if he was buried, he would probably find a way to claw himself out somehow.

He shook his head. "I should just let you die."

"What's stopping you?" I asked. "I can't possibly be worth anything."

Commander Mason and I had been scratching our heads as to why Bruno would hold two of our own prisoners. We speculated that they were a bargaining chip for something or someone. But the commander had inquired with our government's top officials and had come up empty. The only reason we could deduce was that Bruno wanted their blood. After all, he was in the business of blood smuggling. But that didn't measure up since he'd focused more on selling human blood to the vampire community, not the other way around.

"You'd be surprised to know you are worth something, in more ways than one." His hazel eyes grew wide. "Vampire blood is in high demand."

"Is that why we're here? Is that why you captured Quade and

Crowe on our mission in Argentina? You can get all the vampire blood you want from any of us walking the earth."

"Ah, true. But not vampire blood from the infamous sentinels. You guys have powers that none of us can match. We learned a couple of things from capturing Crowe and Quade. One, their blood gives us low-life vampires the ability to manipulate air, earth, water, and fire. And two, it gives us added strength. Hell, it even gives a human added strength. The problem is those powers are short-lived. So, we've been testing, but we haven't been able to find the right mixture to make it permanent." He pinched his chin. "But I think I might've found the solution. Rumor on the street is we have a very powerful vampire among our kind. One who is more powerful than her father. She might be our ticket to riches. Not only could I sell her blood to some very eager vamps, but imagine what money I could make with the human market? Powerful blood could be the new drug over crack and heroin."

I jerked on the chains. "Go anywhere near her, and I'll burn you alive."

"You don't have to worry about that. She'll come to me." He was confident in his delivery. "I learned you two are in love. So she'll do anything to rescue you."

I growled, the sound ominous in the deep recesses of the Alaskan mountains. "I'll be dead soon. So you won't have a bargaining chip." I would die before I would let him or anyone get their hands on Jo. Not to mention, Commander Mason wouldn't allow Jo anywhere near this place.

A shadow flitted by the door before a beast of a bald man filled the doorway. "Sir. The helicopter is inbound."

"I'll be right there," Bruno said to the beast.

My heart sped up at the idea that he was referring to Jo. No way was she there. Then again, I couldn't say for sure how long I'd been under his control. He could've already lured her there, although he'd made it sound as though he hadn't yet. Regardless, my pulse wouldn't slow until I knew. "How long have I been here?"

He painted on a fake frown. "You don't remember anything, do you?"

I remembered back to when my chute opened, and I plummeted through a cluster of trees, but got tangled in a branch. Then I'd pulled out my knife, cut the ropes, and let gravity take me to the ground. As soon as my feet hit the uneven surface, my ankle had twisted before it snapped. The moment I'd reached for a bag of blood, something stung my neck before I'd gotten dizzy. Then I blacked out.

"Let me help you," Bruno said in a giddy tone. "The moment you and your team fell from the sky, my men swooped in and shot all of you with a sedative then hauled you back to the compound, where everyone has become one big happy family in my lab for more than three months."

Anger churned in my gut. "Are you telling me that we've been in a coma-induced state for that long?"

"I wouldn't say coma, but extremely groggy. Anytime any of you came to, we knocked you back out. We've gotten some great data too. I have to say, Patrick Mason is a genius."

My jaw dropped. I vaguely remember hearing my sister Kate's voice. Or maybe I'd dreamt of her. Otherwise, I couldn't remember a fucking thing. I shouldn't be surprised at what I was hearing. Nevertheless, I asked anyway. "You knew we were coming?"

He nodded. "Yes. We planted the seed of Quade and Crowe's location. The sentinels couldn't resist rescuing one of their own. You guys are so predictable."

Before any mission, we made sure that our intel was solid, checking and rechecking our sources. The commander and I had suspected we had a second mole among our team. It was clear now that we did, although the bigger issue was the revelation that Bruno was in bed with Patrick Mason.

"If you're working with Patrick, that means you're working with Edmund. Are they here?" Maybe they were on that helicopter. Or maybe Jo was. I yanked on the chains again. I had to get out of there and warn Jo. *You also have to find your team.* Afterward, I would make it my life's mission to kill Bruno, Edmund, and Patrick. I was tired of their threats. The faster they died, the faster I could get on with my life and get back to the alluring vamp who had caught my attention the moment I'd met her.

"That's none of your concern." He poked his head out into the dimly lit hall before he turned back, studying me as if he was trying to get in my head.

I didn't know what type of vampire powers he had, but I knew he couldn't read minds. And if what he said was true about sentinel blood, he still couldn't yield that result. Commander Mason and Jo were the only two who could read minds. Man, I prayed she was all right, although if I knew her, she was freaking out, especially after three fucking months. She had predicted something would happen on this mission. Actually, she'd seen my death. I wasn't far from it, especially if I didn't get blood soon.

Beast came back. "Sir, we need to go."

Bruno pulled out his phone. "Smile, London. I need proof for your girl."

The flash, his smug voice, him, everything around me set me off. I roared so loud, Beast cringed. "Touch her, and I promise I'll torture you until you're begging for your death."

He lowered his phone. "You'll be dead before she arrives." Then he stalked out.

3

JO

I paced the control room, racking my brain as to why Ben would walk into the enemy's den. Maybe he wanted help. Maybe Edmund sent him. We still didn't know if he was working for Edmund or if he'd just disappeared on his own. I imagined he had to be frightened, especially if he wasn't human anymore. The thought of Ben turning out like Blake Turner made my heart hurt for Ben. If I hadn't killed Blake, he would've died anyway. According to Dr. Vieira, Blake's autopsy revealed that his system couldn't handle the change from human to vampire. Regardless, I didn't want my dad to order Ben's death without first having all the facts. Although I understood all too well my dad's skepticism.

With a potential mole among the SEAL team, we had to be extremely cautious. We'd learned that any one of us could side with the enemy like Kate London had. Her falling into Edmund's bed, figuratively and literally, was hard to swallow, particularly when she had tried to kill her own brother.

The doors flew open, and in walked two sentinels with their guns drawn on Ben. My jaw dropped. Ben had been tall and toned as a human, but now he was more muscular, as though he'd been preparing for a weightlifting competition. Gone was the fear that Ben had once housed whenever he was around vampires. In its place was a bravado that screamed he was ready to fight, although he wasn't putting up much of one at the moment. Instead, his hands were raised as he homed in on me. He smiled, warm and apologetic, showing off his dimples.

Sam was calm as he appraised Ben. Normally, Sam would've thrown himself at Ben with his fists flying. Sure, they'd been best friends, but that was a lifetime ago, it seemed. When Ben had attacked me outside of the gala event at Ms. Costner's estate, Sam had gone ballistic and almost killed his best friend.

As Ben stood on the landing that overlooked the control room, he diverted his gaze from me to my dad. "I need your help," he said in a deep voice.

Wow! Even his voice had changed.

With my heightened senses, I sniffed the air. He smelled human, yet he didn't. I always attributed Ben's scent to burnt sugar. However, he now gave off an acidic odor, reminding me of vinegar.

My father flicked his head to the hulking sentinels garbed in fatigues. "Take him into the war room."

Like good soldiers, they retreated with Ben sandwiched between them.

Driving a rough hand through his black hair, my father stalked toward his office, stopping to talk to a petite computer analyst, whose fingers were flying across her keyboard like a pianist. "Get Dr. Vieira down to the war room," he ordered before he disappeared through the doorway into his little cubbyhole across from her.

Tripp and Sam trudged behind Dad. It took me a minute to shake off the cobwebs after seeing Ben. So many questions were flying through my head, but one stood out. Was he human? That thought quickly vanished when I heard the tail end of Dad's statement.

"We'll need to put him down."

Horrified, I hurried into his office. "You can't kill Ben." Granted, I would have agreed if Ben had suffered the same fate as Blake Turner, but we didn't know yet for sure. "Dr. Vieira needs to run tests on him."

Dad glanced up from his desk. "That's not what I said, Jo. We'll have Dr. Vieira check out Ben. But realize that Edmund's serum hasn't been successful." He turned his attention to Tripp. "Get that private investigator, Diane Wallace, on the phone."

With a sigh, I dropped down into a metal chair next to Sam.

"Sir, it's only four thirty in the morning," Tripp said.

Dad narrowed his green eyes. "I don't give a shit if it was two in the morning. Wake her ass up."

"But you don't like her," I said. Diane Wallace had been instrumental in finding evidence for my lawyer, Mr. Rose, during my trial. Her efforts helped to acquit me of Blake's murder. Still, she'd been coy about who she really was when she'd followed Webb and me up to Webb's house in Maine. Mr. Jackson had hired her to investigate us because he believed we'd had something to do with Ben's disappearance.

"I may not like her, but she's a good investigator. I want to know if she's still working for Mr. Jackson or has any insight into where Ben has been." Dad huffed out a sigh as Tripp left.

"What are you two doing out of bed? It looks like you've been working out," he said more to Sam than me.

"I couldn't sleep," Sam said.

Dad swung his tired gaze to me. "You too?"

"Same problem, different day."

"We'll have to figure out how you can sleep longer than two hours. I would really like to find out if your dreams can tell us anything." Frustration rode Dad's words.

I chewed the inside of my lip as a pang of sympathy gripped my chest. My dad was under an extreme amount of stress. He worried about me constantly. I hated that I contributed to his stress. I understood his need to protect me from our enemies. I also understood how I could be the key to Edmund's sick plan of building a vampire army. But I wanted—no, needed—him to be the father I never had, the father he didn't get a chance to be since Sam and I had been in foster care up until eight months ago. Now that we were with our biological father, we hardly had any time to be a real family. And until our fight with Edmund was over, spending time as a family wasn't possible.

"Dad," I said. "Tripp mentioned that he could put me to sleep for a little while. Maybe we can try that."

His green eyes narrowed. "Absolutely not. There's a risk involved with you drinking his blood. I'm not willing to take that chance."

Clenching my fists, I drilled my gaze into my father's.

Dad almost rolled his eyes. "Stop making the chairs move, Jo."

My anger always kick-started my telekinesis. I unclenched my fists. "Look at this way. If I'm sleeping, that means I'm not in your hair. And a deep sleep could help me dream more."

He leaned back with a look that implied he was considering my request. "No. We'll figure something else out."

"Then let me hang out with Darcy or at least let me get off this base. If I clear my head, maybe that would help."

Sam muttered something under his breath.

"We'll talk after I speak with Ben," Dad said.

He didn't say no, which was a good sign.

Tripp sauntered back in. "Diane is on line four."

Dad lifted the receiver. "Diane, are you still working with Ben's father?"

I homed in on her voice.

"No. After Jo's trial, I broke ties with him, although I heard recently from a colleague within the Fall River Police Department that Mr. Jackson is still trying to get someone to listen to him about you. Did something happen? Do you need my help?" Her voice was sweet and sounded sleepy.

I couldn't blame Mr. Jackson for trying to get the law to investigate Dad and his military operation. If I were in his shoes, I would question why my son was always getting hurt and ending up in our base hospital or why Ben had disappeared without a trace.

Dad's fingers turned white around the receiver. "Ben has been off the radar for the last three months. Can you open a dialogue with Mr. Jackson again?"

"Absolutely. But you didn't get me out of bed to ask me to talk to Mr. Jackson. What else is going on?"

"Ben showed up on base this morning," Dad said. "While I find out more about him, I need someone to keep an eye on Mr. Jackson. Who he's talking to other than the police? Where does he go? You get my drift. He can't know his son is here, either."

"Why not?" she asked.

Dad pressed his fingers to his forehead as though he was trying to ward off a headache. "Look, you don't need to know more than that right now. Can I count on you and your discretion?"

"Sure. I'll do what I can."

"Oh, and one more thing while I have you on the phone. We still haven't found the person who cut the brakes on the limo that almost killed my daughter. I'd like you to look into it, and I would start with Mr. Jackson."

Not that I'd forgotten about that freaky ride down the mountain road in Maine when Webb and I were heading home. That was the night we met Diane a.k.a. Lauren. We'd suspected her, but after reading her mind, I found that she hadn't been the culprit.

Her voice hitched. "You think Mr. Jackson had something to do with running Webb and Jo off the road?"

Dad stood. "I've got a gut instinct. Call me when you find out something on anything we just discussed." Then Dad hung up.

I couldn't see Mr. Jackson trying to kill me. He'd always been a decent man, a good principal, a good father to Ben, and he'd taken Sam and me in when we ran into trouble with our last foster family.

"Pops, you can't be serious about Mr. Jackson cutting the brakes on Webb's car."

"Anything is possible. Tripp, let's see what Ben has to say. In the meantime, Sam and Jo, head back up to the apartment and try to get some sleep."

At the same time, Sam and I said, "No."

Dad's eyes flickered from green to silver for a split second as they always did when his emotions teetered on the edge. The color change was unique, as it was for me. My eyes were silver, but when my fangs dropped or my emotions went haywire, violet replaced the silver. Ninety-nine-point nine percent of the vampire population had eye color that changed to black when their emotions changed. Only one other vampire joined Dad and me in the field of unique vampire eye color, and that was Edmund Rain. His went from brown to red. We weren't quite sure why yet. However, we knew it had something to do with his powers.

"Pops," Sam said. "Jo and I need to be in there. He knows you can read minds, but he doesn't know Jo does. So whether he's human or something else, he'll let his guard down around her, and he won't hurt her with us there."

I pinched my eyebrows. Ever since Sam had learned that Ben was in love with me and tried to kidnap me, he didn't want Ben anywhere near me. Now, he was switching his tune.

Sam looked at me as if he knew what I was thinking. "I don't want you around Ben, but I know you can handle yourself, Sis."

My heart fluttered for a second as I silently did a happy dance. All my life, Sam had been my protector, especially when we had lived in foster care. Most of the time, I welcomed him as my savior, and even though I wouldn't want him to stop taking the lead as my big brother, I stood up a little taller, knowing he had confidence in me that I could fight my own battles.

My father scrubbed a hand over his scruffy jaw. "You have a point, Son."

It didn't matter what Dad's answer was. I would've found a way to eavesdrop. No way was I missing what Ben had to say.

"I'll meet you three in the war room. I need blood." Dad stalked out.

My pulse raced at the idea of confronting Ben. A part of me wanted him to be happy, and he hadn't been happy since learning Sam and I were vampires. He'd always believed that mortality was better than immortality. At first, I'd agreed with him, but now, as a vampire, I wouldn't want to be human again. I liked the idea of spending eternity with my family. Of course, I didn't like all the fighting and kidnapping and worrying about whether our enemies would succeed in killing us. But I couldn't be killed as easily as a human. Not to mention, I had powers that were pretty cool, although reading people's minds wasn't exactly the best one. I didn't like learning others' creepy thoughts.

Memories bombarded me as I entered the amphitheater-like war room. As humans, Ben and I had learned several things the day Webb brought me here. My dad had been missing. Sam had been kidnapped. My dad's half-brother, Patrick Mason, a well-renowned geneticist, had become a traitor. Edmund Rain was the head of a group called the Plutariums. Patrick Mason had been working on a serum to change himself into a vampire. He'd also concocted an endotoxin to attack the DNA of some young vampires. Most of all, I'd learned that I had to give up my humanity to save Sam. All of that felt like eons ago. Yet I couldn't shake how Ben and I had come full circle.

Ben sat stoically in the first row of seats, with his hands in his lap and no expression on his face. It was as though he had resolved all of his demons. I imagined he had many, considering he'd been injected with a new formula of the vampire serum my uncle Patrick had concocted after his original serum hadn't worked on Blake Turner.

Ben waved a hand around. "Brings back memories, doesn't it, Jo?" He raked his bronze gaze over me.

Human Jo would've cowered or blushed at the way a boy was looking at her, but not anymore. The only person I blushed for was

Webb, and my days of cowering were over. Instead, I lifted a shoulder as I rested against a table opposite Ben, keeping my gaze focused on him rather than the sentinel behind him or the one slightly at attention to Ben's right. "Why are you here? Are you doing okay? Where have you been?"

Sam stepped up beside me. "Slow down."

Tripp settled on Ben's left and shoved his hands into the pockets of his workout pants. "Let's wait for Commander Mason."

Ben regarded us. "Isn't it kind of early for you to be working out? Or did you get news on Webb's whereabouts?" His tone held a smidgeon of sarcasm.

I almost choked. Maybe Dad's hypothesis was right, and Ben was working for the enemy. Or maybe he'd spoken to Darcy. She knew Webb's plane had gone down. Besides, it wasn't a secret. The local newspaper had published an article about the plane crash that had claimed Webb and his SEAL team.

The door creaked open and in walked Dad, looking less pale.

"Is that why you're here?" Sam asked. "Do you have information on Webb?"

Dad took a position next to Tripp, raising his eyebrow. "Are you working for Edmund Rain?"

Fisting his hands in his lap, Ben growled as his light-brown eyes flared an orangey red. "I wouldn't work for that asshole if you paid me."

"Then start talking." Dad's tone permitted no argument.

The sentinel behind Ben gripped his shoulder. Ben sneered, his eyes blazing with fire.

"Sentinels, leave us," Dad said.

Both guards obeyed. Once they were gone, Ben's shoulders slumped.

Dad crossed his arms over his chest. "Now, talk."

Ben sighed. "I'm not here to cause trouble. I need your help."

"Why would we help you?" Sam's tone could have sliced a glacier.

Dad glared at Sam for at least a minute. I would bet Dad was reprimanding my brother by telepathic means. I went over and sat next to Ben.

"They're doing that mind thing, aren't they?" Ben asked.

"Probably. So what help do you need?" My tone was soft. I didn't want to argue with Ben. He'd come there of his own free will rather than the sentinels capturing him or tying him down.

Dad gave Ben his full attention as did Sam and Tripp.

Ben fidgeted somewhat before he began. "I've been hiding out in dark places around the city, sleeping in empty buildings, trying to keep my distance from humans." He let out a crazy laugh. "Humans." He shook his head. "It wasn't that long ago that I was a human. I want my life back. I don't know what I am, but I'm not normal. I have strength that goes beyond the physics of humanity, and I have the urge to drink blood." He set his sights on Dad. "You've got to help me. I know I've been a complete jerk, and for that I'm sorry to all of you." He took his time to glance at Dad, Sam, then me, bypassing Tripp. "Especially you, Jo. I wasn't myself that night outside that gala. My mind has been all screwed up."

"You don't have to apologize," I said. "Sam and I know more than anyone how losing your humanity can be. That is if you aren't human anymore." Which I was skeptical about. Edmund had mentioned to Ben and me just before he left us stranded on a yacht that the serum hadn't worked on Ben. Even Dr. Vieira had tested Ben and confirmed that he was in fact human.

"Trust me. I'm not human. But I'm not vampire either. I don't have fangs, although my gums hurt like hell."

That wasn't a good sign. "Do you understand any of this?" I asked Dad. "Edmund injected Ben with his vampire juice almost five months ago."

"Dr. Vieira should be here shortly," Dad said. "Ben, during those five months, had you been experiencing any physical changes?"

"It was slow at first. In the beginning, I found myself throwing a baseball farther than was humanly possible. When I was helping my dad move some furniture, I could lift a dresser all by myself. My dad thought I was on steroids in preparation for that baseball camp he wanted to send me to. But when my eyes changed color, I knew I wasn't normal. And they only change to red when I'm angry or now I'm finding when the urge for blood is strong. I swear this is all so screwed up."

It was also scary because the changes in Ben meant that Edmund was succeeding with his plan to build an army of vampires. The other scary part was that Ben was given the same serum that Blake Turner had been given. Dr. Vieira had testified during my trial that the reason Blake had died was due to his enlarged heart. Apparently, when a natural-born vampire like myself changes from human to vampire, our hearts shrink in size. However, since Blake didn't carry a natural-born vampire gene, his heart had grown larger than his normal human heart. Not to mention, Blake's brain had been shrinking, which wasn't normal even for a vampire. The brain was one organ that didn't change when humans became vampires.

"Have you spoken to your dad?" Tripp asked.

"I can't. I have been watching him, though. He's a mess. He can't lose me. My mother's death years ago almost sent him over the edge. Please, Mr. Mason. You've got to help me."

I grabbed Ben's cold hand. Immediately, his thoughts accosted me. *I can't go on living like this. I need to help my dad. I'm on the verge of killing myself. These people are the only ones who can help me. Please. Please. Say you'll help me.*

Ben squeezed my hand.

"He's telling the truth, Dad." Tears burned my eyes. Poor Ben. He'd been Sam's best friend. He'd saved my life. He'd helped me when Sam had gone missing. He didn't have to put his life on the line for me or any of us, yet he had. Sure, he loved me, which I was certain was one of the reasons he hadn't run when he found out I was a vampire. Still, Dad and his team helped people.

The click of the door drew my attention away from Dad. Dr. Vieira ambled in, pushing up his gold-rimmed glasses with the tip of his forefinger. "Never a dull moment around here," he said with a yawn.

"Damon, thanks for getting out of bed," Dad said. "Ben Jackson needs our help."

Dr. Vieira shoved his hands in the pockets of his lab coat that hung over a pair of plaid pajama bottoms and a T-shirt. "Are you going to let us examine you?" He settled in front of Ben with a scowl on his face.

Sam sauntered over to sit next to me.

"Yes, sir. Anything you need. I'm not going to run or cause trouble this time. Just please tell me what I am," Ben pleaded.

"Very well," Dr. Vieira said. "Let's head up to my lab and get started."

Ben squeezed my hand again as he stood.

I jumped up and hugged him. "You're in good hands. I'll see you soon."

He hugged me back before he left with Dr. Vieira. Once the door shut, the tension in the room dissipated. I was glad Ben hadn't lied.

Dad eyed Sam and me. "Why don't we try and get a couple hours of sleep."

I was kind of tired all of a sudden. Maybe I could try to sleep and maybe dream.

4
———————

JO

I flopped around in my bed like a fish out of water. Less than an hour ago after Ben left with Dr. Vieira, my eyes had become heavy. But as I lay on my back, staring at the white ceiling, my mind wandered to Ben then to Webb then to Darcy then back to Webb. I went back and forth. Was Ben really a vampire? How could I force myself to dream? Would Dad let me visit Darcy? I closed my eyes. I had to try to dream. Or I could help Dr. Vieira run tests on Ben. I had started shadowing Dr. Vieira not long after Webb's plane crashed. For one thing, learning something new took my mind off Webb. For another thing, being in the lab gave me the opportunity to get a feel of medicine and help me decide if studying to become a doctor was something I wanted to do with my life. Granted, I had an infinite amount of time to decide, but I was quite fascinated with how someone like me, who carried a special gene, could change from human to vampire. The genetics alone were jaw-dropping. I could see why my estranged uncle Patrick studied genetics.

Laughing out loud, I opened my eyes. The blades on the ceiling fan spun like my mind. *Argh!* I was tired, yet I wasn't. I took in a deep breath, then another, regulating my breathing as I again

24

lowered my lids. I tuned out the hum of the refrigerator that was situated behind the wall of my headboard, the whirring sound of the fan blades, and every other little noise that my vampire ears were sensitive to. Then I crawled under the blankets, snuggled into my pillow, and imagined Webb holding me. I would give anything to see his stark-blue eyes, run my fingers over his muscular body, or taste him. The last time I got a taste of his lips on mine was minutes before he left on his mission.

His kiss had been soft and gentle, and his eyes had held so much love. "Open those pretty eyes, Jo," he'd said. "I don't want to leave you. Please understand I have to do a job."

Tears spilled out and down my cheeks. As I cried, my mind drifted, farther and farther into the abyss.

The musty decay of earth permeated the air as a familiar place emerged—a place I'd seen a couple of times. I turned to run from the field of coffins and headstones that dotted the landscape. When I did, I ran into the sleek panther.

"Serapis, get out of the way," I said.

He pressed his nose into my leg, trying to get me to move.

I shook my head. "I can't bear to look."

He nudged me again before a soft angelic voice floated somewhere nearby. "You must turn around."

I angled my head toward Serapis, gazing into his topaz-colored eyes. "Are you speaking to me?"

He bowed his head, his black coat shining beneath the moonlight. "You're up against a massive war that's about to unfold. Your enemies are aligning."

I held my breath as I slowly turned. Operating tables had replaced the coffins in a cemetery. I shuffled forward, down the stone path with Serapis at my side.

"Who are all these people? They look alive." All of them had IVs in their arms, and red liquid filled the IV bags.

"Your loved ones are in danger. You are the key to their survival," Serapis said in my head.

"How? What do I need to do?" Holding my breath, I scanned the tables of bodies, looking for Webb or anyone I knew. But I couldn't make out faces.

Serapis rubbed his ear against my leg. "That I can't answer."

A vibration sound caused me to bolt upright. I blinked a few times as sweat coated my body. The vibration sound stopped. I dropped back down on the pillow. As I did, my head landed on my phone. I checked the screen and saw a missed call. I waited for a second to see if the unknown caller would leave a voicemail. One minute ticked by, and nothing.

I closed my eyes. I had more questions for Serapis. Then as my brain cleared, my eyes flew open. The panther was talking to me. The old man who had been in all my dreams wasn't there. That seemed odd because the panther never came without the old man. As I pondered the significance of my dream, my phone vibrated again.

I sat up and answered. "Hello."

"Is this Jo Mason?" the male voice asked.

"Who wants to know?"

"I'll take that as a yes." The man's tone was unique, reminding me of the man who did those Allstate insurance commercials. "Are you still looking for Webb London?"

I went ramrod straight. "Where is he?"

"There's a price," he said.

"Anything." My pulse was all over the place. "Is he alive?"

"He's breathing."

Oh my God. "My dad is going to flip."

"Not so fast. There are conditions. You should know that my name is Bruno, and this deal only involves you and no one else."

I laughed, albeit nervously. Not telling my dad would be impossible since he could read my mind anytime we were in the same room. Not only that, he had me locked down on this military base.

"Are you in, or should I let him die?"

I gasped. I loved Webb. I would do anything to get him back. I had to pause for a moment, though. I'd learned a thing or two about enemies during the time I'd spent on the military base, surrounded by my dad and the sentinels. *Trust no one* was my dad's motto. As a leader who commanded a team and sent them into battle, my dad always weighed everything that could go wrong.

My dad taught me to be cautious, so I realized the man on the phone could be setting me up, but he was offering up Webb, the man I was in love with. I couldn't be blinded by that fact. I'd already experienced a lot in the short time since I'd become a vampire. Edmund had kidnapped me and left me to die in the turbulent Atlantic, and I'd battled him to save Darcy, Webb, and Sam. I would endure all that and more to get Webb back. "I want proof he's alive. I want to talk to him."

"I figured you would say that," Bruno said. "But you can't talk to him. I'll text you proof. Do we have a deal?"

I hopped out of bed and started pacing. I prayed my dad was sleeping or not in the apartment. "Provided I get proof, then yes."

"Good. I'll be sending a private jet for you. Here are the rules. One, come alone. Two, you can't mention our deal to anyone, not even your father, the sentinels, or the vampire government. If you do, then Webb will die. Is that understood?"

My mind raced, trying to figure out how I would get around my father. But I couldn't pass up the opportunity to rescue Webb. "So, you're going to release Webb in exchange for what?" Considering he wanted me to come alone, I had a feeling I knew the answer. But I wanted him to say it.

"I want you," he said in a mocking tone.

"Why? I'm just a vampire with nothing to offer." Unless Bruno wanted the same thing as Edmund—my DNA.

"You have much to offer." He sounded irritated.

This was the first piece of hope I'd had in months. I had to at least follow it through. I would firm up a plan along the way. A crazy laugh broke out in my head. *You're walking into a trap.* Maybe I was, but if Serapis was right, and I was the key to my loved ones' survival, I definitely had to jump at the chance. My dreams had been telling me bits and pieces about the future that didn't make any sense, but the one common thread that had always been present when the old man and Serapis graced my dreams was that I was the key to stopping my enemies. "If I see proof, then what do you want me to do?"

"I'll text you the details within the hour. And Jo, if my team suspects anything when you get to the hangar, then Webb dies. Are we clear?"

"You have my word," I said as a knock sounded, causing me to end the call.

I blew out a breath, trying to clear my mind.

"Jo?" Dad knocked again.

I was screwed. I began chanting the alphabet in my head as I opened the door, something I'd gotten into the habit of doing when I didn't want Dad in my head.

Dad stood there with a crease between his eyebrows. His lids were heavy, and lines creased around his eyes. "Everything okay? Who were you talking to?"

Damn vampire hearing.

"You don't know?" I asked in a flat tone. At least I hoped the guilt and fear didn't resonate in my voice and that he hadn't read my mind.

He studied me. "What don't you want me to know?"

I laughed. "I just had a personal dream about Webb. And not one where he was dead or anything if you get my drift," I said in a rush as heat infused my cheeks.

"Yeah, I don't want to know. I'm going to get some sleep for a few hours." He scratched his head. "You have your tutoring session with Ms. Costner today, right?"

"Yes. After that, I would like to visit Darcy. Please, Dad. I've been cooped up for too long. I'm either in the control room, training room, or the library. I need to get my head clear. It might help me dream more about other things like if Webb is alive. If anything happens, you know I can handle myself."

He briefly closed his eyes. "I guess I can't keep you locked up forever. And you do have some strong abilities." He threaded his fingers through his thick black hair. "Edmund has been quiet too. So I'll allow it under one condition. You listen to your security detail."

I hugged him. "Thank you." I hadn't expected that he would let me go alone.

He hugged me tightly. "Jo, I worry about you. I know I've been quite strict. But now that I have you back, I want to be a good father. I want us to do things as a family. We can't do that when Edmund wants nothing more than to hurt you. I can't lose you."

I eased back, and tears threatened. "I know you go out of your way to protect Sam and me. But we're adults now. Our powers are strong."

He studied me as though he was trying to read my mind. Oh, wait. He probably was.

"How's Ben? Is he staying somewhere on base?" I asked.

"He'll be staying in one of the bunks in the sentinel barracks for now."

"You're not locking him in the prison?" I found that odd. Dad had never trusted Ben. Well, he'd never trusted Ben around me. It was more of a boy and girl thing with Dad. Not to mention, Ben had a police record for inappropriate behavior with a girl. Dad had been leery about Ben ever since he'd read that report.

"He'll cooperate better if he's not locked up. Besides, I have someone watching him. As for you, I want you to be cautious around him. I know your powers are strong, but remember, until we know more about him, he's still human to us."

Here, I'd thought Dad would bring up Ben's police report. I had to smile that my father was trusting me and my powers. Regardless, I still had to ask, "You're not worried about Ben's police record."

"Not anymore. I read his mind. That boy won't hurt you. What I don't want to happen is another murder trial over some human or half human/half vampire person that you killed in self-defense."

"The last thing I want is to go back to court." I wouldn't hurt Ben anyway, unless he hurt me. "Is Ben with Dr. Vieira now?"

He kissed me on the forehead. "He's in the mess hall with Sam.

I'll see you later tonight." He yawned as he vanished into his bedroom.

I quickly changed into jeans, a sweater over a T-shirt, and boots. I grabbed my phone and headed to the mess hall. Once out of the apartment, I let out a huge breath. I was grateful that my conversation with Dad had helped to keep my mind off of Bruno. I wasn't lying when I told him I needed to clear my head, but I was also about to break his trust. I slumped where I stood. After today, Dad would never trust me again. But I couldn't dwell on Dad. If I did, I might chicken out, and I couldn't, not if I wanted to save Webb's life.

I checked my phone. Bruno had said he would get back to me within the hour. Only thirty minutes had passed. All kinds of questions bombarded me as I climbed down the stairs to the third floor, where the mess hall was located. *Why does Bruno have Webb? If Webb is alive, are the rest of the sentinels who were with him alive as well?*

As soon as I pulled open the door, the scent of bacon erased my thoughts for the moment. Breakfast was in full force, which meant the place was filled with vampires. Even though we survived on blood, we also needed protein.

Two long high-top bars lined the right side of the room. The buffet setup of food was immediately to my left, and tables and chairs were scattered around. I cut a path in between the tables on my way to the stainless steel fridge that stood against the back wall. I snagged an orange-cream juice box. Well, it was actually filled with flavored blood. As I inserted the straw, I spotted Sam and Ben at a table near the window that overlooked the courtyard. I sipped my drink as I made my way over to them. Ben rose and pulled out a chair for me.

I smiled. "Thank you." His behavior was such a change from when he'd been so angry for so long with not only me but with the vampire world in general.

He nodded as he sat back down.

"What are you guys talking about?" I continued to sip on sugary blood.

Ben chuckled. "Remember when you first drank one of those blood boxes? You were human."

Sam angled his head.

"Your sister got deathly sick from drinking flavored blood. Wait. Since when can you drink those? Aren't you still on your father's blood?"

"No," Sam said. "We graduated months ago from our newborn status. Now we can drink bagged blood like every other vampire." He scrunched his nose. "I don't like those juice boxes, though."

I couldn't help but think of Webb and how he had been in panic mode the day I'd passed out from drinking a box of blood. Knowing he was alive made me grin.

"You look happy, Sis," Sam said. "What's going on? Did Tripp find out news about Webb? Or did Pops give you the go ahead for Tripp to put you to sleep?"

I eyed Sam warily. He was an empath who could detect feelings, strong ones. Hence, he was always questioning and suspicious of everyone. "I haven't seen Tripp. Dad is letting me visit Darcy today."

Ben fiddled with his fork. "I owe her an apology. Can I tag along?"

Sam glanced at Ben with tired eyes. "That's not a good idea."

"Dr. Vieira will be done with me later on," Ben added.

I set down my empty blood box. "No offense, but I just want to spend girl time with her. Maybe another time." I wagged a finger between Sam and Ben. "You know, I'm surprised that you two are cordial to one another."

"We had a long conversation," Ben said.

"Yeah, we're cool." Sam grinned, but it didn't reach his green eyes. He was so much like our father, untrusting and cautious.

For the next twenty minutes, we chatted about our human days as I pulled out my phone and grasped it as though it was my lifeline. Actually, the phone kind of was. Webb was my life.

Sam's and Ben's voices and the noises from the room in general lowered to a soft hum as I stared at my phone. I was partly afraid to see what proof Bruno would send me. I was also partly excited. It didn't matter how bad Webb looked as long as he was alive.

Sam snapped his fingers. "Sis, you with us?"

I glanced up. "Sorry, I was zoning out. I didn't get enough sleep."

"No worries," Ben said. "I was just saying how badly I missed my dad."

A pang of sympathy coursed through me. Ben had been through hell since the day Sam went missing from the human high school. Ben had stood by my side when he knew I carried a vampire gene. He'd been there for me, helping me find Sam. He'd been attacked by vampires, not once, not twice, but three times. The third time, he'd been used as a test subject for Edmund's human vampire serum. I also empathized with his father. Mr. Jackson had to be on eggshells not knowing where Ben was.

My phone vibrated in my hand. I flinched as I lowered my gaze to the screen. "Excuse me. It's Darcy. I'll be right back." In the event that I freaked out from Bruno's proof, I didn't want to be around anyone, especially my brother. Not only would he stop me, but he would tell Dad for sure.

I ducked out of the mess hall and into a deserted bathroom. The text had a video attached. Once the video began, I stifled a scream. Dirt walls formed the backdrop behind a deathly looking Webb.

"Smile, London," Bruno said.

Webb bared his fangs. "Touch her, and I promise I'll torture you until you're begging for your death." His voice was hoarse, as though he'd been screaming for months on end.

His voice slid over me, but it did nothing to calm me like it always had. I couldn't get past the hollowness of his black vampire eyes or how ashen he looked. *But he's alive. He's talking.*

My phone buzzed with a text. *Confirm you got this and that we have a deal.*

The video could've been taken months ago. *But what if it wasn't? What if Webb is alive? You've got to find out.*

I texted back. *We have a deal.*

Within seconds Bruno replied. *Get to the Fall River Airport by six thirty tonight.*

I blew out a long breath, not sure if I was doing the right thing. I wanted more than anything to save Webb, but maybe it would be best to include Dad in the plan. *Don't get scared. Go to Webb.* Then I was reminded of what Serapis had said to me in my dream. "Your loved ones are in danger. You are the key to their survival." My mind was made up.

5

———

WEBB

My head lolled forward as my eyes closed. I'd been dozing on and off since Bruno graced me with his presence. I couldn't shake the bad feeling that was all-consuming. Maybe it was just the hunger stabbing me in the gut.

Don't fall asleep, London. You won't wake up. I laughed. *You've got to save Jo.* I laughed again, only a little louder. My deep voice traveled around the cavernous cell. I threw my head back. *Think, asshole.* That was my problem. I couldn't think straight.

A rustling sound echoed from somewhere in the cell. I glanced around. A rat emerged from a small opening in the rock wall. He sniffed the air.

"That's it," I said to the rat. "Keep sniffing." Maybe my scent could lure him to me because I smelled downright rotten.

I crawled toward the rat like a starved dog. Rocks and debris punctured my hands and knees, but I couldn't feel any pain. I was numb to it. The chains jerked me to a stop in the middle of the cell, feet from the rodent. *Fuck.*

The rat hesitated, unsure of what to do next.

"This way." Desperation rode me hard. "I just want a drop of blood." Hell, I wanted as much blood as I could get my hands on. The problem was the rat wouldn't come anywhere near satisfying my hunger.

The furry guy started toward me again, stopping every few feet to sniff the air. I scurried back to where the chains had me tethered, hoping I could snatch the rodent when he got closer to me. When I reached my original spot, the rat was a foot within reach. With my hands behind my back, the only way to capture him was with my mouth. I laid flat on my stomach, saliva dripping from my fangs as I willed the fucking rodent to come closer. I had the ability to alter water, fire, and earth, but I could only do that by absorbing and storing energy from the sun and nature. I hadn't been in the sun or around anything remotely close to nature in three months.

My efforts, or lack thereof, for the rat died when the lock on the door clicked. Normally, I would've popped to attention, but I didn't have the energy to move. The rat sure did, though.

Bruno's laughter grated on me as he entered the room. "London, you've resorted to a rat. I have to applaud you, though. You're trying. I'm not sorry to say that it pains me to see you like this. However, I am happy to inform you that your little beauty, Jo, is on her way."

Energy or not, I was on my feet, lunging at Bruno at the mention of Jo's name. Stars danced before me. "You lie." I growled, snarled, and sneered.

He pulled out his phone and stuck it in my face. "Read."

He was so close. I had the opportunity to bite into his wrist if I weren't more drawn to the text on his phone. My heart plummeted to the floor at Jo's response. *We have a deal.* I wouldn't have believed Bruno, except the text came from Jo's phone number. Bruno's response was equally horrifying. *Get to the Fall River Airport by six thirty tonight.*

An inferno started building inside me. The need to kill Bruno far outreached the need to kill Edmund, and the desire to bury Edmund was strong. He'd lured my sister, Kate, into his coven of lies to the point that Kate had tried to kill me. That little plot wasn't resolved yet, but if I made it out of here alive, I would be a killing machine. Fuck doing what was right according to the vampire law or any law. Fuck everyone. Jo and I would disappear until I could follow through on my personal mission. The commander could throw me in prison. The vampire government could sentence me to death. Either way, I was done taking orders, and I'd had enough with everyone wanting a piece of the woman I loved.

"I may be ruthless," Bruno said. "But I wasn't bluffing. She's going to give Edmund and me everything we want. Now, I've come to say good-bye."

Keep him talking. He was still so close that I would bet he'd forgotten how close he was standing to a hungry vampire. "I thought you needed sentinel blood?"

That bald beast stuck his head in the room. "We've got ten minutes to get out of here." Then he disappeared.

One side of Bruno's mouth quirked up. "I have all the blood I need. However, if I need more, then I know where you and your team live."

I counted to three in my head.

"Enjoy the fireworks, London," Bruno said.

Just as he turned, I attacked, sinking my fangs into his shoulder, close to his carotid artery. Immediately, blood spilled into my mouth. I sucked as hard as I could, my eyes rolling back into my head at how my body came alive. I came alive.

Bruno roared as he tugged, trying to get free. But my fangs were deeply embedded in him. He head-butted me before one of his elbows landed in my gut.

I felt nothing except euphoria each time I swallowed his blood. Each pull gave me renewed energy. I could feel my organs awakening. My vision sharpened. My hearing homed in on voices in other cells. I stopped for a split second as I heard Olivia's voice. When I did, Bruno jerked forward and free. Blood spilled down his back. I savored the remaining mouthful of blood as though I was sampling a fine bottle of wine. Hell, his blood was wine in my book. A small amount of dizziness made me sway. Too much, too soon.

After Bruno left, I stood stock-still, taking in a deep breath along with the stench in the air. I breathed in and out as the walls around me spun like a vortex. I definitely ingested too much blood way too soon. I couldn't say for sure how much time had passed when an explosion rocked the cavern, sending me careening backward into the wall. My body splattered, bones shattered, and my head cracked. Before I could react, another explosion went off. The cell walls started to crumble as the ceiling rained down on me.

6

JO

The atmosphere in Darcy's bedroom was just what the doctor ordered, although I'd been trying to come up with a plan on how to sneak past my security detail, who waited outside in the car.

Darcy snapped her fingers. "Earth to Jo."

I blinked, and her big brown eyes came into focus. "Sorry, I'm not great company."

I adjusted myself so I was sitting next to her, up against the headboard. We'd been watching a movie that I couldn't remember the name of. All I kept doing during the movie was looking at the time on my phone and thinking about how in the world I would get to the Fall River Airport, which was a thirty-minute drive from Darcy's house.

She muted the TV on the wall over her dresser. "Why do you keep looking at your phone? Is it time for you to feed? Or are you trying not to bite me?"

I busted out laughing. "Granted, your cotton-candy scent always gets my fangs to drop, but I'm not hungry. You know I've learned how to control myself. Otherwise, my father wouldn't allow me here, and your parents would definitely put up a fight." Well, her father

38

would have. Her mother didn't know about vampires, and Mr. Rose, who represented vampires in court for a living, wanted to keep it that way. So did Darcy. I couldn't tell her about Bruno or what I was about to do. I didn't want to get her involved. She'd been through too much already with vampires. "I meant to tell you. Ben is staying on base. He wants our help."

She tapped me on the arm. "You waited all this time to tell me. Is he okay? Is he human?"

"We don't know. He seems like his old self, though—kind and friendly."

The doorbell rang.

"I think that's your cue to go." Darcy jumped off the bed, her blond ponytail swinging behind her.

My curfew was eight p.m., but I didn't tell her that. I had approximately forty minutes to get to the Fall River Airport and still no clue as to how to coax my guards to take me without alerting my father. I didn't have the ability to compel anyone like Webb or even Sam.

The doorbell rang again.

I darted in front of her. "Let me answer it." I didn't want to take the chance that maybe the person calling wasn't my security detail. I opened my senses, sniffing the air, but Darcy's sugary scent was overpowering.

When I reached the door, I motioned with my hand for her to move behind me. Once she was in place, I slowly opened the door.

The cool fall air breezed in along with Sam.

Darcy pushed me out of the way and threw her arms around him. "Hi."

My muscles tensed. If Sam was here, then something was wrong.

He managed to untangle her from his six-foot frame.

"You cut your hair," Darcy cooed. My best friend had a huge crush on my brother.

He narrowed his green eyes at me, and I checked the street. My guards were gone. "Is everything okay?"

"We need to go." His tone was even.

"Where?" Darcy stepped back. "To a fight. You're all garbed out in one of those black sentinel uniforms."

Black cargo pants, a black T-shirt, and military boots were standard attire for my brother on most days. I hardly saw him in jeans anymore. Regardless, I was now in a pickle. I wouldn't be able to dodge my brother. He knew me too well. He wouldn't let me walk into the hands of an enemy.

My mind raced. "Is it Webb?" Maybe Webb had escaped or word came in alerting my dad to his location. If so, then I wouldn't have to follow Bruno's orders.

Sam fidgeted as he flicked his head toward the black SUV in the driveway. "I'll tell you in the car."

The hairs on the back of my neck stiffened. If he was antsy, then that meant a threat. Maybe Edmund was making his move. If that were the case, then I couldn't be here. I couldn't put Darcy in danger. So I hugged her. "We'll talk soon. Lock the doors."

She let out a nervous laugh. "Locked doors don't stop vampires. But I have my cobalt dagger," she said as her face paled. "I can handle myself, and my dad will be home any minute."

Thank God. Mr. Rose knew a thing or two about how to handle a vampire, and so did Darcy, thanks to Sam. He'd taught her how to protect herself against a vampire.

I gave her a weak smile. "Call if you need us." Then Sam and I left. I hated leaving her, but I relaxed a bit knowing Mr. Rose would be home soon.

Once inside the military issue SUV, Sam turned to me. "When were you going to tell me about Bruno?"

My mouth fell open. "Can you read minds now?" After my excited behavior in front of him and Ben, Sam probably went down to the control room and did a search on who called my phone. Sam had learned how to extract and find information, a feat he'd gotten good at with all the access he had to computers. "Or are you tracking my phone?"

He backed out of the driveway. "Bruno called me."

Gasping, my mind scrambled to figure out why Bruno would clue Sam in on the deal. "What does he want with you?" Sam and I were twins, but our DNA structure as vampires was slightly different. According to Dr. Vieira, I was in more demand since I had a quadruple helix DNA makeup, while Sam had the normal natural-born vampire triple helix makeup.

"Not sure. But he said that we needed to be on his plane at six thirty sharp. And if you weren't with me, he'd not only kill Webb and his team, but Pops too." He negotiated stop signs and traffic lights as we headed toward the Fall River Airport.

"Bruno said the deal was with me and no one else. I don't understand. Something must've happened in order for him to change his mind, unless his plan was to include you all along. But then, why not tell me?"

"Sis, it doesn't matter."

"It does. He wants me for my DNA. I'm sure of it, even though he didn't come out and say it. Our DNA doesn't match. So there's no reason he would need you unless..." I froze as I thought back to the day of our physicals. "Remember when Dr. Vieira told Dad about my unique DNA? And you asked Dr. Vieira if you were normal? His response was 'Your earlier tests are normal.' Then he sent another series of samples from our physicals to that lab in Boston. No sooner than the lab received them, someone broke in and stole our medical records."

He tapped his fingers on the steering wheel. "Are you saying that we have the same DNA?"

"Think about it. You're becoming as powerful as me."

"So this dude Bruno stole our medical records?"

"Either him or Edmund. And they're holding the sentinels hostage now until they get us. This is all making sense now. We're exactly the same. Remember last month when we were practicing our powers down by the shore and we joined hands?"

"Shit. Rocks started to explode, and the water became turbulent while the wind whipped around like a hurricane." His knuckles turned white as he gripped the steering wheel.

Businesses clipped by as we sped down the road.

"When we told Dad, he raised an eyebrow and got all pale. He said that was impossible." I glanced at Sam. "Speaking of Dad, did you tell him about where we were going?" I didn't think he had. If Dad knew, he would've been on Darcy's doorstep rather than Sam.

A muscle jumped along Sam's strong jaw. "Hell no. He'd go commando, and that's the last thing we need. Besides, I've grown rather fond of our father, and I'd like to see him live."

I didn't want to put Sam in danger again. He'd been on his deathbed when we rescued him from Edmund. "I have an idea." I didn't think he would go for it, but I had to try. "Drop me off at the airport. Let me go alone. Give me a head start. Then you can tell Dad what's going on. You can track my whereabouts with my phone." I would bet money that Dad was or would be tracking our every move if we didn't return to the base soon. "Once we land, you'll have a location to send in the cavalry."

"No," he said in a tone that sounded like our dad. "Again, Bruno's instructions were explicit. Any deviation, then the shit storm starts."

The so-called shit storm had already started. "Sam, please. I don't want to lose you. You've been poked with enough needles already by Edmund and our uncle Patrick."

His face reddened. "There is no fucking way you're going alone."

Something wasn't adding up with Sam. "Why aren't you talking me out of this or hauling me back to base?" If Bruno went after Dad, our father would tear him to pieces. After all, Dad was considered the most powerful of all vampires among us.

He growled. "If we tell Pops, then Webb and the others are

dead. At least if we follow Bruno's plan, then we have a chance to save the sentinels. Plus, I can't sit around anymore and wait to hear if the team is alive. I'm suffocating on that base."

My jaw hit my chest. This was the first time in ages that Sam had expressed how he really felt about being barricaded on a military base. My brother had always kept most of his feelings to himself unless someone angered him. But since we'd become vampires, he'd learned how to temper those anger outbursts.

Sam flipped on the blinker, the sound ticking as fast as my heart. Cars zipped by as Sam merged onto the highway.

"Glad to know I'm not the only one," I said. Even before Webb went missing, living under Dad's thumb had been and still was quite exhausting. Not that walking into the arms of the enemy was going to be a party. When I let out a sigh, something occurred to me. "Why do you think Bruno is luring us out of the city?" We still didn't know where we would meet Bruno.

"My guess? He wants us as far away from Pops as possible, somewhere we can't be found."

I shivered at his last sentence. "Maybe this isn't a good idea."

Sam reached over the console and squeezed my hand. "Look, we can survive. We have strong powers on our own but think about the damage we can do together. Plus, Bruno doesn't know the strength we have together. All they may know is we have the same DNA structure, if that's even true."

Sam had mastered the ability to manipulate water, air, earth, and fire just like me. He could read someone's feelings in the blink of an eye. He had an uncanny ability to compel his victims, even the strongest of vampires. What made Sam unique was the ability to compel multiple victims at once. Webb could only compel one person at a time. Somehow, Sam could command a group of people with his mind. Regardless, he was right, especially if we could save Webb.

I sat up straighter. "Then let's kick some ass."

He laughed as the sign for the airport came into view.

"Where do you think Bruno is holding Webb?" I asked.

"I imagine since Webb's plane went down over the Alaskan mountains, that's where we're headed."

He slowed as we exited the highway. When he came to a stop, my phone vibrated in the cupholder. We exchanged a tentative look.

Then I glanced at my screen. "It's Dad." The phone kept dancing. "I'll just tell him we're on our way back."

"Don't answer it," Sam said as he turned left off the exit.

The vibration stopped. My heart didn't, though. My bravado wavered once again as my pulse raced. More than anything, I wanted to see Webb, touch him, help him, kiss him, and do all the boyfriend-girlfriend things that couples do. But doubt niggled in the back of my brain, not only because of what we were walking into, but because I was betraying Dad's trust.

"You know it's probably a trap," I said.

"Always is with our enemies."

After three additional turns, Sam wheeled into the quiet and quaint airport. Two men decked out in camouflage uniforms waved us over to the open hangar in the distance. Beyond them, a small jet sat idle with its stairs down.

My phone vibrated again. Again, Dad's name came across the screen.

Sam slowed to a stop inside the hangar, our tires screeching on the shiny cement floor.

I grabbed my phone and went to pocket it when I heard Dad's voice.

Sam narrowed his eyes, and I shrugged. I guessed I'd accidently hit the answer button. Before I could do anything, one of the men opened my door. "Phone," he said as he held out his calloused hand.

"Sorry, Dad," I said in an elevated voice, not sure if he could hear me.

"Jo," Dad shouted.

The large man dropped my phone then stomped on it with a booted foot the size of Sasquatch.

I tossed a look over my shoulder. The other camouflaged man did the same thing to Sam's phone. There went my plan of Dad tracking our location.

The plane's engines powered up, pushing my pulse into overdrive. If Bruno kept his end of the deal, and Webb was alive, then Sam and I were doing the right thing.

7

WEBB

A boulder sat on my chest, making it difficult to get air into my lungs. Water dripped from high above, splattering every-where but my mouth. The faint sound of voices echoed. Then I remembered Olivia's voice. Suddenly, I bolted upright, or tried. Bruno's blood hadn't given me enough strength to easily pop to attention, but I managed to push the boulder off me. Once free, I sucked in all the dust-filled air I could as I stood and swayed.

As I tried to shake off the dizziness, thoughts of Jo bombarded me. Surely, Bruno wouldn't bring Jo into his den, not when he knew he would be blowing up the place. After all, she was a valuable commodity to him and Edmund. I had to pray I was right. I had to pray she wasn't anywhere near this place.

Voices groaned from somewhere in the earth.

"Olivia," I shouted in a scratchy voice that echoed far and wide through the cavernous dungeon. "Olivia. Sloan. Kraft. Kodiak. Anyone?"

I heard more groans and muffled sounds.

I began moving rocks and debris, cutting a path to nowhere.

The entire area was closed in from the explosion. I tilted my head back and found that a metal bridge connected one side of the rock wall to the other. The good news was that the bridge survived the explosion. The bad news was that the way out was at least twenty stories high with no access from where I stood. I scanned both sides of the bridge for a door but didn't see one. I darted my gaze forward, but I was met with darkness. My vampire eyesight was impeccable in the dark, but I needed more blood to sharpen my senses.

A burning sensation flamed around my wrists. *Damn cobalt cuffs.* I squatted down on a rock then banged my right wrist against the stone to break the lock on the cuff. Once free, I did the same with my other wrist. Then I resumed my search, bellowing, "Sloan. Kraft. Olivia. Kodiak."

A woman groaned again from somewhere in the darkness.

I climbed up one rock then down another. When I reached another pile of debris, a strong animal-like scent hit my nostrils. I licked my dust-crusted lips. If an animal was near, that meant blood was too. I swept the immediate area with a mechanical precision. As I turned back to my right, I found myself standing face-to-face with a wolf, a very large wolf with golden-yellow eyes. He bared his teeth as he growled. I snarled, showing my fangs. I'd fought a wolf or two in my day. They were easy to take down. But this wolf wasn't any ordinary wolf. The one before me was a human who had shifted. Shifters could be large, depending on their human size, although the one I was about to tango with was of medium build.

The muffled sounds continued.

I needed to feed first, then I could continue to search for my team and a way out.

The wolf bowed his head as though he was ready to tackle me to the ground. I stood my ground, ready to battle, when the animal slowly shifted. Bones snapped into place as the wolf lost its reddish-brown fur, golden-yellow eyes, and large fangs, until he was completely human. Only he was a very naked she. The redhead stretched her neck one way then the other as she stuck out her bare breasts, rolling back her shoulders.

"I hate shifting sometimes," she said as she covered up her breasts with her long red hair.

I swept my gaze over her milky skin, which seemed to be a beacon in the darkness surrounding us. But as sexy as she was, all I could focus on was her healthy beating heart and the blood pumping through her arteries. *Thump. Thump. Thump.* Her pulse beat a steady rhythm. I licked my lips as my gaze traveled up to her face, a very familiar face. "Crysta?"

Horror etched her delicate features. "Webb? Where's my cousin, Tripp? Is he here?"

I wracked my brain as to why she would be part of Bruno's army.

"It's not what you think," she said as though she knew what I was thinking. "Can I have your shirt? I left all my clothes outside when I shifted."

I removed my ripped, soiled, and sweat-laden T-shirt then threw it to her. "So you don't work for Bruno?" Man, Tripp would have a cow if she were working for our enemy.

She made quick work of covering her body. "Um, can you put your fangs away?" Her dark-green eyes appraised me as she smoothed down my shirt, which hung low enough to cover her knees.

"Until I get blood, they're not going anywhere."

She raised an eyebrow then erased her expression before a long nail emerged on her forefinger. "Here." She dragged her sharp claw across her wrist. "Only a small amount. I know how you vampires can drain someone."

Immediately, the scent of iron permeated the air. I shook off the urge to take her offer. She needed to stay healthy to help us get out of there. "Save it. I'd prefer you offer blood to my team if we can find them."

She wiped the blood from her wrist as the skin knitted back

together. "I can't supply a whole team of vampires. So where is Tripp? Please tell me he's not here."

"He didn't accompany us on this mission," I said. "Why are you here?"

She flipped her hair behind her. "I'm a private investigator now. Tripp doesn't know yet. The Crowe family hired me. They felt that the vampire government wasn't doing anything to search for him."

The moans lessened. We didn't have much time to save those that needed saving.

I hopped over rocks and debris, following the moans. "Let's start digging."

She followed.

We settled on a small area where we heard two voices, one from a female and the other from a male.

As we moved rock, I said, "The vampire government is wrong. We've been searching for Crowe and Quade since their disappearance. We've never given up."

"Maybe not, but the family isn't seeing any results and hasn't been contacted by the military with an update in months. Do you think your commander is looking for you?"

I couldn't answer that, and at the moment, it didn't matter. What did matter was finding my team, then finding and contacting Jo to stop her, although my gut was telling me she was already in the arms of Bruno.

When we cleared an opening, Olivia's dirty, bloody, and bruised face came into view along with an unconscious Kraft, who had his fangs embedded in his bottom lip.

"They need blood," I said.

Crysta didn't hesitate. She slit her wrist again and shoved it against Olivia's mouth. I did the same to Kraft, although I didn't have much blood in me. Within seconds, Kraft was sucking on my wrist.

"Have you seen Crowe or Quade since you've been here?" Crysta asked as Olivia fed from her.

"Can't say I have. I've been drugged for the last three months."

She pulled her wrist away from Olivia. "Sorry, but pace yourself," she said to Olivia, whose pale face began to fill with color.

I tried to release Kraft, but the strong vampire wouldn't let go. "Kraft, enough," I ordered. "I haven't had much blood myself."

He growled then retracted his fangs before sitting up. "What happened? The last thing I remember was some grunt throwing me into my cell." Then he narrowed his eyes at Crysta. "What the hell are you doing here?"

Tension stretched between them.

"Nice to see you too, Kraft." Crysta's tone was sarcastic. "But we don't have time for ten questions. We need to find the others, and then get out of here. Before I shifted, I heard someone say that three explosions would occur. Bruno wanted to make sure there were no survivors."

And no evidence.

I helped Olivia to her feet. "There have been two so far."

Olivia wiped her lips as she wobbled. "We need to get to the lab that's topside. That's the last place I remember seeing Sloan and Kodiak."

"What about Crowe?" Crysta asked.

Olivia shrugged, and Crysta eyed Kraft.

"Don't look at me." Kraft's voice was scratchy. "I don't remember much except I thought I saw Edmund in the lab, standing over me while I was high on some drug."

I glanced up at the bridge. "Well, your eyes weren't seeing things. Bruno and Edmund are working together."

"Edmund Rain?" Crysta asked. "I heard about Jo Mason's court hearing. The chatter after that hearing was that Edmund is trying to build a vampire army."

"With Jo Mason's DNA," I said. Then I turned to Olivia and Kraft. "The bigger problem is Bruno has lured Jo to him. She's on her way to Alaska."

Olivia barely chuckled. "And how is she going to get away from her father?"

That was the million-dollar question since the commander kept her under lock and key. I couldn't worry about Jo for the moment. I had to pray she knew what she was doing. My goal was to get the fuck out of there and find that lab.

"Here's the plan," I said. "We need to quickly search the rocks and rubble for any signs of life. Then we'll need to build a staircase with rocks up to that bridge." I pointed up.

Crysta stabbed her thumb to my right. "There's sort of one near the far end. That's how I climbed down here to begin with."

Kraft sniffed the air as he sized her up. "You shifted. Is that Webb's shirt?"

I held up my hand. "Kraft, whatever you two have going on, deal with it later." It was clear they had some sort of relationship with "had" being the accurate conclusion. "Olivia and Kraft, scour the area ahead of us. Crysta and I will take this half. We'll meet at the base of the bridge. Make it quick."

Olivia and Kraft obeyed, even though Kraft growled his annoyance.

Crysta and I combed our area. "Do you have a phone anywhere?" I knew she didn't have one on her, but she should have one with her clothes.

"I do, but it's in my jacket outside."

That was the best news I'd had in a while. The phone meant a lifeline to Jo. "So how did you know where to find Crowe?"

"Got a tip from a colleague." She sniffed. "He heard some chatter on the streets in Miami that a shipment of powerful sentinel blood was due in soon. I started digging further with some of the lieutenants who run the gangs in Miami. One of them talked. He said Bruno was hiding out in Alaska. I've been living up here, watching and taking notes for months, until I got a break the other night at a club in Anchorage. Some human dude was drunk and spilled that he could get his hands on some powerful vampire blood. I tracked him here two days ago."

"Mm. I guess Bruno has been educating humans about vampires." That news wasn't something I needed to be worrying about.

I moved rocks, trying to listen for any signs of life, but I heard nothing. I prayed Kodiak and Sloan were still alive. I didn't hold out too much hope that Crowe and Quade were, not if Bruno had been draining blood out of them for over a year. Then another horrifying thought hit me like a fucking hurricane. Jo could be facing the same fate as Quade and Crowe.

8

—————

JO

I wanted to jump out of the deathtrap of an airplane. I'd never been in one before, and given that Webb's plane had crashed, I wasn't all that enamored with being in one.

Yet there I was, holding on to the armrests for dear life, as Sam looked completely calm across from me. The plane had seats that faced each other and a table that was bolted to the floor in between us.

"What are you thinking?" I asked. We hadn't said much since we were shoved into the private jet.

He tossed a look over his shoulder to where the guards sat, playing cards. They hadn't given us so much as the time of day. We couldn't exactly escape, although the thought of hijacking the plane had crossed my mind. The only thing stopping me was the fact neither Sam nor I could fly a plane.

Sam turned his attention back to me. "What trap are we walking into? This Bruno guy isn't just going to hand over Webb or the sentinels if they're alive."

I mashed my lips together hard. Webb better be alive or else people were going to die.

The guard facing me, who I called beard man, glanced up from his cards. It was hard to tell the men apart since both had large builds, buzz cuts, and rough-looking features. I'd asked both of them their names, and all they had done was raise an eyebrow. So bearded man it was.

"Hey beard man, do you know if Webb and the sentinels are alive?" I didn't think he would answer or know, but it wouldn't hurt to ask.

He grimaced. "Don't know. Don't care. Our mission is to deliver you both to Bruno."

Sam popped to his feet. "If you can."

Rising, the other guard laughed. "You do know we're on an airplane. So you're not getting out of here."

Sam and the non-bearded guard got into the other's face.

"Easy, Howell. Remember, we need them alive *for now*." Bearded man emphasized the last two words.

Growling, Howell bared his fangs before he disappeared into the bathroom in the back of the plane. Sam leaned against a seat.

"So we now know Howell's name," I said. "Care to clue us in on yours?"

He huffed almost like a child. "All you need to know is Smith."

"Well, Smith," I said. "Get word to your boss that we want to see Webb London alive and standing on the tarmac when we land. If not, you'll wish you never met us."

A muscle jumped in his jaw. "Are you threatening me?"

Sam chuckled, although the sound was demeaning. "It's more of a promise."

Smith shook his head. "Why not? It's your death, not mine." He unfolded his large body then pounded up the tight aisle, brushing Sam's shoulder.

Sam dropped his fangs, his eyes turning to a molten black. My brother looked downright scary when he was angry and about to attack.

"Calm down, Sam," I said.

Smith ignored Sam and kept going until he reached the galley, where he picked up the receiver. "Get Bruno on the phone." A beat passed before Smith said, "Yeah, Boss. The girl wanted me to relay a message."

"Put her on. Let me hear it from her." Bruno's voice blasted in the small cabin, or maybe it was my sensitive hearing.

I hurried to pluck the phone from Smith. "I—"

"Your precious Webb is alive if that's what you're worried about," Bruno said evenly.

"Then make sure Webb is standing beside you when we land."

Bruno roared with laughter. "Or what?"

"Do you know much about me?" I asked in a soft tone, trying to hold back my anger. With any little outburst, I could bring down the plane, and I wasn't ready to do that. So I blew out a breath.

"I know more than you think." Bruno sounded proud.

My ears began to pop. "Then tell me."

"I know you have a unique DNA makeup that Edmund Rain wants. I know that I'm about to make millions just delivering you to Edmund."

Not if I could help it. "So why my brother?"

"Ah. You don't know, do you? He doesn't either, I take it." He laughed. "The medical records we stole from the lab show your brother has almost the same DNA makeup as you. In fact, he just might be more powerful than you and your father combined."

My eyes found Sam's now green ones. He angled his head before his voice was in my head. *He just confirmed our suspicions.*

I fidgeted where I stood. "We had a deal, Bruno. Me for Webb. My brother has no stake in the game."

Bruno raised his voice. "Tell that to Edmund."

My fangs descended as I bit my lower lip. Suddenly, the plane dropped several hundred feet.

Smith's face paled as he grabbed onto the stainless counter. "What was that?"

"Jo," Sam said. "Relax."

"What's going on?" Bruno asked.

The plane dropped again as I tried to rein in the rage coursing through me.

The pilot came on the overhead speaker. "Take your seats. I'm not sure what's happening, but the plane is out of control."

"Are you the cause of the turbulence?" Smith asked, his voice breaking up.

"Bruno, have Webb on the tarmac or else you won't get your millions." I hung up and stared at Smith. "Seriously, you have no idea the power I can wield."

He puffed out his pale white cheeks as I headed for my seat. When I sat down, the turbulence stopped.

"I know you won't kill us but cool it. I'm not exactly fond of flying," Sam said.

Smith staggered down the aisle then banged on the bathroom door. "Howell, are you okay?"

I smiled. I shouldn't be so smug since my stomach was trying to recover from the roller-coaster ride.

"Okay," the pilot said. "We're ten minutes out, so stay seated."

The snowcapped mountains drew closer as the plane lowered in the sky. I gazed out the window, thinking of a plan we didn't have. My heart kicked into gear as the vast terrain got closer and closer. Then doubt took hold for the third or fourth time. I'd lost count. All I kept thinking about was my dad and how furious he would be or already was. I wanted to laugh. I was more worried about how my dad would react than whatever craziness Sam and I were walking into. *Stop thinking of the worst. Webb is alive. You're doing this for him. Your father will understand.* I wasn't so sure.

You need to do whatever you can to get away, I said telepathically to Sam. I didn't want him in any danger.

No. You heard Bruno. Edmund wants us both.

Do you believe him about your DNA? They could be bluffing.

Sam rubbed a hand down his thigh. *They're not. Edmund wouldn't include me unless he knew for sure my DNA matched yours.*

As the plane came in for a landing, Howell and Smith hurried into their seats.

I gripped the armrests as nausea swished around in my stomach. From my window, I couldn't see anything except mountains.

No sooner had the tires screeched on the runway, than Smith bolted out of his seat with Howell on his heels. They converged in the galley area as they waited for the plane to stop taxiing down the runway.

My brain scrambled for a plan while Sam unsnapped his seat belt, ducked into the row across from us, and peeked out the window. Then he tossed a look of despair over his shoulder. I joined him as a chill skated over my spine. The tarmac was empty. No cars. No Bruno. I went to every window to see if civilization even existed beyond the mountains. Nothing.

"Where's Bruno?" I demanded as I closed my hands, digging my nails into my palms. The plane shook lightly.

Howell crossed his large arms over his chest. "Sit down."

I drilled my gaze into Howell's dark eyes. The longer I glared at him, the more the plane rocked from one side to the other.

"Stop." Smith said as he pushed Howell out of the way. "Bruno will be here shortly."

"Was that hard?" My words dripped with sarcasm as I unclenched my fists and the plane stopped rocking like a boat in rough seas.

We heard two clicks, and the cockpit door opened.

I sniffed the air. The short squat pilot was human. Human blood always smelled sweeter than vampire blood. Humans also had a slight sense of fear around us as though they knew what we were. Maybe the pilot did, although in my world, a vampire could get thrown in jail if they educated humans on our species.

I have an idea, I said to Sam. *Can you compel everyone?*

Normally, a vampire's compelling power was done through eye contact. But Sam had mastered the ability to compel the mind with a magic spell made of a series of numbers, thanks in part to our classes with Ms. Costner. She'd taught us that one could spark different spells with the right combination of numbers.

You know it takes the energy from me, and I need to be able to fight.

We're not fighting, I returned. *We're hijacking the plane.*

Smith unlatched the door, pushed a button, and the stairs lowered. Brisk air seeped in.

"Get ready," I said to Sam as I walked up to Howell.

"In a hurry to die?" Howell asked excitedly.

"Maybe. I want to see if Bruno met my demands. Do you mind?"

He backed away with his hands in the air. "Your funeral."

I laughed. "Then bring flowers."

Smith and the pilot also didn't stop me as I shuffled up to the open door. A black SUV rolled to a stop, and a tall, white-haired vampire slid out.

I held up my hand and unleashed my power, building an invisible wall between us.

"Where's Webb?" I asked, trying to see into the SUV.

The white-haired vampire drew close. "It's nice to finally meet you, Jo." His voice confirmed that he was Bruno.

Aside from a man inside the vehicle, I didn't see anyone else— no Webb and definitely no sentinels. I darted my gaze in all directions. No other cars were approaching or anywhere in sight.

Bruno put his foot on the first step. "Don't worry. Edmund isn't here yet. I have one thing to do before I turn you and your brother over to him."

"I told you to bring Webb. Where is he?"

Bruno climbed to the second step. When he did, his head hit the invisible wall. He stumbled backward. "Nice one. I see you are as powerful as Edmund says."

"Answer the question." With my hand still in the air, I brought my fingers together to form a fist.

Bruno grabbed hold of his neck with his gnarly fingers. "Stop, and I'll tell you." His voice was strained.

A bald man jumped out of the SUV and ran to Bruno's side.

I loosened my fist. "Answer me." My tone was hard as I quickly checked behind me.

Smith, Howell, and the pilot had faraway glints in their eyes.

Sam dropped his shoulders then shook his head. "Compelling zaps my energy."

"Get the pilot ready," I said to Sam then turned my attention back to Bruno. "You didn't bring Webb with you?"

Bruno coughed, still holding his neck. "You have no recourse, Jo."

"And you don't either. If you want your millions, then I suggest you find it elsewhere because I will kill you before you or Edmund get your hands on us."

Bruno ran up the stairs only to be thrown backward.

"Close the doors," Sam said to someone.

Within a second, the stairs began to close.

"Your vampire is dead," Bruno shouted. "All of them. Dead."

I sucked in a sharp breath as the plane's engines sounded.

"There's not enough fuel for you to get very far," Bruno shouted again.

We had enough to get away from him. As soon as the stairs were tucked in and the door closed, the plane taxied down the runaway along with my heart.

Sam drew me in for a hug. "Webb isn't dead."

I wished I could believe him, but all my senses told me Bruno wasn't bluffing.

9

WEBB

The bone-chilling air and graying sky were welcome reliefs to the dark and suffocating air of the dungeon. I dropped to the ground and almost kissed the black pavement. Behind me, Olivia, Crysta, and Kraft emerged through a metal door that had been carved into the mountainside.

Olivia labored for breath as she bent over. "Oh my God. We made it."

"Yeah," Kraft chimed in. "I didn't think we could scale the rocks to get to that bridge."

I pushed to my feet, inhaling all the cold air I could. "Thanks to Crysta." Without her, we wouldn't have made it out. She was the only one who was strong enough to finish piling the rocks to form stairs up to the bridge. Olivia, Kraft, and I needed blood badly. Otherwise, we would be of no use in saving ourselves.

A quick scan of the area showed that a wide dirt road dissected the snow-covered forest across from us. A metal-sided building sat about a quarter mile to my right, and the scent of death lingered somewhere close by.

"I'll be right back." Crysta darted across the road then disappeared into the woods.

I pointed to the building. "Let's see what's inside. Maybe we can find blood and supplies and a phone. I have to get to Jo."

"She'll be fine," Olivia said. "I know that won't soothe your nerves, but you've got to trust that she can handle herself."

The softness of her voice did nothing to soothe my nerves. "Let's go." I had to keep moving and believe in Olivia's words. Otherwise, I wouldn't be able to think straight.

Kraft's long legs ate up the pavement. "There better be some blood in that building."

Olivia chuckled. "Can I wish that maybe we would find a shower in there?"

Kraft slapped her on the back. "I'm wishing too."

Fuck showers. Phone, blood, and supplies were the only things on my mind. Not to mention, the need to kill my enemies. As I trudged across the open lot to the ominous building, my decision to drop off the radar burned brightly in my mind. Stealth was the key to taking down Bruno and Edmund. *But you will be considered AWOL if you disappear.* I didn't care. I'd always been a good soldier, trained to serve and protect. I'd always taken orders from Commander Mason even though I might not have agreed with his decisions. But Jo's life was in danger. She was my life, and I would do anything to save her.

A hard wind blew, stinging my face and drawing my attention to the dark clouds rolling in.

"We may have to stay put for the night," I said. "Looks like a storm is on the horizon."

The wind whipped Olivia's long brown hair in all directions. "Not a good idea, Lieutenant. Find blood and anyone alive then get our asses out of here. I get the eerie feeling someone is watching us."

"We also have to be aware of that third explosion that Crysta mentioned," Kraft said.

Crysta bounded up to my side, dressed in jeans and bundled in a parka.

"Where's your phone?" I asked.

She gave me a weak smile. "Sorry, dude. No signal."

Raking a hand through my dirty hair, I uttered several curse words. It could be days or weeks before we hiked out of the mountains.

Olivia lightly touched my arm. "Lieutenant, the faster we check the building for blood and supplies, the faster we can get moving. We need to feed or else we won't get far. And if there's nothing in that building for us, then we hunt. But we've got to do it now."

I wanted to punch something. But she was right. We wouldn't be able to do much if we weren't one hundred percent. Once we were, our vampire senses and powers would get us farther quicker.

I sighed heavily. "Check every room for bodies and survival gear. We operate as though the building is set to blow. Get in. Get out. Then we'll find a place in the forest to settle for the night."

"There's an abandoned cabin five miles south of here," Crysta said. "I used it to lay low until this morning."

"We'll rendezvous back here in ten minutes. Got it?" I pinned a look on each of them, and everyone gave me a nod.

I glanced at Crysta. "In case we find a phone that works, what part of Alaska are we in?"

"We're southwest of Fairbanks in the Denali National Park."

"Our intel on Bruno had been the Chugach Mountains, which is why we haven't been rescued," Olivia said.

Even if the commander had searched the area of the Chugach Mountains, it would have been difficult to find anyone. Before I led the team inside, I checked the doorway and immediate vicinity for any signs of a tripwire. Once I was sure the coast was clear, I stepped into the U-shaped hallway, where a stairwell divided the building in half.

"Kraft and Crysta, you two go up. Olivia, take the hall to our left. I'll head right. Again, make it quick," I ordered a little too curtly.

With no weapons, we had no way of protecting ourselves. Not only that, our vampire strength was greatly diminished until we fed. I cautiously poked my head into the first room I came to. Boxes filled with IV bags, needles, gauze pads, and other medical supplies littered the room. I found a smaller box containing syringes filled with clear liquid. I stuffed a few in my pocket. I had no idea what type of medicine was in them, but my guess was that it was a sedative of sorts. They could come in handy as a weapon.

The next room had a counter and a chair that people would sit in to give blood. On the wall beside the chair was a phone. I was about to pick it up when Olivia shouted.

I bolted out of the room and took off, following Olivia's scream. When I ran into the room she had found, I froze. Olivia's mouth was agape as she stood over Kodiak, who was laid out on a stretcher.

Kraft and Crysta came running in. They both stopped dead in their tracks beside me.

"What the fuck?" Kraft asked.

I shook off the shock, taking in my surroundings. Operating-type tables dotted the room, and sheets were draped over what appeared to be dead bodies. I prayed like a priest that Sloan wasn't under one of those sheets, or Quade and Crowe for that matter. I didn't have time to let my emotions get the best of me. So I snapped into soldier mode. We had to get the fuck out of this place. That thought was cemented even more so when I spotted a timer bolted to the back wall. I followed the wire down to the floor, and my eyes bugged out at the pile of C-4.

I began removing sheets from the dead bodies. "We got three minutes before this place blows. Kraft, snap to it. Help me check these tables. Crysta, see if you can find any blood or food supplies in that fridge in the corner. Olivia, is Kodiak alive?"

As Kraft and I tore sheets from dead bodies, Olivia pulled out the IV from Kodiak's arm. When she did, the hulking vampire bolted upright before he fell back.

I ran to her. "Get one side of him. I'll get the other." We lifted the pale-faced vampire off the table. As we did, his fangs shot out, and he roared like a beast that had just been woken from a winter slumber. Then he bit Olivia on the arm.

She punched him directly in the head. "Well, he's alive."

I grabbed him by the hair and pulled. "Kodiak, it's Olivia and Webb. We're here to help."

Kodiak whirled around, baring his fangs at me.

I let go of him, raising my hands in the air. "It's me, man."

He shook his head, growling, his vampire black eyes burning with the need for blood.

"We need to get out of here," I said to him.

His Adam's apple bobbed before he blinked several times. "I'm going to kill Bruno."

"Get in line," Olivia said. "Now, give me your arm so I can help you out of here."

I checked the timer. "One minute and thirty seconds. Get moving."

Crysta had two bags of blood in her hands. Kraft had managed to uncover every body. Out of the ten, I only recognized one.

I swallowed hard. "Is Sloan dead?"

Kraft pressed his ear to Sloan's chest then slapped Sloan hard in the face—once, then twice. "He's not responding."

I scanned the bodies but didn't see Quade or Crowe.

"Shit. No sign of Crowe," Crysta said as she backed away to the door.

"Kraft, help Olivia with Kodiak. All of you, get out."

Kraft ran to Olivia and Kodiak, then all of them hobbled out.

"Come on, Webb." Crysta's voice was hard.

"I'm right behind you. I need to get Sloan." We never left a man behind, dead or alive. With all the strength I had left in me, I hauled him off the table and slung him over my shoulder. Then I ran as fast as I could out of the room and down the hall. No sooner had I opened the door to the outside world, than the building shook. The ceiling rained down as shards of glass embedded in my skin. The last thing I heard was Olivia scream my name before I was propelled through the air. Then everything went black.

10

JO

I sat in the cockpit next to the gray-haired pilot, who stared out the window as if he were a zombie. In actuality, he was. Whenever anyone was compelled, their eyes glazed over. The good thing, though, was that they followed any and all orders given to them. The whole process mimicked hypnosis, although unlike hypnosis, where the subject was drawn out of his state by the snap of the fingers, the compelling spell would wear off gradually in an hour at most.

Sam came in. "Howell and Smith are playing cards like good soldiers. Also, Howell said that Bruno was keeping prisoners at some place in the Denali forest. Is that true?" Sam asked the pilot.

The best part of compelling someone was that they always obeyed as though they were injected with a truth serum. Unfortunately, I couldn't command the subjects since I didn't cast the spell.

"It is," the pilot said. "But Bruno had the place wired to blow. You're out of luck." His tone was somewhat sarcastic as though he was about to come out of Sam's control.

I pinched my eyebrows at Sam as my heart sputtered. Webb was dead. I shook off the thought. I had to see for myself. "Tell the pilot to take us there," I said to Sam.

"You heard him," Sam said to me in a flat tone. "Bruno blew up the place. Probably no survivors."

"I don't care. I want to check it out." As vampires, we were resilient at most times or could heal quickly when hurt. I was hoping that was the case with Webb or anyone from his team.

Sam studied me for a second. "Do we have enough fuel?"

"We have enough to get us to the compound," the pilot said out of nowhere.

I almost hugged the pilot.

"Then take us there," Sam ordered.

The pilot banked right like a good soldier. As he did, I fell into the side of the cockpit's window. When he leveled out the plane, smoke rose in the distance. An eerie sense of déjà vu blanketed me. It wasn't that long ago when I was rescued from sea that I'd come home to fire and devastation, thinking that my family was dead.

The plane slowly lowered, but it was teetering like a playground seesaw. I knew I wasn't the cause. My anger was nowhere in sight.

"It's windy," the pilot said, gripping the wheel.

A gust of wind rocked the plane hard, and my stomach rocked with it as we approached a narrow dirt road.

My pulse began sprinting. "You can't land there."

"I do it all the time." Even in a zombie state, the pilot was cool and confident.

Trees crowded both sides of the landing strip, and I swore I could touch them from where I sat.

I held my breath while Sam paled. I opened all my senses as I set my sights on the smoke and fire.

One side of the pilot's mouth quirked up. "Well, it looks like you're out of luck."

The wheels touched down before we bounced once, twice, then a third time. As the plane came to a stop, a beautiful woman emerged through the smoke as though she was expecting us. Her red hair billowed behind her as though the smoke had claws and was pulling her back into the melee.

Sam disappeared for a second then stuck his head back into the cockpit. "Howell and Smith are still under my command, but not for long, and I can't compel them again, at least not without losing more energy." He glanced out the cockpit window. "What in the world?" Then he banked around the bathroom toward the door.

I jumped out of my seat. "Sam, don't open that door." We had to take every precaution. "She may be one of Bruno's people."

He pressed a button on the wall. "We can't just sit here." The door slowly opened, and the stairs began to unfold.

"Let me at least build an invisible wall until we can confirm if she's with Bruno or not."

The redhead approached.

I held up my hands, emitting the energy I needed to build an invisible wall—a feat I was super good at now. "Stop right there."

She climbed the stairs or at least tried to until her head hit the wall. She narrowed her green gaze at us. "What the hell? How in the world did you do that?"

My nostrils flared. "That's not important."

"Who are you?" Sam asked.

She glanced up, her green eyes ablaze with concern. "My name is Crysta. I don't want any trouble."

"Do you work for Bruno?" I asked.

"Look, I don't have time for ten questions. I need help. We have a man badly hurt."

I climbed down the stairs, lowering the invisible wall. Then I reached out and took her hand. She flinched. I sniffed before I dipped into her mind. She wasn't human, but she wasn't vampire either. Her scent smelled like a dog that one of my foster families had. Since I hadn't been a vampire that long, I didn't know of all the other species that lived among us, although I knew Tripp had mentioned he came from a lineage of wolf shifters.

"Is she telling the truth?" Sam asked.

Her mind was filled with dead bodies. As I sifted through her brain, I gasped. "She was with Webb."

All of sudden, Sam barreled into me like a bowling ball, almost knocking Crysta and me over. I stumbled before I steadied myself. When I turned, Howell was standing at the entrance to the plane with a smirk on his face.

Just as he was about to stalk down to us, Smith caught him. "Leave them. They'll die out here. There's nothing left. The storm will slow them down, anyway."

A snowflake fell before me.

"The spell wore off," Sam muttered.

The stairs folded up.

Sam launched at the stairs. "We need that plane to get out of here."

I caught up to him. "Don't. They won't get far. Remember, not enough fuel. Besides, this girl knows about Webb."

Another snowflake fluttered to the ground.

Howell sneered. "I pray our paths cross again, vampire."

Sam flipped him the finger. "Until we meet again."

The door shut as the engines roared to life.

Crysta grabbed us both and ushered us into the woods.

The plane's engine grew softer as it taxied out of sight.

Without a word, Sam clamped a hand on Crysta's throat. "What do you know about Webb?"

I tugged on my brother's shirt. "Sam, let her go."

When he walked away, she rubbed her long neck. I grasped her free hand and resumed reading her mind. Her thoughts were all about Sam and how good-looking she thought my brother was. Okay, I wasn't divulging that information. Not that it was a secret, but it was her admission to tell, not mine. On top of Sam's good looks, she kept replaying a scene that made me want to puke. Webb had been walking out of a building when it exploded. His body flew through the air until his head hit a rock.

"Talk," Sam said with a bite to his tone.

All her thoughts of Webb vanished.

Huffing, I let go of her. "I almost had the information we needed."

"You read minds?" Her perfectly shaped eyebrows drew down. "You must be Jo Mason."

I shouldn't have been surprised she knew my name. Most of the vampire world did. I'd become a bit famous within the vampire community after my murder hearing. Word had gotten around that I had unique powers. Well, that, and I'd been acquitted of all murder charges. Dad wasn't exactly jumping up and down with joy about any of it, although he was happy that I hadn't ended up in a vampire prison off the coast of Puerto Rico, where they sent vampires who were convicted of murdering one of their own.

A branch snapped, drawing our attention to the dense forest behind us. I stiffened and readied my hands to wield my one go-to power that would stop anyone without killing them. As I blinked, Olivia came into focus. Her long dark hair was wild as though she'd been in a fight with an animal. Her clothes were ripped in most places, and her fangs were dripping with blood.

"Jo? Sam?" she said before she yelled, "Kraft, over here."

I ran, stopping inches from her. "Is Webb alive? Tell me." My heartbeat was erratic.

Her chest heaved. Then she dropped her gaze.

Kraft swatted at branches with his tattooed arms as he emerged. Blood covered his mouth as though he'd been feeding. Like Olivia, his clothes were shredded in most places. His once shoulder-length blond hair had grown longer, and he sported a thick beard.

"Where's Webb?" I asked again as my stomach curdled with nausea.

Kraft and Olivia exchanged a forlorn glance.

More branches snapped before Kodiak stalked out from in between the trees. "Webb isn't going to make it."

"Why would you say that?" Olivia snarled.

Kodiak lifted a large shoulder as his lifeless green eyes scanned my face. "It's the truth."

Sam grabbed my hand. "Where is he?"

Thank God for my brother. I was tongue-tied for some reason as I continued to stare at Kodiak. He'd never been one to beat around the bush about anything. My dad had had a couple of problems with Kodiak's crass attitude.

Crysta took hold of my other hand. "Come with us, Jo. Maybe Webb will respond to you. He hit his head pretty hard, and he's lost a lot of blood." Her soothing voice did nothing to quell the uneasiness inside me.

My pulse pounded in my ears as we trudged through the falling snow and thick leaves. *Please let Webb live.* I kept repeating that in my head.

Olivia and Kraft led the way, while Kodiak took up the rear.

"Can someone fill us in on what's happened to you guys since you left the base three months ago?" Sam asked.

"Bruno," Kodiak said his name as though Bruno was the devil. "That man has a target on his forehead. I don't care if I spend the rest of my life looking for him; I will kill him."

"Get in line," Olivia and Kraft said in unison.

I had my own reasons to see that Bruno got what was coming to him, but first, we had to take care of Webb. I couldn't lose him. I couldn't go on in life without him. The last three months had been unbearable, not knowing if he was dead or alive. The only thing that had kept me from losing my sanity was hope. The old cliché that no news was good news certainly helped me get out of bed every day. Even now as we wound through the forest, hope still bloomed along with despair. What if Kodiak was right? What if Webb didn't make it? Vampires had very few ways they could die, and Webb hitting his head on a rock wasn't one of them, although losing a lot of blood could contribute to his demise.

"Why haven't any of you given him blood?" I asked as my brain began to awaken with tons of questions. In my world, we normally didn't drink from other vampires unless it was an emergency or, as Webb had schooled me, when two vampires had an intimate connection.

Butterflies took flight as I remembered back to the night I had to drink from Webb in the woods behind the base. I'd just been rescued from sea and was in desperate need of blood. But at the time, I was a newborn vampire and could only drink my father's blood. Webb had considered my dire need for blood an extreme emergency. I'd argued with him, albeit weakly. I'd lost the argument, and as soon as his blood touched my tongue, sweet and sinful, my body came alive. Heat rushed upward and pinched my cheeks as though a hot fireplace poker had touched them. Then his emotions poured into me. It was at that moment that I knew Webb was mine forever.

Sam nudged me, catapulting me back to the present. "Look." He dipped his head to a bed of leaves.

I tore from Crysta and Sam's hold and ran to Webb. He lay on the ground with his hands resting on his bare muscular stomach. His pale skin beamed in the darkening forest. Tears rushed out as I dropped to the ground. "Hey, it's me. I'm here now." I placed a trembling hand over his heart. His pulse was faint, but I could hear the blood pumping through him.

Olivia knelt down beside me. "We didn't feed him because we're all very weak from Bruno draining us for three months. We found a few bags of blood, but we lost them in the explosion. So we were hunting to replenish our system. Crysta can't give him any either. He would drain her."

"It looks like the three of you found blood," I said. "So we need to start a line. Let's force blood into him little by little. That way, we don't weaken anyone. Sam and I will go first since we're healthy." We would do whatever we had to do. I didn't care if Webb drained me, as long as he lived.

Sam joined me on my left near Webb's head. "I'll go first." He pulled a knife out of his boot then slit his wrist.

I was about to ask him where he got the knife, but I was certain it was from one of the guards. Besides, it didn't matter. The scent of blood wafted around us. Crysta came around and settled across from us before she opened Webb's mouth. Sam's blood dripped onto Webb's tongue, and with each drop, my heart broke into pieces and knitted back together at the same time. It was odd how my emotions were mixed. It pained me to see Webb almost comatose, but I was also elated that he was alive. My soaring pulse was a testament to my wild emotions.

Kraft walked up to stand near Webb's head then stole the knife from Sam. "It's my turn."

I was about to protest, when Kraft pinned his mahogany-colored gaze on me, indicating not to challenge him. If I'd learned anything about military life, it was that SEALs wanted to protect and save their brethren. Once Kraft had sliced open his skin, he pressed his wrist to Webb's mouth.

Crysta stood, pulled out her phone, and tapped the screen. "Still no signal. We need to get to higher ground."

All of us ignored Crysta as Kodiak and Olivia took their turns feeding Webb. I was about to slit my wrist when Webb's eyes flew open. Immediately, he homed in on me. Then with vampire speed, he jumped up, grabbed me, then darted into the woods.

"Webb?" Crysta shouted.

"Give him a few minutes," Olivia said. "He's not going far."

I wasn't protesting. Webb was on his feet, and I was in his arms. I'd prayed for so long that this moment would come. Happy tears coursed down my face as Webb ran deeper into the forest. I held onto his neck tightly, listening to his heartbeat. The sound made my own heart soar. God, he felt like heaven against me, although he needed a shower. But that didn't matter. I would take him any way, any how, and with any scent. The man of my dreams, the one I was so deeply in love with, was holding me.

Then, as though the wind died and life around us stopped, so did the voices in the distance. Webb came to a halt under a massive tree. Without a word, he anchored me against the tree trunk and scanned every part of my face, as though he was programming me. I grabbed my hair and pulled it to one side, exposing my neck. His fangs shot out as he pressed his body into mine. It was all I could do not to squirm. I nodded as my body heated from head to toe. Webb had never taken my blood, and I'd never given my blood to anyone either. I didn't know if I would feel pain. Then again, I would take all the pain if it meant that Webb and I were together.

My breathing grew shallow as he raked his cloudy blue gaze over my face and neck. I almost laughed at the irony of where we were. When I drank from him, we'd been in the woods. When he told me he loved me, we had been in the woods. Now, he held me as though he was holding onto a lifeline, and we were once again in a dense forest. I suddenly realized that if we ever got married, I just might consider a wooded ceremony.

His rough palm touched my cheek as his gaze rested on my neck.

I leaned into him. "It's okay. You won't hurt me."

His fangs grazed just below my ear. I shivered in delight. Then he pressed his entire body farther into me. Bark poked into my back, but all I felt were lots and lots of tingles. Before I could move, Webb struck, his fangs piercing my skin. If there was supposed to be pain, I didn't feel it. The world around me narrowed. More tingles slid down to settle in my belly. Suddenly, it was as though I was careening down a waterfall, flying, free as a bird with stars twinkling above me. If this was euphoria, then I wanted more. I wanted to stay glued to Webb as my blood flowed into him.

I opened a telepathic connection. When I did, two things hit me. His voice was as smooth as silk in my head. *I'm so in love with you.* Then I was reading his mind. He was flitting through all the nastiness that Bruno had put him through. How he was chained to a wall. How he was near death, angry, and gave up hope that he would ever see me again.

Tears burned hot and bright as I took his journey with him. He wanted to kill Bruno for what he'd done. He wanted to hide me away until all our enemies were dead. His heart pumped faster than it ever had. His cells were coming alive. Hell, I was alive with more need for him than ever before.

Your father has no say in us anymore. His tone in my head was lethal.

The word father made me flinch. He was probably furious. No, scratch that. Dad was certainly beyond furious. But this wasn't the moment to worry about my father. I was with Webb, and I would take all my father's rage for disappearing without telling him.

Webb retracted his fangs then peppered kisses along my neck before he edged back. Gone was the pale vampire I'd seen when I first dropped to my knees. A sparkle shimmered in his blue eyes as he licked the remaining blood from his chapped lips.

I flattened my palms on the sides of his rough bearded face. "Better?"

He answered by plunging his tongue into my mouth. His kiss was desperate, frantic, and oh, so good. I met him, tasting and taking what I'd daydreamed about for the past three months.

Someone cleared her throat. Webb growled as he released my lips.

"We need to find shelter for the night," Crysta said. "The snow is getting worse."

Webb kept me close to him. "Where's Sloan's body?"

Kraft, Sam, Kodiak, and Olivia fanned out behind Crysta as though she was their leader. Big flakes were falling at a rapid rate, but the trees caught most of the snow.

Olivia stepped around Crysta. "We set his body down five yards back."

"We carry him with us," Webb said, firm and strong.

"What happened to Sloan? Is he alive?" I'd forgotten he'd been part of the mission.

"What about the two sentinels that you were supposed to rescue?" Sam asked.

Webb peered down at me. "Sloan didn't make it."

A pain shot through my heart. Soldiers always went into battle with the threat of death. Still, war or no war, it didn't make it any easier to hear that Sloan was dead.

"We can't carry him as we find our way out of here," Crysta said. She was the only one among us who had a coat and hat and was bundled for this type of weather.

Since I hadn't experienced extreme cold temperatures as a vampire, I wasn't sure how my body would react to only wearing a sweater. At that thought, I shivered.

"He comes with us until we can bury him," Webb said firmly. "Besides, would you want us to leave your cousin, Tripp, behind if he were dead?"

Sam and I exchanged a wide-eyed look.

"Are you the cousin that Tripp put into a coma?" I asked, remembering the conversation Sam and I had had with Tripp. He'd given his cousin some of his blood, and the aftereffects had caused her to drop into a coma for over a year.

Crysta's dark-green eyes grew big. "He told you about that?"

"Focus," Webb said. "Sam, you take the first leg and carry Sloan. Right now, you're the strongest."

Sam nodded.

Crysta didn't argue. I imagined Webb's point about Tripp had hit her right in the gut.

Sam and the rest of the sentinels took off, leaving Webb, Crysta, and me alone.

Crysta sidled up to Webb and touched his arm. "I'm sorry. I don't want to leave anyone behind either, but the conditions and the environment we're in don't give us the latitude to save everyone. The longer we're in these mountains with winter setting in, the less chance of survival for any of us."

Webb hugged me to him. "Let's not forget that we're at the top of the food chain. You can shift to protect yourself. As far as the rest of us, we can withstand the cold. Plus, the wildlife in the area is food for all of us."

I wasn't stoked about drinking blood from an animal. I'd tried to snag a wolf once, but I hadn't been successful.

"One encounter with a bear, and he'll rip your head off," she countered.

I tensed. Up until now, I would die to save Webb. But now that he was alive and I was securely tucked into his arms, fear coursed through me. I would die fighting the enemy, but a bear? That idea froze the blood in my veins.

Webb narrowed his eyes at Crysta. "You said yourself there's a cabin five miles from here. We head for that cabin before the snow gets too heavy. We'll settle there for the night. End of discussion."

Sam and the sentinels emerged with Sloan draped over Sam's shoulder. Once we were all together, we set out, following Crysta, who took the lead. Webb held my hand as we trailed behind the group. All was right in my world for the moment, although that feeling of weightlessness wouldn't last long, especially once we contacted my father.

11

WEBB

The boarded-up cabin came into view, and the log building was a sight for sore eyes. The five-mile trek there had been excruciatingly painful, both physically and mentally. I still hungered for blood, but I also had this desperate need to whisk Jo away. During the entire hike, I'd wanted to hear how Sam and Jo escaped Bruno, but I couldn't concentrate. One, I was elated that she was even with me. I wanted to enjoy how her soft hand felt in mine and how she smelled of lavender and all woman. Fuck, was she a woman. She'd filled out in all the right places, more so since I'd last seen her. And two, my head was cloudy, almost dizzy from ingesting Jo's blood, and I wanted a clear head to ask questions. I was beginning to understand why Bruno was stealing vampire blood. Sure, I'd taken blood from other sentinels when I'd needed it in battle, but it had never affected me the way Jo's had. Even now as I put one foot in front of the other, I had to shake off the high. I swayed as I tried to clear my vision.

"Hey," Jo said, her silky voice sliding along my arms. "Are you okay? That head injury got to you, didn't it?"

Without a doubt, I knew my semi-drunken state was due to her blood. I'd felt the tingly feeling the moment her blood filled my mouth. The more I'd drunk from her, the more the dizzy feeling blanketed me. I'd also started to see her visions. When I drank her blood, it was as though I was seeing things through her eyes. I'd seen her sitting next to Ben Jackson, laughing and having a good time. That sight was enough to make my blood boil, and not because she was laughing. Ben wanted her in a girlfriend-boyfriend kind of relationship. I wasn't about to deny that I was jealous. As a vampire, I was very territorial. All vampires were. We went to extremes to protect those we loved, more so when we had an intimate connection. I'd never had this strong of a pull to someone in my life, but the need to love, protect, and kill for Jo was stronger than ever.

Crysta ran up the porch steps to the cabin and knocked.

Kraft drew up alongside her. "Really, wolf?" He kicked in the door without any hesitation. "After you."

"Ass," Crysta muttered as she entered the cabin.

With the exception of Jo and me, the rest of the group trampled in behind Crysta. Kodiak trailed with Sloan draped over his shoulder. The men had taken turns carrying Sloan. I'd offered, but all agreed that I was too weak. I hadn't argued. I would've dropped Sloan with the first step I took.

Just as Jo climbed the steps to the porch, I grabbed her arm. She gave me one of her award-winning smiles as her silver eyes glistened beneath the darkened sky. I ran a hand through her wet hair as I continued to drink in every inch of her beauty. I had fucking missed her. I wanted to curl up with her and sleep. Who was I kidding? I wanted to do more than sleep. Yet at the moment, I couldn't get past the determination in her eyes that said she was ready to take on the world.

"What's different about you?" I wanted nothing more than to run the backs of my fingers over her naked stomach, much like I'd done when we were lying in my living room at my house in Maine. That night was so serene with the ocean's waves crashing along the shore, the sound trickling in through the windows.

Her eyes flashed from silver to violet, a color change like no other vampire, a sign that she was the chosen one in our world. Her father worried constantly about her and how her powers would change our lives. At first, I didn't believe a vampire could be stronger than Commander Mason. Part of me still didn't. He was feared among our kind for the mere fact that he was capable of elemental magic. As a sentinel, I had the ability to control three of the elements. But control of all four was reserved for the commander. Not even Jo had the power to control all four, at least not that I was aware of. When I'd left for my mission, she'd only been able to manipulate three of the four elements.

Her tongue darted out to coat her pink lips. "I'm still the same person."

I flattened my palms on the sides of her delicate face. "No. You're stronger and more beautiful."

Her gaze shot up to mine. "How do you know I'm stronger?"

I couldn't help but smile. "I feel your energy. I see it in your eyes, and as stubborn as you are, you would've never disobeyed your father."

"That's not true. You know I don't always do as my father says."

"That might've been true at first, but the more you've been living with him, the more you and Sam do as he says."

She shrugged. "I would do anything and everything to save you. And it's true. I did listen to my father. But I was given an opportunity, and I took it."

An opportunity I wanted to scold her for. Again, she was safe and with me, and that was all that mattered. Not to mention, if I had been in her shoes, I would have done everything in my power to save her. Yet I had questions, but one stood out at the moment. "Why is Sam here?" Bruno wanted Jo, not Sam. Not that I was complaining about her brother accompanying her. But Sam had been a good soldier as of late, obeying everything his father doled out.

"Webb, why are we talking about this? We're together. That's all that matters."

I slid my hands down to her shoulders. "Look, angel. Before I left, we suspected a mole within our organization. Now, I'm not saying that person is Sam. In fact, while I'm not all that happy that you risked your life to get here, I am glad that Sam is with you. I'm just trying to figure out our enemy, and I have to take everyone into consideration."

"Even me?" she asked with a frown.

I touched her chin, searching the hurt in her eyes. "Never you. But Sam doesn't go against your father. Not to mention, he would've never let you walk into the hands of the enemy."

"I think that head injury is clouding your brain."

Suspicion settled in my veins. "How did you get here? Where's Bruno? Did he let you go?" I couldn't believe that Jo and Sam could fight Bruno's army of men and win unless Bruno wanted them to find us. *But Bruno thinks you're dead. You're not making sense.*

Her pretty eyebrows pinched together.

"You think I'm the mole?" Sam's boots clamored on the wooden porch. "If you believe that, then you're a moron, London."

I drew my attention away from the woman I loved to her twin. His black hair was cut short, and strength and intelligence swam in his green gaze. He too was stronger, and he'd also grown up and out. I felt as though I'd been gone for years, but I knew better. Newborn vampires grew rapidly and settled into their permanent physique within a year of changing. But it had only been six or seven months since the twins had turned.

"You never go against your old man, Sam," I said.

"I would to protect my sister," he said in a scathing tone.

I glared at him. "You've been siding with your old man when it comes to Jo. Neither you nor him will let her breathe."

Jo gasped, whipping her gaze to her brother. "Is that true? You never stuck up for me?"

Sam held up his hands. "Sis?"

"Let's not forget that my own sister tried to kill me," I said. "So I trust no one these days." Ninety-nine percent of me didn't believe Sam was the mole, but something wasn't sitting well with me.

Jo huffed as she stormed past Sam, bumping his shoulder on her way into the cabin.

"Smooth, London. Now she's angry with both of us. You know, I'm not going to get upset. I actually disobeyed my father because he didn't put enough effort into finding you and the others. So before you become judge and jury, I want you to know that I'm here not only for my sister, but for you. I owe you for saving my life. And you of all people should know that my old man can be a dick. He doesn't see the forest through the trees sometimes." He shook his head. "I'll be inside when you're ready to hear how we got here." Then he disappeared.

I stood in the snow, searching everywhere, but nowhere. The world tilted slightly. I made a mental note not to drink any more of Jo's blood. I was beginning to think her blood made me delirious.

"Lieutenant." Olivia's voice was soft. "We need to plan."

I took in a huge gulp of cold mountain air then blew it out before I joined her on the porch. "We need to hunt. We're not going to get far tomorrow if we don't. Get Kraft and Kodiak." Animal blood would be bitter and nasty, but the way I was feeling, I needed something other than the sweet taste of Jo's blood.

"You think it's safe for Crysta, Sam, and Jo to be here without us?"

"There was no one alive back at that compound, and I didn't sense anyone following us here. Besides, all three of them are strong." I was confident they could handle themselves.

"I'll get Kraft and Kodiak." Olivia went inside as Jo came out.

"You need to rest," Jo said with a pained expression on her face.

"We need blood. We won't be long." I pulled her to me and planted my lips on hers.

She froze for a second before she relaxed. "I'm not going to fight with you. But I am hurt that you don't trust any of us."

"I know without a doubt I can trust you. I read your thoughts."

She edged back with wide violet eyes, her fangs extended. I had to smile. She was beautiful as a human, but when her eye color changed and she showed me her fangs, my body burned for her.

"Your blood," I said.

"Can you read my mind now?"

I shook my head. "Only when I drink your blood."

The sentinels emerged.

I kissed her hair. "We'll talk as soon as we get back."

She slid out of the way, staring at me the whole time. As I jogged away, I opened up a telepathic connection to her. *I love you.*

12

———

JO

Cold lips pressed to mine, pulling me from my same old dream with the panther. I blinked to find Webb standing over me. While the sentinels hunted, Sam had been standing watch so Crysta and I could get some rest. It had taken me a good ten minutes to fall asleep. I couldn't get past the hurt that was tugging at my heart over Webb's admission that he didn't trust Sam or me, although he'd retracted his statement about me. I realized his trust factor wasn't that strong since his sister, Kate, had tried to kill him. Not to mention, he was a soldier who was trained not to trust. It also didn't help that he was a super alpha male vampire that never threw caution to the wind. Aside from all that, I was still hurt because he suspected Sam.

He smiled as he knelt down. "We brought food."

I wasn't the least bit hungry for blood or human food. I touched his scraggly beard. He looked ten times better than when I'd first found him. "You must've eaten well."

Webb smiled. "We wrestled a bear. It took all four of us, though."

The sound of pots and pans clanged from the kitchen. I sat up to find the sentinels cutting up meat. Sam sat on a stool at the bar, watching in quiet fascination.

"Where's Crysta?" I asked.

"She needed to run. She'll return for dinner," Kraft said with an impish smirk as though I'd missed the joke.

Webb traded the floor for the couch. As soon as he was comfortable, he draped an arm around me. Curling into him, I planted a hand on his warm, hard, and bare chest. Sexy thoughts skipped through my head of my hand dancing over every part of him and my lips following suit. Suddenly, my cheeks were hotter than the fire crackling in the fireplace.

"I'm sorry about earlier," Webb said against my hair. "We've been through hell the last three months, and our enemies are getting smarter."

I gazed up into his cobalt-blue eyes. "I'm not your enemy, and neither is Sam."

"I know. Now, I want to hear about your journey and how you and Sam escaped Bruno. But before that, tell us about what's going on back at home."

Sam started. "When you first went missing, we sent out search teams. My father called in support to the military base in Anchorage, even. But after three weeks, he ordered a stop to the search teams. He'd said the terrain and vast landscape of Alaska made it impossible to find anyone. So we kept our ears to the computers, the chatter on the radios, and we checked in with Anchorage every now and then."

Kodiak wiped his bloody hands on his shredded T-shirt. We had no running water or electricity. The only light we had came from the fireplace. Luckily, vampires didn't need light to see well. Still, the fire provided a good amount in the small living room and kitchen area.

"I've been trying to dream," I said. "I was hoping I could at least dream to see if Webb was alive. But I could hardly sleep, let alone dream about anything. Then I got a call from Bruno. His terms were to come alone. It wasn't until I was trying to devise a plan to get away from the base that Sam showed up at Darcy's house. Well, before then, Ben came to us for help."

Olivia stopped slicing through the meat that Kraft had handed her. "Ben Jackson?" Her tone sounded suspicious.

Sam turned on the stool so he was facing the cabin door. "Yeah. He wants us to help him figure out what he is now."

Webb muttered under his breath.

"Ben needs our help," I said in a measured tone. Webb could get jealous all he wanted. We didn't turn away people who needed help, regardless of their affections.

Kraft skirted the kitchen island and found a spot to sit on the stone fireplace. "One thing is certain. The commander will have your head and Sam's. Don't be surprised if he throws you in prison when you get back to the base."

I shivered in Webb's arms. I had no doubt my dad would filet Sam and me. He'd thrown me in the base prison before when I killed Blake Turner.

"Look," Sam said. "Jo and I are stronger together—literally, that is. If we join hands, we can do some serious damage."

"He's right," I said. "We've been learning magic spells from Ms. Costner, but Sam and I have also been practicing our powers for the last three months. We've found that together, our powers are unlike anything you've ever seen."

Webb rubbed my arm. "That's great. But our powers will not stop bullets laced with sedatives." He dipped into his pants pocket, removed four syringes filled with clear liquid, and set them on the pockmarked coffee table. "I found these in the building that blew up. I don't know if these are filled with the same stuff that's in the bullets or not. They're our only weapons at the moment."

Kodiak carried a pan full of bear meat to the fireplace. "If I get one more of those fuckers in me, I'm going to snap necks."

"So Bruno called you both," Webb continued. "Then what happened?"

Sam raked his hand through his short black hair. "We got on the plane. Then we hijacked the plane."

Olivia climbed on the stool next to Sam. "How?"

"Sam has learned how to compel an entire group. So he compelled the two guards and the pilot," I said as a matter of fact.

Webb unfolded his hard body and began pacing behind the couch. "Man, a lot has happened since we've been gone. I won't even ask how your powers have grown so fast. Still, your father is going to blow shit up until he finds you both."

"That's good," Sam said.

Webb's brown hair had grown past his shoulders, and with his beard, he looked like a bear. I wasn't complaining. He looked kind of badass with all the hair. Kraft and Kodiak had the same look going on.

Webb darted his gaze to Sam. "It's not. In order to take out our enemies, it's best if the sentinels and I drop off the radar. We operate better in stealth mode, especially if we have a mole within the SEAL team. Did we find the mole, or do we still suspect?"

"I believe my father still believes we have someone working for Edmund within the organization," Sam said.

The sentinels all muttered under their breaths.

Webb nodded, his face determined. "Then no one can know we're alive. Bruno thinks we're dead. I'd like to keep it that way. Edmund will think the same. That way, our surprise attack will be more effective."

"And us?" I asked. My heart felt as though it was sprinting around a racetrack. In no way was I leaving Webb. "Don't tell me that Sam and I have to return to the base. We're strong. We can fight. I also don't care about sedatives and bullets." I mashed my lips together.

Webb grinned like an ass. If he were about to patronize me, then I would unleash my powers. Maybe Sam and I should give him a sample of what we were capable of.

The door burst open. Every one of us jumped up, ready to attack, until Crysta walked in, smelling like a wet dog.

"Woman," Kraft said, "a little warning."

She snarled. "Can't you smell me a mile away?"

Suddenly, I realized as the two stared each other down that Crysta was the girl in my vision when I drank Kraft's blood. "That's her," I blurted out, setting my sights on Kraft. "She's the girl I saw when I drank your blood."

Kraft lifted his shoulder and grinned like a proud man. "If you so much as tell Tripp, I'll—"

"Can it," Webb snapped. "I could give a shit about you two, and so could Tripp."

Crysta rolled her eyes. "Tripp knows, anyway."

Kraft's eyebrows went up. "All this time, I've been walking on eggshells around him."

"It's not like we're seeing each other." Her tone dripped with sarcasm.

Webb tugged on his beard. "Okay, enough. We were getting ready to discuss a plan."

Crysta crossed the room to the fireplace and rubbed her hands together. "It's easy. Get to my truck. It's parked on the other side of the north ridge. From there, we can regroup at my place in Fairbanks."

"So what about Sam and me?" I asked. "We're not going back to the base."

No sooner had the words left my mouth, than glass shattered. Webb dove over the couch and tackled me to the floor. Cold air rushed in, then a spotlight lit up the room.

"Stay down, Jo," Webb said as he covered me with his body.

I squirmed. "Let me up. I can stop them."

"Kodiak." Webb's voice was hard.

"I've got it under control," Kodiak said.

Webb rolled off me and took my hand. "Come on, Jo. Crawl with me into the bathroom."

I popped to my feet. "Look, I can stop them."

Webb let out a low growl. The vampire would have to take a chill pill. I got there on my own with no injuries.

"Sam, grab my hand," I said.

A bullet flew past me as I ducked, taking Sam's hand. Immediately, an electrical charge zapped down my arm, indicating our connection.

Olivia ran down the hall, and Crysta followed her. Kodiak threw fireballs out the window near the main door. At any second, the cabin would go up in flames.

"Ready," Sam said.

We bowed our heads. Bullets were flying. Streams of fire were coming from Kodiak and now Webb. I didn't see Kraft anywhere. Then Webb was yelling in my head. *Stop. You'll get shot. All the elemental magic can't stop those bullets.*

Sam and I drew in a large breath, then we released it as we lifted our gazes. When we did, two men in black emerged through fire that emblazoned the doorway. Their guns were pointed directly at Sam and me.

Webb shouted something in my head when the walls began to shake. Sam and I drilled our gazes into the men as though our eyes could pierce holes through them. Their faces blanched, and their bodies began to shake. Then one dropped his gun and fell backward out the door. The other man in black pushed forward, wincing as he fought the lack of oxygen.

"Now," I said to Sam.

We lifted our arms, the electricity bouncing between us. Then a feeling of weightlessness washed over me. My skin prickled. The fire engulfed the entire side of the cabin as Sam and I closed our free hands into fists. When we did, the second man collapsed. But another soldier appeared in the doorway.

"Get down, Jo," Webb yelled.

Then a body flew in front of Sam and me. At the same time, the soldier fired his gun. Instantly, warmth traveled through my veins at a high speed. My arms went limp, my one hand falling away from Sam's. I peered down at the dart-like bullet in my chest then checked on my brother. He listed to one side. Or maybe the room was spinning. Slowly, I turned my attention to my attacker. Webb had his hands on my attacker's head. When I blinked, the man's head fell off his body. I bent over, not knowing whether to puke or pass out. But blackness crept into my periphery, and as it closed in, the only thing I could hear was Webb's voice.

"Fuck," he said as his arms wrapped around me.

Then I was falling into a black hole.

13

WEBB

I wore a hole in the scuffed wooden floor of the cabin. Jo had been out for most of the night. I glanced at her as she slept peacefully on the couch. Bullets with sedatives could knock a vampire out for days, and we didn't have days. We needed to get the fuck out of here. If our enemy found us, it wouldn't be long before more came.

The only good things from our attackers were clothes, weapons, and radios. We still hadn't figured out how they knew where we were. I suspected Crysta. She'd been the only one with a phone, and she'd gone for a run, while we stayed back at the cabin. Or she might have been tracked by the GPS in her phone. Then again, I didn't think Bruno knew of Crysta or that she'd been in the area. Still, I hadn't had a chance to ask her. After we'd killed five soldiers, I sent everyone out to scour the area.

I twirled one of the daggers in my hand, wanting nothing more than to drive the blade into Bruno's and Edmund's hearts along with anyone else who dared to make an attempt on Jo's life. My vision had blurred when I saw the bullet heading for her chest. I

"

couldn't get in between her and that bullet fast enough. Then when I saw the bullet lodged in her, I saw death. Not hers, but the soldier's. I'd shucked the syringe I'd been holding and tore off his head.

If I had any doubts about going off the radar, I didn't anymore. Fuck the commander, vampire laws, and military rules.

Sam poked in his head through the charred doorway. "Is she awake yet?" He'd been fortunate not to take a bullet, but the power he and Jo had used had drained him of energy. Regardless, the kid was strong. He just shook off the effects and helped us kill.

"No. But I'm going to try and wake her." Since she was under a strong sedative, I wouldn't be surprised if I couldn't get her to wake up. "Dawn is breaking, and we need to get moving. If I have to carry her, I will." I dropped down on the barstool. "Did you find anyone?"

"The area to the west is clear. Crysta shifted, and she's circling the perimeter on the east and south."

"Good. She can gain more ground in wolf form." Not that vampires couldn't run fast, but knowing our enemy, they were only looking for vampires, not wolves. "You and Jo have certainly grown. I knew she could deplete the oxygen in the room, but how did you both learn to target one person at a time?" When she'd been with me at my house in Maine, she'd come face-to-face with Nicki, a former girlfriend of mine. They'd exchanged some words, and Jo unleashed her power, sucking the oxygen out of the room. Only then, I'd been affected by it along with Nicki.

"Honestly, I don't know," Sam said. "And I really don't care. It works. Although when Jo and I grab hold of each other, an amazing amount of energy flows through the both of us. Ms. Costner suspects our combined powers have something to do with Jo and me being twins."

Whatever worked. But the fact remained that all that energy couldn't stop a bullet. I shook my head. The girl was going to be the death of me.

A wolf howled in the distance.

Sam gave me a tentative look. "Crysta said that she'd give us a signal if the area was clear. I can't tell if that's her signal."

"Probably is." I wasn't exactly sure. I went over to Jo and tapped her on the face. God, she looked so beautiful and peaceful. Her skin was silky. Her lips were soft, and she had somewhat of a smile on her face as though she was dreaming of fairies and good times. I hoped she was because last night was just a taste of what was to come.

Sam took up a position behind the couch. "Don't get upset with her. She just wanted to show you that she's capable of fighting. I wouldn't have let her get on that plane with me if I didn't think she could fight. She's been through hell with you missing. But she's also been fine-tuning her powers and fighting skills. She's quite the fighter."

I dragged the backs of my knuckles over her soft cheek. "Does she know how to use a weapon?"

Sam chuckled. "She's one of the best when it comes to daggers. She practiced every day when you were gone."

Now I laughed, remembering the day she and I were in the woods and I was teaching her how to throw a dagger. She hadn't wanted to learn. That was also the day I told her I loved her. I'd been reluctant to tell her for months. The first time I laid eyes on her in Principal Jackson's office at that human high school was the day I knew my life wouldn't be the same.

She squirmed, distracting me from my thoughts. "Angel," I whispered.

Her eyelids opened then closed then opened up again, showing me those stunning silver eyes, although I preferred her vampire violet eyes. Either way, she was exquisite, whether human or vampire.

Her fangs descended, slow and lethal. "I'm hungry. My throat is parched."

I snagged a knife from the sheath around my leg and was about to slit my wrist.

"I want your neck," she whined in a tone that consumed me and heated every cell in me.

I wanted her mouth on my neck too, but the act alone was too intimate, and we didn't have time to get lost in each other.

I opened a telepathic connection. *Not now. Too intimate for the setting.* So I slit my wrist then placed the open wound to her slightly upturned lips. Without any arguments, she clamped down on my skin and began to suck.

"Sis, are you okay?" Sam asked.

She blinked.

Voices trickled in. Sam turned his attention outside.

"Why don't you meet them outside," I said to Sam. "I'd like a minute alone with Jo."

She continued to drink. I wasn't worried about my own blood supply. After we'd killed our enemies, we'd stocked up on as much blood as we could. Olivia had found mason jars in the cabinet. Hopefully, we had enough for at least a two-day supply. Maybe by then, we would have found our way out of the mountains and to Crysta's truck.

Jo's fangs retracted, then she licked my wound before she sat up, threading her fingers through her long black hair. "I feel dizzy."

"I warned you about those bullets."

Her face twisted as her eyes narrowed. "You're not sending me back to the base. I refuse to return. I can fight." She pouted, and I had the urge to kiss her. If I did, we wouldn't get out of there.

"Who said I was sending you back?" I grabbed her hands. "I want you to fight. I want you by my side. I'm not your father. And if you've ever felt I treated you that way, I'm sorry. I only want to protect you."

Her mouth fell open. "You're not going to stow me away like my dad?"

"Angel, why did you think I was trying to teach you how to

throw daggers? It was always my suggestion that you learn to fight." From day one, I had pushed the commander to make sure that Sam and Jo learned. "But in some cases, you have to listen to me. The vampire world is not just about our metaphysical abilities. You won't kill with your powers. Remember what Ms. Costner has taught you. Your spells and other powers will stop or slow down your enemy. But to kill a vampire—"

"You have to behead them, burn them, or drive a cobalt dagger through their heart." She pinched her eyebrows. "You ripped off that guy's head."

I lifted a shoulder. "That's war. Besides, I didn't have a dagger."

"Why didn't you just push him into the flames or sedate him?" she asked so innocently.

She had more to learn, and if she was going to fight alongside me, then she needed a strong stomach and a quick lesson. "In a nutshell, you have to keep the vampire from escaping the fire, which means tie him down. Otherwise, we're not dying." I stood and grabbed the remaining flak vest, which had two daggers strapped to it. "Put this on." I handed her the vest.

She rose. "Where's yours?"

"I don't need one." Then I pointed to my belt, which held bullets and two grenades, then to the sheath on my leg. "I have what I need. As we find our way out, I want you to listen to me. If I'm not around, then take orders from one of the sentinels," I said softly. "Okay?" I wasn't trying to be her superior, but until she was as good at fighting as Olivia was, then she needed to listen and learn.

She smiled so wide, I thought my knees would buckle. The woman had a way of making my stomach do all kinds of somersaults. Before I could brace myself, she was in my arms, planting her sweet lips on mine. "Thank you," she said.

I anchored her to me, holding on to her butt. "I mean it, Jo. You have to listen to me."

She stuck her tongue in my mouth. I was about to kiss the hell out of her when my team clomped up on the dilapidated porch.

I set Jo down on two feet. We would have plenty of time to do all sorts of intimate things when we were somewhere safe. I couldn't guarantee we would be safe for a long time. But I'd waited years to find my soul mate. I could wait another day or two to get her alone with no distractions.

14

JO

Crysta's place in Fairbanks was a tiny motel room that certainly didn't fit the seven us. The men in the group barely fit in height. The room was the standard setup, with a bed, desk, table, chair, and bathroom. The wall above the bed had a crack in it, and the air smelled as though someone had sprinkled mothballs around the stained green shag carpet.

All of us were tired and beaten up from the day-long hike out of the mountains, which had been quite a challenge. With snow up to our knees, the hike was even more difficult, especially with the men taking turns carrying Sloan's dead body. My heart still hurt, knowing he was dead.

"Are we going to bury Sloan?" I asked, breaking the silence among us.

Everyone was scattered around the room. Olivia stood watch at the window, Kodiak sat on one edge of the bed, Sam was on the other side, and Crysta perched at the foot of the bed. Webb leaned against the ugly green door, while Kraft rested his shoulder against the bathroom doorjamb. I sat on the desk chair adjacent to Webb.

97

"We will." Webb was focused on Crysta's phone that she was clutching in her hands.

After we'd driven about twenty miles down the mountain range, she had finally gotten a signal. She had been ready to make a call when Webb stopped her. "No calls," he'd said. "Somehow, the men found us at the cabin. I don't want to risk our location again." I imagined he was contemplating calling my father. Then again, he'd mentioned he wanted to drop off the radar.

Crysta didn't take her eyes off her phone. "I can't leave him in my truck. He'll start to decompose any day."

"First things first," Sam piped in. "We need to get our hands on some civilian clothes if we want to blend in."

Crysta and I were the only ones in jeans.

Kraft ripped off the sleeves of his shirt, exposing his tatted arms. "Sam's right. These don't fit, anyway."

I giggled. Webb, Kraft, and Kodiak looked like misfits in the tight-fitting uniforms they had confiscated from our attackers.

Olivia hiked up her loose-fitting pants. "What's the plan?"

"Where can we get clothes?" Kodiak asked.

Everyone looked to Webb. He was still fixated on Crysta's phone. Suddenly, he snatched the phone from her hands with light-ning speed.

She jumped to her feet.

Webb held up his hand.

"I thought you weren't going to call the commander?" Kraft asked.

"I'm not," Webb said. "Something has been bugging me since we were attacked at the cabin."

The vein in Crysta's neck pulsed rapidly. "You can't suspect me."

Webb towered over her. "It's not a coincidence that when you came back to the cabin from your run, we were attacked. I'll give you one chance to explain. I'll also caution you not to lie."

She stuck out her chin. "I swear I'm not working with Bruno."

"Then you won't mind if Jo reads your mind?" Webb said as a statement, not a question.

She extended her hand to me. "Read away. I'm Tripp's cousin. Why the hell would I be working with your enemy? I told you the truth. I'm a private investigator, and I'm here to find Crowe."

I didn't believe Crysta was working for Bruno, although I could understand Webb's suspicion. I got up and captured her warm, soft palm in mine, then I knitted my eyebrows as I closed my eyes.

"You should be questioning the twins," Crysta said. "Aren't you curious how they hijacked the plane to get here?"

"We told Webb," Sam said. "When you were running."

"Everyone quiet, please," I said in frustration. I had learned that when people talked while I was trying to read their minds, it caused their thoughts to be erratic.

"Kraft, are you going to let them treat me like this?" Crysta's voice rose.

"Darling, our personal relationship, whatever that might be, has no place in this room." Kraft's tone was even. "This is business."

"Can it," Webb ordered.

I dove into her mind and was hit with a repeating thought. *I can't wait to tell Tripp how horrible his comrades have been. The gall of them to even think that I would work for the enemy against my cousin. All I'm here to do is find out about Crowe.*

I opened my eyes and studied Crysta. "When I don't want my father to read my mind, I repeat the same phrase over and over. So what are you hiding?"

Webb stalked over to her, grabbed her arm, and ushered her to the desk chair. "Kraft, hand me one of those syringes I gave you." Webb's face was devoid of any compassion. The man was outright oozing with rage.

I wrapped my fingers around Webb's tense arm. "Hey, she may be lying, but don't hurt her." SEALs had scare tactics that I didn't care to see or learn.

Tears pricked Crysta's stark-green eyes. "I'm telling the truth."

Kraft plucked one of the needles from the side pocket of his cargo pants. "Darling, tell us what you're hiding."

She bared her teeth at Kraft. "You're an asshole."

A muscle twitched in Kraft's jaw as it did in Webb's. The others were watching intently, almost holding their breath.

Webb took the needle. "I'm not sure what's in this. It could be the sedative used to knock out vampires. If it is, then the question is what does the sedative do to a wolf shifter?"

Surely, it wouldn't kill her.

She laughed. "You're going to knock me out?"

Then I remembered. "It's the best way to read minds," I said, at least according to my father. "As you fall into a slumber, your mind relaxes, and I can get more info."

Crysta's eyes narrowed. "Fine. When I went for a run, I found a spot on the mountain where I was able to get a signal on my phone. I called Tripp. He's on his way to Alaska."

"Was that so difficult?" Kraft asked, relaxing his hard features, clearly relieved that Webb hadn't hurt his girl.

Webb grabbed the back of his neck. "Let me guess. You told him we were alive."

"Yeah," she said. "Isn't that what you wanted?"

"At first. But not now," Webb said. "Plans have changed."

Crysta hadn't been there when Webb decided that all of us would drop off the radar.

Kodiak unfolded his bulk. "So if Crysta isn't working for Bruno, then how did they know we were at the cabin?"

"Those men were there for Sam and me," I said. "The two guards on the plane knew we were somewhere in the woods. They probably got lucky."

Webb pinned a glare on Crysta. "Or she could've been followed when she returned to the cabin."

"Lieutenant, we need to get out of here if you still want to go off the grid," Olivia said.

"Does it really matter if Bruno, Edmund, or anyone knows

that you're alive?" I didn't see how it would make a difference to Bruno if Webb and his team were dead or alive. Bruno wanted to deliver Sam and me to Edmund and collect his ransom money.

Webb scrubbed both his large hands down his face.

A sense of foreboding washed over me. My father was on his way here, or maybe he was in town already. If he took me back home, then I would never see the light of day. I couldn't be a prisoner in my own home. I had to fight. My dad would never allow me to be part of the plan or the fight. *He let you once.* Considering I had disobeyed him and taken off, the chances of being part of anything were extremely slim.

"If Bruno assumes we're dead, then he relaxes, which makes him more vulnerable," Olivia explained. Her dark eyes flashed with excitement as though she loved the thrill of the hunt. No doubt she did since she was a Navy SEAL.

"Also, if we go back to the base, then we have to follow the red tape of orders unless the commander allows us to go off the grid," Kraft added.

"He would never let us go off the grid without permission from the vampire government," Webb said. "The less the commander knows, the better. He and I have always suspected, but aren't completely sure, that Edmund has someone on his side within the Council of Eternal Affairs. Hence, Edmund is always one step ahead of us."

"So you're saying that the second mole we suspect could be on the council and not on the base?" Sam asked.

Webb nodded. "Possibly, but we could also have one on base."

"Yeah, but Mr. Rose, my attorney, uncovered that already. Maddox Tinsley, the solicitor for the prosecution, was helping Edmund. She confessed to that."

"She's not one of the elders on the council, though," Webb said sadly. "I'm talking about one of the elders. Your father has to report to them. So anything he tells them can leak out, including our missions." Webb turned his attention to Crysta. "Did you give Tripp your location?"

Crysta picked at her nails. "I told him it might be a few days before I could navigate our way out of the mountains. I wasn't certain if we were going to be able to even make the hike, given the snow. He said since we were safe for the moment, he and the commander would devise a plan and head out today. I suspect they'll be here tonight. Look, I'm sorry. Tripp didn't want me to say anything to you. He knows you. He knows you'll drop off the grid. And according to him, the commander will be pissed if you do that."

Webb laughed, a sound I loved hearing, even more so since I hadn't in quite some time. "Your cousin does know me well. He also knows when I get pissed, I don't listen well."

Then Crysta set her attention on Sam and me. "And your father is out of his mind pissed that both of you took off."

No surprise there.

Sam smirked then plastered on a serious expression. "Webb, if what you say is true and my father alerts the council on coming to Alaska, that would mean Edmund and Bruno already know you're alive and where we are."

Olivia peeked out the window again. "Coast is clear."

"Why does Edmund want you, Sam?" Webb pinched his eyebrows. "I thought he just wanted Jo."

I went to sit on the bed. "Bruno told me that he was the one who stole our lab data, and that tests showed that Sam has the same DNA structure as me."

"Which means that you're both powerful," Olivia said, the words rushing out.

"Now it makes sense how both of you were capable of depleting the oxygen in the room last night," Webb added.

"What I don't get," Sam said, "is that my eyes don't turn purple or silver or even red like Jo, my dad, and Edmund."

We were all still scratching our heads as to why Edmund's eyes changed to red in vampire guise. But that wasn't the topic at hand or something for us to worry about just yet.

"I think the point here," Webb said, "is that you're powerful. The question I have is can both of you manipulate all four elements?"

I smiled like a proud student. "I can now."

"Me too," Sam said.

I scanned the faces of the sentinels. With the exception of Webb, their eyes were wide.

"Holy shit," Kraft blurted out. "We have three vampires that have elemental magic, which means your father isn't the most powerful vampire anymore."

Sam's face blanched with fear. "Hence, the reason Edmund wants us badly."

I would guess he was remembering how Edmund and my uncle Patrick had drained his human blood. I certainly would never forget how I'd found my brother on a sterile table in a glass room on his deathbed. The only way for Sam to survive was for me to change from human to vampire so he could drink my vampire blood.

"Given everything we just discussed, the twins are more exposed if they're with their father," Olivia said.

Crysta rose. "I have an idea."

All heads turned toward the pretty wolf.

"I'll hide the twins. They can leave with me. I have the perfect place in mind, where no one will find them, not even my cousin. And if Edmund or Bruno do, then they'll meet their deaths."

I raised an eyebrow. I didn't want to go back to the base, where my father would lock me up tight until he could kill Edmund, and it could be years before our battle with Edmund was over. I also didn't want to be hidden away where no one could find me. I wanted to fight. I wanted revenge more than any of the sentinels or anyone in the vampire community.

Edmund had made my life miserable. He'd almost killed my brother. He'd almost killed Ben and Darcy. Not to mention,

Edmund had left me to die in a bad storm at sea. Then he'd tortured Sam and Webb at the mansion in Newport. And the icing on the cake was that I had almost gone to jail for murdering a boy whom Edmund had changed into a monster. The man wasn't stopping until he built his army of vampires. We couldn't let that happen. I couldn't let that happen. Mere humans who didn't carry the natural-born vampire gene didn't deserve to be lab experiments or die. For that matter, no one did, whether born with the vampire gene or not. The only way to stop Edmund was to kill him. And since the only way to do that was to get close to him, I had an idea. But Webb wasn't going to like it.

I took in a breath. "If we want to kill Edmund, then let him capture me."

Dead silence filled the room as everyone turned to me.

"The plan is simple," I continued. "He takes me. I kill him."

Sam finally blinked. "Are you out of your fucking mind?"

"He'll kill you," Olivia said.

Webb stood statue-still with his lips pressed into a thin line. His blue eyes changed to black, and his face darkened to a deep red.

Then everyone shifted their gaze to Webb, including Crysta, who didn't have that *What the hell* look like the rest of them.

I stepped up to Webb then placed my hand over his racing heart. "We can't keep running. They want Sam and me. So let's give him one of us. My powers are strong."

Webb peered down at me. "How will you combat the sedative? That will be the first thing they do so you don't use your powers." His voice was soft, but his expression was anything but.

"I've been thinking about that. Dr. Vieira has been working on an antidote to stave off the effects of the sedative. When I haven't been practicing my powers, I've been learning things in the lab. That USB drive that we confiscated from our raid on the mansion showed the ingredients of the sedative."

"Does he have the antidote ready to go? Is this something we are given before or after we're hit with the sedative?" Excitement laced Webb's tone.

"I'd forgotten about that," Sam said.

I had as well. Even when Webb had brought up the sedative at the cabin, I wasn't thinking straight. My concern had been focused on not being shipped back to my father.

I lifted one shoulder. I only knew a little about it since I wasn't in the lab with Dr. Vieira and Dr. Case every day. "I don't know. Dr. Vieira and Dr. Case are testing out the formula on rats at the moment. But it is working."

"While that is great news," Olivia said, "remember your powers won't kill vampires."

I didn't take my eyes off of Webb. "True, but if I can arm myself with the antidote, then I can kill. I'll take my human uncle out first since he's the brainchild. Without him, Edmund won't have a serum. Therefore, he can't build his perfect vampire army."

Kraft finally spoke. "We could plant a GPS chip in her."

Both Kraft and Kodiak had been super quiet. My guess was they were still surprised at learning that Sam and I were just as powerful as our father.

Webb released a breath. "Enough. Jo isn't walking into the hands of the enemy, and we're not planting a chip in her."

"Thank you," Sam blurted out. "Look, we appreciate everyone's concern for us. Jo and I are strong, physically and mentally." Sam set his stern expression on Webb. "I know you love my sister. I know you want to protect her. I do too. But she has amazing fighting skills. Give her a set of daggers, and she'll kill."

I wanted to hug my brother. For so long, he had protected me while we were in foster care. He'd beaten a foster dad or two. He'd gotten into fights with boys in school to the point where he was carted off to jail. He hadn't wanted me to fight. But now, we were equals.

"Crysta," Webb said. "Thank you. But the twins stay with us. In fact, Jo, Sam, and I will drop off the radar. I want you three"—

Webb pointed to Olivia, Kraft, and Kodiak—"to stay and meet Tripp and the commander. Crysta, I need your truck and some cash."

Olivia narrowed her dark gaze at Webb. "The commander will throw you in the brig for going AWOL."

With no expression on his handsome face, he continued to look at Crysta. She nodded.

"We have your back," Kraft and Kodiak said together.

I didn't care what Webb had planned. He considered me an equal, and that made me puff out my chest. Even my brother believed in me. I couldn't ask for anything more, except maybe convincing my father that I was capable of holding my own. But that feat would have to wait.

15

WEBB

I stood under the scalding shower at my house in Maine while the water pounded down on my back. It would take multiple showers to rid myself of the crud that had taken up a permanent home on my skin. The water felt amazing as the pressure beat my muscles. After the plane crash and being drugged for three solid months, I was exhausted—even more so since I hadn't slept in more than four days. We'd laid low in the event that we ran into Commander Mason or our enemies. When I had felt that the coast was clear, I finally contacted the pilot that Crysta had recommended.

I tipped my head back and let the water massage my face when footsteps padded in. The scent of musk told me it wasn't Jo, although her lavender scent lingered. She'd taken a shower earlier. Man, I would give anything to have her in here with me. But I wasn't certain she was ready for more than my kisses. I also needed some alone time to think of the plan that had been brewing since she'd told me about Dr. Vieira's breakthrough in an antidote to combat the effects of the sedative.

"Webb," George said.

The man was my champion and lifelong family friend, who stuck by me every step of the way. He was the only person outside of one or two of my team members who I trusted implicitly, and he was the only one who knew me better than I knew myself.

I turned off the shower, pulled the towel down from the stone barricade that separated me from the bathroom, then wrapped the terry fabric around my waist before I emerged.

George's tall and lanky body blocked the mirror over the sink. "You look like yourself again."

I rubbed my clean-shaven jaw, basking in the freeness of losing the beard.

His brown eyes appraised me. "You even cut your hair."

"First thing I did before I stepped into the shower." I grabbed a leather tie off the shelf near the sink and pulled my shoulder-length hair into a low ponytail. "I feel a thousand times better. Where are the twins?" I wasn't exactly worried about them. Our enemies were in Alaska. Their father was too. At least I assumed they were all still there. And this town on the coast of Maine was tight-knit. The residents knew when someone out of the ordinary graced the streets and roads of the sleepy community. Plus, I had a good friend who was the sheriff in town, and Stan would alert me if he suspected trouble.

George's smooth features belied the fact that he was a century-old vampire. "Did you tell your team where you were going?"

"Negative." I knew my team wouldn't give me up, but the commander had mind-reading capabilities. "The commander will think I'm somewhere in Alaska, and Sam planted that in Crysta's mind just before he erased her memory of her telling me about her pilot friend." The kid had some unique abilities to be able to erase one memory, which was a large feat in itself. His father had the ability to wipe out all of someone's memories, but not just one.

Shaking his head, George chuckled. "Sam did the same to the pilot after I paid him, which is what I came in to tell you. The pilot is all taken care of. He shouldn't be a problem."

I'd thought to use Sam to compel the pilot into flying us across the country then decided against it. Even though he had been successful with Crysta, I'd wanted to be cautious. Questions would have mounted if the pilot had gone home to a wife and family he didn't know.

I snagged my clothes from the counter and dressed. "So the pilot took the hundred thousand without the blink of an eye?"

A door clicked open and shut before Sam's and Jo's voices trickled upstairs.

"Affirmative," George said. "So are you worried that you'll get court-martialed for disappearing?" Concern glistened in his brown eyes.

"If my fate is to be behind bars for the remainder of my life, then so be it. As long as Jo is safe, that's all I care about. Besides, at the moment, I'm more worried about Jo's infallibility. She's developed this enormous amount of bravery overnight." Not that she'd been lacking in confidence before, but when I'd first met her, she was timid and shy. Even so, she was new at fighting. She needed to learn that strategy was just as important as the tactical part of a battle. Nonetheless, whatever my fate would be, it was time to make some changes in my life.

"I believe the twins are the ones who will be giving orders in our world," George said. "They're the ones that the elders will be looking up to."

I slipped on my watch. "I don't want Jo in the middle of chaos. I don't want her ruling the vampire nation." Sure, I was being selfish. I wanted the vampire beauty all to myself. "I want to retire from the military and live a quiet life."

Pushing off the counter, he chuckled. "Good luck with that. You know, Sam and Jo might do some good. It's been ages since the vampire government has made any changes. Human society is evolving, and we need to change with them. We can't be stuck in laws and rules that were put in place a century ago."

Buckling my belt, I let out a heavy sigh. I didn't know if I agreed with him. Our laws protected us as well as humans. If anything, I would mandate stricter laws. I headed for my bedroom. The French doors were open, and the cool saltwater air wafted in.

George sidled up to me. "I love when the ocean is calm and the moon is rising."

I couldn't argue. The Atlantic was peaceful as the waves rolled in lazily. I missed spending time here. I missed the sound of the waves lulling me to sleep. I also missed quiet nights as I sat out on the deck and chatted with George and Stan.

Sam laughed.

"Let them know I'll be down in a minute," I said.

"Sure." George padded across the honeyed wood floor and out the door.

I abandoned the serene view for the inside of my walk-in closet. I moved shoeboxes out of the way then dialed the combination to my safe.

Jo giggled at something George was saying.

I smiled as I removed a burner cell phone. The sound of her voice had a way of calming me. Tonight, I would soak up all her energy and lightheartedness before I put my plan into place. Once I pushed that proverbial button, all the calm and quiet would be history. Hopefully, when the battle was done, I would still be alive and free to whisk Jo away to a secluded place.

I pocketed the burner phone then snatched a cobalt dagger. I always liked to keep a weapon on me just in case. I removed it from its leather housing and ran my finger over the blade on one side then the other. Satisfied that both sides of the blade were sharp, I replaced it back into its housing. Once the dagger was securely tucked into the back of my jeans, I closed the safe then went downstairs to join the others.

Jo was sprawled out on the cushioned window bench that faced the Atlantic. The entire back of my house was lined with accordion glass doors except the large comfy seat that Jo occupied in the living room.

Sam was lounging on one end of the couch opposite Jo, and George sat at the other end.

"What's all the laughing about? Is George telling jokes again?" I made a beeline toward Jo. Her long black hair spilled around her shoulders. Her silver eyes beamed with happiness, and her tight-fitting sweater accentuated her curves, making my heart tick a bit faster as I approached.

She swung her legs off the couch, giving me room to sit. I cuddled up next to her as she tangled her legs with mine. Now this, I could definitely get used to. Only I wanted to be alone with her.

"So what's the plan?" Sam asked with a crease in between his thick eyebrows.

Sam had grown on me since I'd first met him. He hadn't wanted me anywhere near his sister, and I couldn't blame him. He hadn't known me from the next vampire. As we had gotten to know each other, the walls he had built around him and Jo slowly crumbled. He'd begun to realize that my feelings for Jo were genuine, thanks in part to his ability to read emotions. More than that, he was a natural with weapons. The kid could fight. If what Sam had said was true about Jo's ability to throw a dagger, then I would take my worry factor down two notches.

"I'm going to call my sister, Kate," I said as a matter of fact. It was time to have a one-on-one conversation with her.

Jo's legs flew off me as though I had some sort of virus. "She tried to kill you. Why would you call her?"

George wasn't surprised. Sam didn't display any signs that he was either.

Jo chewed on her lip as her sexy violet eyes emerged.

"Since Kate is with Edmund, I want to gauge her mood." The situation called for a truce, at least for a family discussion. I'd lost sleep at night over many things, but none more than the scene where my sister had driven a cobalt sword into my chest, narrowly missing my heart. I wanted to strangle her for letting her emotions for a man get in the way of family. I couldn't order her to fall out of love with Edmund. When it came to love, there were no rules, although Jo's father would have argued otherwise. He wanted to control not only her life, but her heart too. I wasn't surprised. After all, she was his little girl.

Jo tapped me on the leg. "Are you with us?"

I blinked.

"Do you think Kate will tell you where Edmund is?" Tears clouded her vibrant-colored eyes. "She'll try to kill you again."

I cupped her cheek. "Angel, slow down. First, I understand that if Kate tried to kill me once she could do it again. I also think she wants to talk to me. Before you ask, no, we haven't spoken. But when I was in one of my groggy states under Bruno's control, I swore I heard her voice. I can't be sure, though. Anyway, she said that she had to clear the air with me before he killed me. Then Bruno laughed. I don't know what to think. I might have imagined the entire conversation."

"What do you hope to get out of talking to your sister?" Sam asked, still lounging leisurely on the couch, while Jo was tense as a tightrope.

"If she knows I'm not working for your father anymore, she might loosen up. I need to do this, and I need to talk to her alone." Up until she had switched sides, I could always get my sister to tell me anything. Granted, she had sided with Edmund, so I didn't hold out too much hope that she would tell me what he was up to. But at the very least, I could plant a tracking device on her.

"I still vote for sending me in," Jo said without an ounce of fear in her voice.

George ran a nervous hand over his jaw. "You're okay with Edmund getting your DNA and building that army of his?"

Jo snuggled into me. "No. But Edmund is building an army with or without us. I could kill him then my uncle Patrick."

I dragged my fingers along Jo's arm. She wasn't thinking clearly. "It's not that simple." I so wished it was as easy as the words rolling off her lips.

Sam heaved a sigh. "Then what's the plan?"

"When I speak with Kate, I'll somehow plant a tracking device on her. Then we'll find out where they're operating from, and then we can plan an attack. Of course, that depends on whether or not she agrees to meet me." My gut told me she would.

Jo huffed.

"Not a bad plan," Sam said. "Then we can attack when they least expect it."

George smirked. "I was worried for a minute that you would do something crazy."

The crazy thing to do would have been to kidnap my sister and throw her to Commander Mason. But I needed her to get to Edmund.

"What makes you think Kate will meet you?" Jo asked. "Or that she's even in New England?"

"I don't to either question. But if I know my sister, she'll be curious, and therefore, will make a point to meet me."

Her expression softened. "I can't lose you again."

"You're not," I said softly.

George cleared his throat. "Webb, I made a few phone calls when you told me about Bruno. A buddy of mine has a nephew who he believes started working for Bruno about a month ago. I'll confirm if that's the case and see if I can get more information."

"Be careful," I said. "I don't want you getting too deep into this mess." I couldn't lose George. Sure, he could handle himself, but he was like a dad to me.

Sam adjusted himself so he was resting his elbows on his knees. "Does his nephew happen to be Howell or Smith?" A look of disgust washed over his face.

George chuckled. "I believe my friend mentioned the name of Howell."

Sam's eyes flashed vampire.

Jo interlaced her fingers with mine. "Howell was one of the guards that escorted us to Bruno."

"All the more reason to contact your buddy," I said to George. "Look, let's get some rest. Tomorrow is a new day. We'll take things one step at a time." At that moment, I wanted alone time with Jo. I wanted to plant kisses all over her body. I wanted to absorb her energy, her light, and all that was her. Time was precious, and depending on how my plan unfolded, I might not get a chance again for a long time.

Her cheeks flushed. "Don't think like that."

I cocked an eyebrow. "Are you reading my mind?"

"I'm sorry, but it's hard not to," she said.

It didn't bother me so much, but some memories had to stay private. "I know how to block you."

"How?" she asked in a challenging tone.

I grinned. "My secret."

She narrowed her eyes.

"Do you like when your father is in your head?" I asked.

She slouched. "No."

"Then don't read minds unless you have to." My tone wasn't exactly soft.

She pouted as she leaned into me.

Silence filled the room until I glanced at George and Sam. "Any last thoughts before we call it a night?"

Sam pushed to his feet. "Not from me. I'm going to bed to think up all the ways I can kill Edmund, oh, and maybe Howell." He strode down the hall to the guest bedroom.

"Jo, why don't you go up to my room? I want to speak to George. I'll be up in a minute." I didn't know if she wanted me to stay with her in my bed or not. At the very least, I would kiss her good night.

She unfolded her curvy body, kissed me on the lips, then on her way by George, she stopped to kiss him on the cheek. "It's good to be here and to see you. I've missed our talks." Her bare feet slapped on the hardwood steps.

Once my bedroom door clicked shut, I let out a huge sigh.

George crossed one leg over the other. "You have your hands full with both of them. How are you going to plant a tracking device on Kate? You know your sister is smart. She worked in intelligence for the commander. Or what if she agrees, and it's an ambush?"

"Then I'll deal with whatever she has to dish out. If I'm captured, I'll do my best to convince Edmund that I have something he wants."

"He wants the twins," George said.

"He does. But he also wants power. He's always wanted Steven's position. He's always wanted to command an army. So why not command the military instead of harming humans to build his own army."

"How are you going to facilitate all that?"

"First things first. I talk with Kate. If Edmund is there, then I'll offer up Steven, who has the same DNA makeup, and with him out of the picture, then the elders would be in a position to appoint a new commander. And if Edmund does have one of the elders on his side, then it should be an easy decision." I was shooting at the stars on this one. The decision to appoint Edmund to command the Vampire SEALs would take more than one elder's vote. Not to mention, I would kill Edmund before he even had a chance to step into Steven's position.

"Remind me again why Edmund isn't trying to kidnap Steven for his DNA. Isn't his just as potent as the twins?" George asked.

"According to Dr. Vieira, Steven's body doesn't produce as much of the specific enzymes needed for vampires." I couldn't exactly remember all the details.

"So he's too old."

"In a sense, yes, but I don't see why Patrick couldn't experiment with Steven's DNA." I suddenly felt like an ass for even considering turning on Steven. Going AWOL was one thing. Serving him up to the enemy was quite another, and I didn't hate the man. I only disagreed with his decisions.

"I don't like your plan," George said.

"I know there are several roadblocks, and I don't have it all figured out yet. But Kate is first on my list. Then I'll regroup."

"You really should talk to the commander, Webb. He's been good to you over the years."

"I know. But I want to do this on my own. That way, I don't risk any leaks from my side or someone on the council who may be working for Edmund."

"You're throwing away your military career. I know your decisions are driven by your feelings for Jo, but you should never make decisions based on a loved one. They can cloud your judgment. But remember, Steven is her father. Put yourself in his shoes. What would you do if your children disappeared?"

"I told Olivia to let the commander know that the twins are safe." I knew George was right, and my heart was getting in the way of my brain. Maybe I wasn't so different from Steven. Regardless, I knew without a doubt that if the twins returned to the base, the commander would throw them into a jail cell like he had when Jo killed Blake Turner. I couldn't see her in that jail cell again. She'd been deathly afraid with no one to help her. "Look, George. I love her so much it hurts. It hurts me to see the way her father treats her sometimes, and I can't say anything because I'm his soldier. It hurts to know that our enemy wants to use her as his lab rat. I'm tired of the way she's been treated. I'm tired of the commander not listening to me when I suggest other alternatives. I get that Jo's actions to disappear from her father and run into the arms of Bruno wasn't the best decision to make. But a part of me is glad she did. Sam is right. She's strong. She's confident, and I would die without her. I can't let anything happen to her."

"Love always drives people and their actions. I've only been in love once, and I have to say I understand completely. After Debra died, I wanted to kill the vampire who murdered her, then I wanted to kill myself. As vampires, we sometimes feel more than the average human. We're fierce in our dedication to our loved ones and family.

But don't let your love for her get in the way of her safety, and Sam's too."

I never knew his wife, and he hardly talked about her. I also didn't probe. Some things were better left in the past. "I'm sorry about Debra."

He nodded. "I'm going to bed."

"George, thank you. I will take what you said and sleep on it. The last thing I want to do is put Jo in harm's way. I would not forgive myself if something happened to her."

"Then consider calling the commander tomorrow. At least let him hear from Jo and Sam that they're okay." On that note, he trudged down the hall to his bedroom.

Grabbing my temples, I closed my eyes. A headache loomed. He was right on so many levels. Maybe my decision to flee with the twins wasn't the best one. Maybe I should call the commander and return Sam and Jo to their father. Then I would be free to take out Edmund without worrying about anyone's safety.

I got up, almost punching my fists through the window. Instead, I went into the kitchen and grabbed a container of blood out of the fridge. Then I found my medicine bottle that Alia Costner had given me. She'd made a magical potion that blocked Steven from reading my mind. Now it came in handy with Jo. I squirted two drops of the concoction onto my tongue. The bitter taste made me wince. I couldn't see Jo without blocking her from reading my mind because the moment she touched me, she would know all my thoughts. And in turn, her anger would no doubt bring down my house. I wanted a peaceful night, where it was only her and me.

After I downed the blood, I tossed the container in the trash then climbed the stairs. I found Jo sitting cross-legged on the bed as she chomped on a nail, staring out at the cool night. The ocean breeze seeped in as the moon cast a bright glow, lighting up the glass surface of the water.

"I love it here," I said as I extended my hand. "Let's sit out on the deck."

Her pretty face was pinched as though she was lost at sea. My guess was that she was thinking about how Edmund had left her to die in a violent storm at sea. Or maybe she was irritated with my decision to talk with my sister.

She licked her lips. "Will we ever get Edmund out of our lives?"

"Come. Let's forget about everything but us for tonight."

She smiled as she followed me out to the deck. After we settled into a cushioned lounge chair, she lay her head on my chest.

I inhaled her lavender scent as I rubbed a path up and down her arm. "You know, you're all I thought about while I was chained to the wall in that dungeon. I honestly thought I'd never see you again."

She nuzzled her nose into my chest as though she wanted to crawl inside me and hide. "I'm sorry for reading your mind."

"Angel, I don't mind that you get in my head, but only when we're making love."

She tensed.

I chuckled. "I know you're not ready. Tonight, we'll sleep out here." I wanted her in my arms the entire night.

"It's not that I'm not ready. I want to. Boy, do I want to. I just… I guess I'm scared."

I kissed her head. "I promise when you're ready, I'll be gentle." I wouldn't be anything else. She deserved soft, slow, and tenderness.

"Your heart is beating fast," she whispered.

"It always does around you," I said.

I closed my eyes, absorbing her, the ocean breeze, the sounds of the waves, and her soft breathing. I could stay like this forever.

"Back in Alaska, you said my father doesn't have any say in us anymore. What did you mean by that? Has he been telling you not to see me?"

"Yes and no." I wasn't going to lie to her. "Your father loves and cares about you very much. He just likes to control things."

"But he can't control me. He can't tell me who I can love and who I can't."

"You're right. In my opinion, he feels he just got you back in his life, and then you fall for one of his soldiers. He hasn't spent time with you."

"That's not your fault," she said.

"I know. Let me handle your father."

"No. We're in this together."

She had a point. Maybe we both should clear the air with him. Not likely if we were in a prison cell.

"What I don't understand is he always seems to be okay when we're together," Jo said. "He trusts you too."

With me going off the grid and taking the twins with me, I doubted that Commander Mason would ever trust me again.

She dragged her fingernails down my chest. "Let's not talk anymore."

Fine by me. I lowered my head and took possession of her lips, soft and sweet. Her tongue touched mine, and all the control I had vanished. I became a wild man. I lifted her with ease so she was straddling my lap. My entire body hardened.

Our tongues fought for control. I wanted nothing more than to make love to her all night. Her chest rose and fell, as did mine. She squirmed in my lap, and fireworks went off behind my eyelids. *Damn.* She was making it hard to not rip off her clothes. I pulled back, breathing heavily.

Hurt flashed in her eyes. "What's wrong?"

I gently grabbed her cheeks as I stared at the beautiful girl I wanted to spend the rest of my eternal life with. "From the moment I laid eyes on you, my life hasn't been the same. I go to bed thinking about you. I wake up thinking about you. And when I was in that dungeon, I thought I would never see you again. Marry me."

She reeled back, her mouth falling open. Then she shook her head as she brought her hand to her heart.

The soothing sound of the waves along the shore filled the air as my heart pounded in my ears. "Say something, angel."

"Oh my God." She crushed her lips to mine, pushing her

tongue inside my mouth. She spewed little noises, controlling the kiss, slow yet fast. She explored my mouth as electricity ricocheted to every part of my body.

"Is that a yes?" I asked against her lips. I tried to break the kiss, but she kept my face firmly planted between the soft palms of her hands.

She eased back, tears clogging those violet eyes that I wanted to look into forever.

She shook her head. "No. It's not a yes."

My heart fell out of my chest.

"It's a hell yes." Before I could react, her fangs slid out, and she bit into my neck, drawing my life's energy into her.

Man, I desperately wanted to take her right there. But first, I wanted her as my wife before we consummated our union. We didn't have any laws stating we had to be married before we had sex. It was my choice. I also wanted to show her father that I was committed to Jo and that I was the right man for her, not that I needed his blessing. But a wedding ceremony would certainly appease Steven's old-fashioned beliefs.

Jo continued to suck, and I continued to rub her everywhere my hands would go. I wanted her to take as much of me as she could. She moved her hips back and forth over me.

Fuck. My jeans tightened and tightened.

I tapped her on her arm. "Angel?"

She retracted her fangs then licked my neck as she kissed her way to my lips. "You're certain you want to marry me?"

At the moment, I wanted to take her right there under the moonlight. I lightly bit her chin as we locked gazes. "I've never been more certain of anything in all my life." Then it was my turn to take possession of her supple lips.

Fireworks sparked when my tongue touched hers. I got lost in her, in us, in the bubble we had created around us, at least for a night.

16

WEBB

Complete quietness enveloped me as I sat on the deck just outside the kitchen. After hours of kissing, talking, and snuggling with Jo, she'd fallen asleep. I carried her to bed then made my way downstairs. My mind was too active to sleep. I wanted to plan where Jo and I would get married and how our first night together would be. I had all sorts of ideas on how to please her. But with the looming problems we were facing ahead of us, I couldn't shake my conversation with George. It replayed over and over in my head like a broken record. I was beginning to realize that maybe I'd made the wrong decision to drop off the grid.

Fuck.

My need to kill my enemies and disobey the commander was getting in the way of Jo's safety. I would never forgive myself if Edmund took her under my watch. Sure, I was resolute that I was the only one who could protect her. But I was also a fool if I thought her father couldn't watch over her. He had so far. Hell, we all had so far. The entire sentinel team did nothing but guard her, and she was alive because of it.

My burner phone lay in my lap as my stomach churned like a

storm at sea. I picked it up and dialed as I fixated on the waning night sky. The line rang once.

"Hello." Steven's deep voice was clear as though he hadn't gone to bed yet.

"It's me."

"Mm."

I couldn't tell from that one word if he was surprised or not. I assumed he would tear into me as soon as he heard my voice.

"The twins are safe." Four seconds of silence. I checked the screen. The line was still connected. "Commander?" Maybe he was trying to track my whereabouts. "You won't be able to get a lead on me. I'm on an old burner phone that doesn't have tracking on it." The most he could do was pinpoint a cell tower or two, but that would only lead him to nowhere. I was a SEAL after all. I knew how to drop off the radar.

"I'm not tracking you. I know you, Webb. I taught you how to go off the grid. What I am doing is trying not to lose my shit. You and the twins return to base today, and I won't throw you in the brig."

I raised my eyebrows. His tone was quite mellow for someone trying not to blow his top, especially Steven Mason. "What gives? No offense, Steven. You're never forgiving or nice when someone disobeys you."

"One, I know you would protect my kids. Two, I'm grateful that you decided to disappear with them because we encountered Bruno and Edmund in Alaska. We almost lost the wolf shifter, but she's alive and a little bruised. Unfortunately, we weren't successful in killing either Bruno or Edmund."

It was good to hear that Crysta was okay. "Where are they now?" I asked.

"Don't know. Our intel tells me that there's been a ton of activity at a warehouse in Anchorage. Please tell me you're not in Anchorage."

"I'm not."

He let out a heavy breath. "Look, my kids need to atone for disappearing. So meet me on base at four this afternoon. We're flying in today. We can regroup."

"On one condition. As mad as you are at Jo and Sam, you can't throw them in a cell."

"That was a stupid move on my part when I did that to Jo. I'm new at this father thing, and I'm learning, but there are consequences for their actions and yours. Just be on base at four with them."

"One more thing, Steven. Was my sister part of the fight with Edmund?"

"She wasn't anywhere in sight." Then the phone went dead.

Okay, that call went better than I'd expected. I wasn't about to analyze things. Instead, I made the next call. Acid settled in my stomach as I dialed Nicki's number. Jo would be furious if she knew I was about to speak to my ex-girlfriend.

"Hello," Nicki said in a sleepy voice.

"It's Webb."

"It's five in the morning. Were you dreaming about me?"

I wished she could see me rolling my eyes. "I need Kate's number."

"Who's that?" a male voice asked in the background.

"Go back to sleep," Nicki said to the man.

"Kate's number." My tone was firm.

Nicki yawned. "She'll kill me if I give it to you."

"Nicki, I'll kill you if you don't." I was serious. The woman had caused too much trouble in my life. I had to ban her from even coming within a mile of the military base.

She huffed. "Fine. Are you ready to write it down?"

"Go." I didn't need to write it down. My memory was good.

She spewed the number then said, "I miss you."

"Good-bye, Nicki." I clicked the phone off. I didn't want to hear her sing the same old tune about how we were meant to be together.

I made the next call. It rang three times.

"This better be good," Kate said.

"It's not," I replied.

Silence ticked for five seconds.

"What do you want?" Her voice was even.

"You don't sound surprised to hear from your only brother. Aren't you going to ask how I survived?" My nervousness carried me from the lounge to the deck railing.

"I don't know what you're talking about," she said.

Again, I couldn't tell if she was sincere or not. She'd always been good at masking her feelings—one of the reasons why she had been so good at working intelligence for the commander. Anytime we had needed someone to meet with an adversary, we'd always sent Kate.

"Are you still with Edmund?" Maybe they weren't together anymore. A brother could hope.

"That's none of your business. Cut to the chase."

I shoved my back into the railing as I gripped the phone, hoping the act would squeeze some sense back into my sister. "We need to have a family discussion."

The slider opened. My gaze shot up as Jo's lavender scent carried on the wind. She rubbed her heavy silver eyes as she ambled over to me. She was dressed in one of my T-shirts that fell to her knees. Beneath the waning moon, she was absolutely stunning with her long black hair a mess around her face and shoulders. My heart stopped for a second as she wrapped her arms around me, batting her long eyelashes.

I put my finger to my mouth. The last thing I wanted was for Kate to hear Jo. Not that they hadn't gotten along when they'd first met, but I was more afraid Jo would act out and cause Kate to hang up on me.

Jo gave me one of her smiles that always made my jeans tight.

I threaded my fingers through her hair, waiting for Kate to respond. "Kate?"

A glass clinked on her end of the line. "We have nothing to discuss."

"It's about time we clear the air. I want to hear why you would go to great lengths to kill your own brother. And don't give me any bullshit about you did it because you love Edmund." I didn't buy that reason. As much as I loved Jo, I would never kill my own flesh and blood for her, and she wouldn't for me.

"Seriously, brother, I tried to kill our own father for a man. What don't you believe?"

"Kate," I said quietly. It wouldn't help if I raised my tone, even though I was itching to scream at her. "I heard you tell Bruno you wanted to talk to me before I die. Now is your chance." I wasn't completely sure if I'd been hallucinating or not when I heard Kate's voice.

Again, silence ticked over the line. "Fine. We meet at a public place. There's a Dunkin' Donuts on Main Street in Fall River. Meet me there at three this afternoon."

"Thank you," I said. "Oh, and Kate? Come alone. No body-guards or Edmund. This is strictly family business."

"Well, make sure you follow your own rules, then. No sentinels or a mass army to surround me." Then she hung up.

I pocketed my phone then hoisted Jo in my arms. As I carried her to the lounge chair, she planted kisses along my neck, her fangs scraping my skin. Chills shot up my arms and everywhere else on my body. I wanted so badly to get lost in her. She nibbled on my ear as I settled both of us on the chair with her in between my legs, her back pressing against my chest.

I moved her hair to one side as I began my assault on her delicate skin, peppering kisses along her shoulder until I was suckling on her neck. She angled her head more, giving me full access to do as I pleased. Hunger, raw and pure, burned in ways I'd never felt in my entire life. My throat was on fire not only for her blood, but also to taste her in other ways I'd dreamt about. At that thought, my fangs lowered. I dragged the tips ever so lightly along her creamy skin.

Goose bumps popped up as she trembled, spewing little moans that sent my groin into a blazing inferno. Waiting for marriage was going to be near impossible.

"Webb." She said my name with so much want and need.

"Yes, angel?"

"Do we have to wait until we're married to make love?" She reached up to flatten her soft palm against my face.

"It's best if we do," I whispered before I captured her finger in my mouth.

She squirmed against me, and all sense of where we were and what was ahead of us vanished as I sank my fangs into her neck. I growled lowly as her blood filled my mouth, sweet like sugar and so fucking potent that a heady feeling consumed me. What I had to do later today evaporated with the wind.

Right here. Right now. The woman I was going to marry was taking me on the highest roller-coaster ride I'd ever been on. So much love encapsulated her as she thought about us, running on the beach, swimming in the ocean, and… I stiffened at her last thought. She was hoping our first time making love would be on the beach. *Fuck me.* I flicked my gaze to the sand, which was only feet from the deck. I could take her now. I could take away all the bad in her life and mine, even if for just an hour.

My hand found her breast before she covered my hand with hers, guiding me to play and explore areas of her body that would only lead to her under me naked. But I couldn't deny what she wanted. I couldn't deny that I wanted to please her in ways I was certain she'd never experienced. She kept guiding my hand in a slow sinuous path down her body until my hand was seated at the apex of her legs.

Holy fuck.

I retracted my fangs, swallowing the last mouthful of her blood as my own breathing grew erratic. Her legs were silkier than I'd imagined, but the feel of her skin wasn't what had me about to explode. Her panties were soaked. I stopped, trying to control my manly urges, trying like hell to do the right thing.

"I want you, Webb," she whispered. "Touch me."

My resolve broke. I was a man, a very virile man in need of her and only her. I sucked lightly on the hollow of her neck, her ear, anywhere my lips would go. Her legs fell open, and my body trembled. I was impossibly hard, ready to burst out of my jeans.

She turned her head up. "Kiss me."

"Angel, you're making it tough for me to control myself."

"We love each other. We're not doing anything wrong."

Kissing her wasn't wrong. Nothing about our relationship was wrong. I was the one who wanted to wait until we were married. I wanted to be a gentleman. Not only that, I wanted weeks on end with her where I had time to play, explore, and tease her into oblivion.

I lowered my lips to hers as I found her sweet spot between her legs. I stilled. *Breathe, man. Breathe.* When her tongue dipped into my mouth, I lost it. I became a wild man, feeling her everywhere and nowhere.

She nipped. I bit. She pressed her butt into my groin, and I saw stars, and not the ones that were twinkling in the sky. My fingers danced all over her. Her nipples were rock hard, but I had to stop. I wanted our lovemaking to be perfect, and while I wasn't complaining about our awkward position on the lounge chair, I wanted a soft blanket on the sand, with us completely naked and tangled together.

I broke the kiss then smoothed down her shirt. "Sleep, angel."

She didn't protest. Instead, she snuggled into me as I slowly regulated my breathing. Then she went limp in my arms.

I kissed her softly on her cheek then her ear. "I love you so much. Please forgive me for what I'm about to do later today."

17

WEBB

I parked behind a church that was situated about two blocks from the coffee shop. I didn't want to leave Jo and Sam alone. I could've dropped them off on base first, but we weren't scheduled to meet with their father until four, and I wanted to be with them when the three of us turned ourselves in. I didn't exactly trust Steven even though he'd told me he wouldn't throw Jo into a cell. I knew him too well. I knew if he got mad enough, he would do just about anything.

"Webb?" Jo's voice tore me away from the war I was having with my conscience.

I cut the engine and felt as though I was slicing through my gut. I had an awful feeling for some reason, and I couldn't quite put my finger on why. Maybe because my mind had been replaying last night when Jo and I were together. *Stop thinking about that, London. You got shit to do.*

"I don't like leaving you and Sam here." The truck was secluded on two sides by a high cement wall, and the church building was on the third side. Since it was a weekday, I didn't think anyone would be attending church, at least not through the backdoor.

"We'll be fine. We know how to fight," she said with confidence.

"And if a priest or anyone with the church shows up, Sam can compel them."

"Again, remember the bullets with the sedative." I reached over the console and took her hand. First thing I was going to do after I took my licks with the commander was speak to Dr. Vieira about that antidote Jo had spoken of. "In no uncertain terms do you leave this truck. If you suspect anything, then I want you to head home. The base is only ten minutes away." I had to trust that both of them could watch out for one another and kick some ass if they had to. What was I even thinking? They had hijacked a plane, a fucking plane. My muscles loosened slightly. I also couldn't suffocate Jo like her father had and not trust her. After all, I wanted her to fight. "Sam, hop in the driver's seat when I leave."

"The plan is to chat with Kate then somehow plant a tracking device, right?" Jo asked, her voice not sounding as confident.

I kissed her hand. "I'll be fine. She won't try to kill me in public." That much, I was certain of. Kate had always believed that humans didn't need to know about our kind. Or at least, that had been her belief at one time in her life.

"What if something happens to you? Or Edmund shows up and takes you?" Jo's voice was on the brink of destruction. "We won't know if we're sitting here without cell phones."

I lifted the console and removed a cell phone. "Take this one. I programmed my number into it. If something happens, I'll call you."

Fear danced in her eyes. To say I wasn't nervous would be wrong. Knots formed in my stomach at the thought of anything happening to Jo. "Also, if I'm not back in thirty minutes, then I want you to alert your father."

"I'm not leaving you," Jo said emphatically.

Sam snarled. "And I'm not returning to my father. He'll lock us up."

I silently cringed at Sam's statement. In another hour, Jo and Sam would hate me. Hell, marriage might be off the table. I prayed

Jo wouldn't go to that extreme, but again, I would never forgive myself if Edmund got his grubby hands on her.

"Sam? I'm ordering you to return to base if I'm not back in thirty minutes or if you suspect trouble. Because if something happens to me, then you two will be next. Are we clear?" I used my lieutenant voice. If Sam wanted any type of military career, then he would need to learn to obey orders.

"We will," Jo said, nodding her head. Her eyes spoke the truth. "Just be careful."

I curled my fingers around Jo's neck. Her blood pumped through at a rapid rate. Or maybe it was my own heart that pounded louder than a high school band on a football field. "I love you." Then I kissed her with all the energy I had, as though it was our last kiss.

As I eased away, I caught a tear that was about to slide down her cheek. "Nothing will happen." I sounded as though I was trying to convince myself more than Jo.

Then with all the strength I could muster, I climbed out of the truck and started walking, making sure not to look back. If I did, I would cave. It didn't matter that I was a strong man, a tough soldier who fought battle after battle, a leader, a lieutenant who led a SEAL team of powerful men and women. When it came to Jo Mason, I was not that man. She had the ability to reduce me to nothing. But we were talking about life or death, and for that, I had to roll back my shoulders, shove my emotions aside, and fight like the soldier I was trained to be.

I set the timer on my watch for thirty minutes then opened my senses, scanning, listening, and sniffing. Engines blasted in my ears as cars passed along Main Street. Humans walked leisurely in the park across from me. A jogger panted out his breath with each step he took, passing humans sitting on the park bench. I focused straight ahead, taking long strides, almost hurrying to get the meeting over with. I had an hour before I had to meet with Steven. I had thirty minutes to talk with Kate.

I fingered the tracking device inside my jacket pocket. My plan was to drop the device into her purse. That was, if she was carrying one, and if I could distract her long enough to plant it. Maybe I would get lucky, and she would ask to come back to our side.

The hair on my arms stood at attention. I was fearful that every car that passed would be driven by Edmund or Bruno. Not that I was afraid of them, but Jo and Sam were in the vicinity. In my other pocket, I grabbed a hold of the dagger. A car slowed to let me cross the driveway to the entrance of the gas station. I checked my watch. Twenty-seven minutes and counting.

The lot surrounding the coffee shop was rather empty except for a black SUV with tinted windows. I shook my head. The government and criminals had to rethink their choice of vehicles. I wondered for a moment if Kate had stuck to our agreement to come alone. The way the SUV was parked, I could only see the back end, which made me a little fidgety.

As soon as I walked into the coffee shop, the bell dinged. The smell of donuts filled my nostrils along with that of two humans who were sipping coffee at the L-shaped bar. The good news so far was that the only vampire other than me in the shop was Kate, who sat in a booth that was tucked away in the far back corner.

I passed a young waitress, who helped an old woman with her selection of donuts. Her bright hazel gaze lit up when she looked my way. I listened intently for others who could be hiding in the back of the shop. I heard a man behind the door that read "employees only" arguing with someone. Another quick sniff of the air resulted in nothing related to vampires.

Once I banked around the counter, Kate and I locked eyes. She sat regally, with her fingers interlaced as though she was at Sunday mass. The hint of a glimmer sparked in her blue eyes. If I weren't mistaken, I would've thought she was happy to see me. *Interesting.*

I folded myself into the seat across from her. I didn't like my back to the door. Nor did I like that I was exposed with the window on my right side.

"Twin brother, how are you?" Her voice was pleasant.

Again, she was giving me some weak signals that she was happy I was there. My gut warned me to tread with caution.

I tipped my head to the window. "That SUV yours?"

She rubbed one thumb over the other. "Maybe."

"Are you nervous? Is someone in the car? I thought we agreed to bring no one."

She let out an audible sigh. "What do you want?"

I laughed. "You drive a cobalt sword through me, narrowly missing a major part of my heart, and you ask me what I want. You're a piece of work."

"I—"

I held up my hand. "Save it. I thought a lot about why my own sister would try to kill me. But as I sit here, I suddenly don't care. Because no matter what you tell me, it won't change the fact that you want me dead." Seeing her made me realize two things. One, I did love my sister. Hell, I turned vampire to save her, just like Jo had to save Sam. The other epiphany that barreled through me as I searched her face was regret. I hadn't been there for her when she needed me the most. After our parents had been killed, I joined the military. She'd protested. She'd wanted me home with her. But I couldn't go back and change things. I also knew that once my sister made a decision, she usually stuck to her guns.

She sucked in her lips as though she was trying to hold back her emotions. I wasn't an empath like Sam, but eyes never lie. Regret shone in her blue depths. The sad part was that her feelings didn't change how I felt.

"I did love you, Webb." Her features softened. "But you were never there when I needed you. You always pushed me away. You always bowed down to Steven Mason, a man I despise. I see how you look up to him, and I hate it. Who the hell is he to run your life? Or mine? I was tired of taking orders from him."

"What if I told you that I feel the same way about Steven?" I told a half-truth. I didn't despise him. I just didn't agree with some of his decisions, one in particular. Instead of beheading Edmund when he was a SEAL for killing an innocent human out of spite, Steven had petitioned the government to discharge him from the military. Now look where we were.

She pinched her smooth eyebrows together. "Since when?"

Choose your words carefully. As I thought for a minute, I glanced down at her purse that was sitting in between her and the wall. "The time doesn't matter. I never said anything to you because you seemed happy with the intelligence job he had you managing." That was the truth.

"You know, Steven might be the most powerful of our species, but not for long," she said proudly.

I angled my head. "Are you saying you think Edmund will rise above Steven?" I didn't see how since Edmund didn't have the powers Steven had. Unless she meant that Edmund would one day run the government, which was the sole purpose of Edmund's drive. He wanted to lead the vampire nation. He wanted to make the rules and enforce them. He'd always been hungry for power. But a voice niggled in the back of my mind that she wasn't referring to government power.

She stuck out her chin, her defiance belying the *oh shit* look in her eyes. "You did hear me in that dungeon in Alaska."

"Don't change the subject. Answer the question, Kate," I growled a little too loudly.

She had said something she wasn't supposed to let out of the bag. I couldn't tell if she was warning me or not.

Kate's gaze darted to the humans at the counter. She gave them a weak smile. "A brother and sister fight."

The bell on the door jangled.

I cautiously slid a look over my shoulder. A human teenager stared at the sign above the case of donuts.

"You've been nervous since I sat down," I said. "Are you waiting for someone?"

She was still fidgeting with her hands. "I told you I came alone."

Something wasn't right. Again, I sniffed, sweeping the shop like the soldier I was trained to be. The human who entered a minute ago was paying for her box of donuts.

I started to stand. "It's been nice, Kate." Something told me to get out of there and back to Jo and Sam. To hell with planting the device.

"Wait," she said, sliding a hand across the table.

She was stalling.

"For what? I got what I came here for, unless you want to come home."

For a brief second, she looked away as though she was considering my last statement.

If she did want out of Edmund's stronghold, I would help her, but it would take more time than the fifteen minutes I had before I had to return to the truck. "Look at me, Kate. You want out of Edmund's rule, don't you?"

When she lifted her head, remorse washed over her face before she banked it. "I'm curious. Does Steven know you're here?" she asked in a sharp tone.

"Kate, what's going on? You're all over the map with your emotions. You're giving me signals that tell me you want out. You're nervous. Unless you're playing me."

She lifted a shoulder as she gave me a satisfied smile.

As I pushed to my feet, someone knocked on the window. I switched my attention from my sister to Nicki. *What the fuck?*

Nicki nodded at Kate.

I shook my head. "Came alone, huh? You're a great actress, Kate."

She peered up at me with a smug expression. "Do you know where your precious Jo is?"

My vision blurred as nausea took hold.

"I have to thank you," she said. "I was not expecting your call, but you did set up our plan perfectly." She stood, picked up her purse, and hiked it over her shoulder.

We faced off as I fingered the dagger in my pocket. "If you value your life, sister, I would highly suggest you speak now."

She placed a hand on my chest. "Oh, brother. We have the twins, thanks to you."

My heart stopped. "Impossible."

She shook her brown head. "Your precious Jo is clouding your intelligent brain. Bruno put a GPS chip in all the sentinels just in case you survived the explosion. He knows how hard it is to kill a vampire. So, surprise. We've known your location all along." She puffed out her chest. "Nicki and I followed you back from Alaska, while Edmund stayed to fight. We were just waiting for the right time. Now, thanks to you, we've picked up the twins from behind the church up the street."

"So you think you won." Now it was my turn to smile smugly. "If what you say is true"—I knew she wasn't lying since she'd just mentioned the church—"then what? You kill me once and for all?" *Fuck.* Bile rose to settle in my throat. I had fucking led Sam and Jo to slaughter. I was supposed to protect them. I had promised Jo nothing would happen. I'd promised Steven the twins were safe. I clenched my fists as I narrowed my eyes, trying to hold back my fangs from dropping.

Think, London. The problem was I couldn't think. I wanted to kill my own sister.

"While the thought excites me to kill you, I'll save that for another day. Right now, you're going to let me walk out of here. I'm sure you of all people don't want to cause a scene. I would hate to cut off your head in front of humans."

I let out a roaring laugh. "That's not your style."

The two people in the shop scurried away. Sometimes, I thought humans could tell that people like Kate and me weren't human.

I gripped her shoulders. "So if you want to kill me, then do it. In fact, I'm sure if you take me with you, Edmund would gladly drive a blade through my heart once and for all." Somehow, I had to get in that vehicle with her. I had to get to Jo and Sam. Even if that meant

I might die in the process, at least I would feel as though I gave my all to try to save the twins.

But if she takes you hostage, then your chances of saving anyone might be zero. They will drug you again for months on end. Bruno would siphon all the blood out of you then let you die like he did Sloan.

Her fangs dropped. "My orders are to bring in Jo and Sam and no one else."

I angled my head. At that moment, I wished I had the ability to read minds. Bruno had tried to kill me in Alaska, but there I was, standing in front of the enemy, and they weren't interested in taking me in. "So do you want to kill or not?"

A horn blew.

"Your death will be on my hands and my hands only. But today isn't that day. So if Nicki and I don't return, then Edmund will be sure to kill Jo first."

My mind was trying to process her admission. My own sister still wanted me dead. Sometimes, I believed she had been brainwashed by Edmund. I searched her eyes. She didn't have the glossed-over look in them like victims who had been compelled. She made her decisions on her own.

"He won't. He's been waiting for months to get her. He's not going to give up the one thing that is stopping him from building the perfect army. Why can't you see that you're just a pawn in his game? Edmund is so much worse than Steven."

She set her jaw. "Edmund loves me, and Steven didn't want me in his bed."

The room spun for a split second. "Say what?" Her motives were becoming clear. "Are you telling me that you and Steven were lovers?" Hell, I had on blinders. "You want revenge against Steven because he didn't want you in his bed? You think by killing me, you would hurt Steven?" For now, I had to shake off the revelation. Jo's and Sam's lives were at stake. "Here's the plan. You and I will walk out calmly. Then you'll tell Nicki to drive away, that we're not done talking about family business, and that you'll call her when you're ready." Kate was coming with me. It was time my sister was locked up and tortured until she told us where the twins were. It was time to end our feud once and for all.

"She won't believe you. Besides, you can't go anywhere without us tracking you."

"Then Nicki won't mind leaving you with me." I didn't give a fuck about the chip embedded in me because I was on my way to the base, anyway. With one hand, I grasped Kate's arm, and with my other, I took out the tiny tracking device just in case the shit hit the fan. "We're going to walk out of here calmly."

As we shuffled to the door with Kate slightly ahead of me, I dropped the tracking device into a side pocket of her purse. Once outside, I removed my dagger with my free hand and pressed the blade to Kate's neck, pulling her to me so her back was to my front.

Nicki rolled down the window on the black SUV. We stared at each other for a long second. Her gray eyes seemed to smile as though I was screwed. Then she leaned over from the driver's side and opened the door. "Let her go, Webb. You don't stand a chance."

"I have a dagger to her throat," I said calmly. "So drive away."

Kate kicked my shin and tried to wriggle out of my hold. The blade scored her neck.

"I have no problem killing my sister," I added.

Cars sped by, oblivious to what was happening, at least from what I could tell. Then an identical-looking SUV careened into the lot, and the door opened. A brute of a vampire pointed a gun at Kate and me. As though the situation were synchronized like a smooth orchestra, Kate bent forward just as a gun went off. Suddenly, I became dizzy.

Fuck.

I couldn't pass out. I dropped the dagger as Kate ran to Nicki. Then I reached for the dart-like bullet and yanked it out of my throat. Warmth began to spill into my veins, making me sway on my feet. Tires screeched, and I squinted to read the license plate. But my vision was too blurry.

Fuck was on repeat in my head as I fell to my knees, my eyelids becoming heavy. I shook my head vigorously, hoping to keep from passing out. I needed blood. Maybe drinking blood would counteract the effects of whatever they'd shot me up with.

A small human hand touched my arm, her scent so delicious that my gums burned with the need to sink my fangs into her. "Sir, are you all right? I'll call the cops."

I squinted at the young girl who smelled like donuts—the same girl who had been behind the counter. "Don't." I inhaled a deep breath, which wasn't the best idea since her sweet scent was driving my need to sink my fangs into her.

"Are you sure?" the girl asked as a teenage boy walked up, smoking a cigarette. The disgusting scent masked anything else.

My vision teetered in and out of blurriness.

"Cee Cee, what's going on? Is this dude bothering you?" the teenage boy asked.

"No. He just got shot," she said, her voice hitching.

The teenage boy with spiked black hair snuffed out his cigarette then picked up my bloody dagger. "No shit? You're not bleeding, but your hand is covered in blood and so is the blade. Did someone stab you?"

"I'm fine. It was just a drill. I work for the military." I planted shaky hands on the ground and pushed myself to stand. When I did, I wobbled.

The boy caught me.

I swiped the dagger from him and pocketed it. "I'll give you a thousand dollars if you get me out of here," I said, towering over the spiky-haired boy.

His dark eyes lit up. "What the fuck are we waiting for? Cee Cee, go back inside. I'll call you later."

If people were watching or saw what had happened, I couldn't tell. I could only see a foot in front of me.

"My truck is up the street." Blackness encroached. My eyelids fluttered shut, and again, I listed. I shook my head a few more times as I clutched the bullet in one hand.

"I hope you'll be all right," Cee Cee bellowed as the spiky-haired boy and I walked away.

Sweat beaded on my forehead, and the entire city spun while the boy helped me to my truck. When we rounded the church, my truck blurred in the distance.

"Seems like someone broke into your truck," the boy said. "Do you have the keys?"

I shook my head.

"That's okay. I know how to hot-wire a car."

When he helped me into the passenger seat, I closed my eyes briefly, trying to ward off the dizziness. When I opened them, I saw a note taped to the dashboard, but the words blurred.

The boy got into the driver's seat. "Oh, the keys are in the ignition."

"What's your name?" My speech slurred.

"Diego."

"Well, Diego, can you read that note?"

"It says 'thank you.'"

"Any name on it?" I asked.

"No." He started the engine. "Where to?"

"The military base on the water."

As he navigated out of the parking lot, I rested my head back and closed my eyes. I was trying to think, but I was a second away from dropping into a deep sleep.

"Diego, I need you to punch me in the face."

He chuckled. "No offense, dude, but you're a mile taller than me, and you're kind of scary."

I sucked on my tongue to get some saliva to coat my throat. "I have to stay awake." I also had to keep my fangs from shooting out. While Cee Cee smelled like a jelly donut, Diego smelled like a juicy steak.

"We're almost there," Diego said.

I opened my eyes as wide as I could, even though they felt as though I had a ten-pound weight on each eyelid.

Diego came to an abrupt halt at the guard shack. He rolled down the window when a sentinel approached.

The guard, who was dressed in fatigues and had his hand on his holster, peered into the truck. His bronze gaze met mine. "Lieutenant? What happened?"

"I got shot with a sedative-laced bullet. I need to get up to the infirmary," I said in a lazy tone. "Lane, can you drive me in? And make sure Diego here gets a ride to wherever he needs to go."

"You owe me money, man," Diego said.

Oh, right. I fumbled with the glove compartment, where I kept emergency money hidden. Then I pulled out ten large bills and handed Diego the thousand dollars.

Lane opened the door. "Diego, step out, please, and have a seat in the guardhouse."

"Thank you, man. I hope you're okay," Diego said as he traded places with Lane.

Lane barked words into his radio as he sped through the military base.

"I can't keep my eyes open any longer." My words slurred. "Tell Dr. Vieira to inject me with the antidote."

As Lane pinched his eyebrows, my head lolled forward, and blackness finally consumed me.

18

JO

The scent of bleach tickled my nostrils as my eyes slowly opened then closed. Voices hummed around me as metal clanked on metal. I went to turn over to continue my restful sleep, when something tugged at my arm before a pain seared my wrists. I sat straight up, or at least tried to. I gasped when I checked my body and found that I was anchored to a cold, metal table. I pulled on both my wrists to no avail. I tried kicking, but my ankles were strapped down, and the burning sensation of the cobalt metal was working its way up my legs.

"That won't do you any good," a familiar voice said.

I lifted my head.

My uncle Patrick sauntered toward me, looking deathly since the last time I'd seen him in the base prison months ago. Black circles marred the underside of his sky-blue eyes. His brown hair was a mess as though he hadn't combed it in over a year. He settled on the side of the table, angling his head. "You've grown. You've turned into a beautiful woman."

I bared my fangs at him. "Is the compliment supposed to soothe my anger?"

"I wished that my brother, your father, and I could've gotten along. I wished he would've taken me seriously."

"You're still jealous that you decided not to become a vampire when you had the chance." I rolled my eyes. "Give it up. Any serum you come up with is not going to change a mere human into a perfect vampire. We all saw what happened to Blake Turner."

"Ah, but we've come a long way in just a few short months," he said proudly. "I'm only missing one ingredient that I believe will do the trick."

"Let me guess—me and Sam." I glanced to my right then left. "Where's my brother?"

Patrick smiled as if he'd caught the canary. "Imagine my surprise when I discovered that Sam has the same DNA makeup as you. Well, one or two small differences, but when I combine your blood and marrow, the results will be powerful. I'll create vampires that supersede your father, your brother, and even you." Confidence oozed off him. "I'll return shortly to take you into my lab."

I stared up at the metal ceiling.

The door squeaked open. "Oh, and Jo? Your powers don't work in here. So even if you get loose, you won't be able to take down the building." The door shut with a resounding thud.

Great! I was dead in the water. I scanned the room. The walls, floor, and ceiling were metal, and probably cobalt. It was the one metal that could kill vampires and the one substance that could prevent us from wielding our powers. I knew firsthand since the cells in the base prison were made out of the same metal.

I relaxed as my breathing slowed. Panicking wouldn't get me off the table. I had to think. But all I could think about was how Webb was probably losing his mind by now. As soon as he'd left the truck, an eerie feeling had come over me before the scent of vampires floated in the air. Sam had tried to start the truck's engine, but for some reason, it wouldn't start. Then before we could even get out of the truck, men came up from behind, pulled us out, stuck needles into us, then threw us into a black SUV. Now I was between a rock and a hard place with no way out. Tears welled up as the urge to scream sat heavily within me. The urge to kill was stronger, though.

Your powers won't work in here. Maybe not, but I had to try. I remembered when I had found Edmund in the base prison. The one thing he'd been able to do amid the cobalt walls was telepathy. Maybe I could get into Sam's head and find out where he was.

"Sam." I said his name out loud and repeated his name in my head. "If you can hear me, I'm okay. How about you?"

As I waited, I heard voices, although they were faint. Someone was almost yelling.

"You owe me that money," the male said. That was Bruno. I couldn't forget his distinct baritone voice.

"You didn't deliver Jo and Sam," Edmund said. "My team did."

I shivered at the sound of Edmund's voice as excitement blanketed me. Maybe I would have the chance to get my revenge on him.

"I put that GPS tracking chip in London," Bruno returned. "I did everything you asked me to."

"You were supposed to kill London. That was your first order."

Bruno raised his voice. "The outcome is still the same. You got what you wanted."

"No, I didn't. You were supposed to deliver the Mason twins. And what are you crying about? You stand to make more selling sentinel blood than the mere million you would have made from me," Edmund said. "Now, get out. Don't make me kill you."

Bruno laughed before a door slammed shut.

Footsteps drew near. A beep sounded before the door opened. I lifted up. Lo and behold, Edmund strutted in, his long legs encased in jeans. A crisp white button-up shirt covered his chest, and his black hair was perfectly coiffed as though he was getting ready to model for a men's magazine. Edmund wasn't ugly by any means. I could see why Kate was drawn to him.

He smiled, showing white sharp fangs, as he settled next to me. "How are you?" His voice was sweet.

I laughed. "My enemy wants to know how I am? Do you care?"

"Jo, that hurts," he said. "You should be excited that you and your brother will be part of something epic in our world. The elders will be ecstatic when they see firsthand what we can do with science. Then the military will be answering to me and not your father."

The only thing that I was excited about was driving a dagger through his heart. Better yet, burning him before I cut off his head. He didn't deserve to have a cobalt blade through the heart. That would be too easy. No, Edmund Rain needed to be tortured to a slow death.

I snarled. I wanted to spit in his face, but that wouldn't have gotten me far. "So you're going to build an army and show the elders you're better at leading than my father. Why would I care about that?" I didn't see what benefit his mission held for me. Sure, he would command the military. But I wasn't in the military. Frankly, I wanted to be far away from any military base. I wanted to live at Webb's house in Maine. As I studied the man, I had a fleeting thought. "If I were your daughter, and I was kidnapped by your enemy, what would you do?"

Grasping my hand, he cocked his dark head as though he was trying to read my mind. Which I knew was impossible. He didn't have that capability. "I would hunt down the asshole and kill him."

I choked. He would flip out then if he knew he had a daughter.

He let go of my hand. "What did you say?"

My face had to be pale. "I didn't say anything." I clenched my fists as all my muscles tightened. I swore to my dad I wouldn't say a word about Abbey. Her mom wanted to keep Abbey from Edmund. She feared as did my dad that Edmund would experiment on his own flesh and blood.

"You said 'had a daughter.'"

No, I only thought that, unless those last few words had actually come out. "I said I was glad I wasn't your daughter." *Liar.*

His eyes changed from light brown to red. "Mm."

Immediately, I thought of Ben. "Why do your eyes change to red?" Again, my curiosity was piqued.

"Why do your eyes change to violet?" he countered.

"I assume that the unique color is due to the fact that I have strong powers."

"Then you've answered your own question. I just wanted to say hi before Patrick starts his testing."

"Are you going to kill Sam and me?"

He patted my hand. "I'll see you later." Then he left the room.

I blew out a breath. That entire conversation had been weird and scary. He'd been nice, not the creepy man I'd met in the basement of Highland Memorial Hospital. He certainly didn't give off the same vibe he had when he'd left me on the boat to die. Sure, that evil man was still inside him. But part of me thought I'd thrown him a curveball when I asked him what he would do if he had a daughter. Not only that, but I swallowed my panic when I seriously thought he'd read my mind, because I knew without a doubt that I hadn't spoken a word of his daughter, Abbey.

Patrick returned, giddy. "Now it's your turn." He pressed something on the table before I found myself on the move.

I started chanting *Sam* in my head. I had to get through to him, although I wasn't sure what good it would do. Talking to him telepathically wouldn't free me.

The bright white ceiling whizzed by. Machines hummed as we passed by rooms along the narrow hallway. A scent of a vampire permeated the hall.

"Patrick," Bruno called.

I raised my head. The white-haired vampire pointed a gun as he stalked toward us. I yanked on the restraints.

"What in the world?" Patrick started pushing the table in the opposite direction.

"Let me off this thing," I shouted.

"I can't," Patrick said. "The key is in my lab, and my lab is the other way." Fear laced his tone.

"You can't run with me." I was on a freaking table.

All of sudden, Patrick fell. His head hit the table before he splattered to the floor. Then Bruno was at my side. "You're mine." He had a key in his hand then worked to get me out of the restraints.

As he lifted me in his arms, I glanced at my uncle, whose body was lifeless. If he were dead, then that meant the key to Edmund's plan was gone. My hope died when I didn't see any blood.

"Is he dead?" I asked as Bruno adjusted me in his arms.

He ran for the exit door. "I wish."

"Wait. You can't take me. I need to get my brother."

The alarms blared when he barreled through the exit.

"No time."

I kicked and screamed, but my voice died when he threw me into the passenger seat of a van then knocked me out.

19

WEBB

Licking my lips, I rubbed my head as I blinked to orient myself. One look around, and I saw two sets of eyes staring at me.

Steven stood against a wall in the small medical room, looking as though someone had pissed in his cereal. I should be shaking, but I wasn't one to cower before anyone, not even the most powerful of vampires. His eyes shifted colors several times, a sign he was trying to rein in his power.

Dr. Vieira, who was at my bedside, gave me a pitiful look.

I almost laughed, but instead I said, "Nice to see you, Doc."

"Damon, leave us." Steven's voice boomed, the sound practically shaking the walls.

"Let me check one thing." Dr. Vieira flashed his penlight in my eyes. "How do you feel? I gave you an injection of something I'm working on to counteract the sedative in those bullets."

"I have a pounding headache. Is that one of the side effects?"

"Possibly. You're the first vampire I've tried it on. I'll make note of that. The good news is that you were only out for three hours instead of twenty-four." He pressed his stethoscope to my chest. "Your heart rate is normal. Interesting. In the lab rats, their hearts

147

raced when I injected them with my experimental drug." He wrapped the tubing of his stethoscope around his neck. "Good to see you. I'm glad you're alive." He turned to leave.

"Wait, Doc. Bruno implanted a GPS chip in me and the other sentinels that were on the mission with me."

Steven straightened. "Where?"

"I don't know. Kate gave me the tip just before I got shot."

"You were with Kate?" Steven growled loudly, showing fangs. A chair rattled next to him.

Man, Jo and Steven were so much alike when they got angry. *Oh, fuck. Jo.* I winced at the thought of Edmund having a field day with her.

"I'll get the metal detector." Dr. Vieira rushed out of the room.

I couldn't tell if he was worried about the chip or afraid of Steven. Then again, everyone was afraid of Steven when he got angry, with the exception of me. I swung my legs over the bed before I stood. As I did, I wobbled slightly. *Fucking sedative.* "Steven, before you shatter the windows, hear me out."

"Hear you out," he shouted, his chest heaving. "You take my kids, disappear, don't even tell your team what you're doing, and you want me to stay calm. Oh, and where are my kids? Let me guess. Kate took them." He got in my face, then out of nowhere, landed a punch that broke my fucking nose before he sent me into a wall.

My spine cracked. I bent over then straightened as my spine snapped back into place. No sooner was I upright, than he came at me again. This time, I caught his fist. I had a strong urge to return blow after blow, but that wouldn't do any good at the moment. It certainly wouldn't bring back Jo and Sam.

He stalked away, muttering expletives. "The last fucking thing I wanted to happen was for Edmund to get his hands on my daughter. Not only does he have Jo, but Sam. Olivia tells me that they have the same DNA makeup, and that Bruno was responsible for stealing their data from the lab in Boston. Is that correct?"

"Yes." I moved my nose back and forth, the bone righting itself.

"Steven, I had no idea I had a chip embedded in me. I had no idea they were tracking me. My goal when I met with Kate was to plant a tracking device on her so we could pinpoint Edmund's location. The plan backfired." Just like the two missions Steven had led had backfired. He should've cut off Edmund's head for killing a human.

"Did you plant the tracking device on Kate?" His voice lowered, but his tone was hard as granite.

"Yes."

He chewed on his cheek as he paced the small room with his fists clenched at his sides. "My worst nightmare came true. Jo and Sam should've never left this base."

"You can't keep them locked up forever. They're strong. They're good fighters. They'll survive this." They had to. Jo had to. If she didn't, I would kill myself. Hell, I would kill no matter what. No way was Edmund or Bruno getting away with what they'd done.

Steven whipped out his phone. "Get a secure laptop up to the infirmary."

"I need some blood." I blew past him and into the main part of Dr. Vieira's lab. I headed straight for the fridge, but as I passed one of the lab benches, I froze. The heads of Crowe and Quade were encased in glass boxes as though they had been preserved forever.

"They were delivered this morning." Dr. Vieira walked up with a small metal detector in his hand. "Sad, isn't it?"

My stomach pitched. I understood that soldiers took risks every time they left for a mission. Death was a risk. Getting captured and tortured by the enemy was always prevalent. Still, it didn't make dealing with the death of our brethren any easier. More importantly, breaking the news to their loved ones was harder, especially when I knew their families. Quade's little girl, Abbey, would be devastated. Actually, Abbey wasn't biologically Quade's daughter, but he had raised her as his own.

"Get some blood, Webb," Dr. Vieira said. "You need it."

What I needed was to find Jo and Sam. What I needed was to kill Edmund and Bruno. What I needed was to get the fuck out of there and never look back. After Jo was safe, I was done with the military. We were getting married and living a quiet life. George's voice rang in my head. "Good luck with that. I believe the twins are the ones who will be giving orders in our world."

Fuck our world.

The door burst open. "Webb." Olivia ran in with a laptop. "Christ, I was worried sick."

"I'm glad you guys made it back in one piece." I was slowly putting on my lieutenant hat. "How is Crysta?"

"She's fine. She's downstairs in the control room, arguing with Tripp and Kraft." Olivia beamed from ear to ear. Not to mention, she was back to her old self. The dirt, grime, and bruises were gone, and she appeared ready to fight. "The twins?"

"Kate got them."

"Speaking of which," Dr. Vieira said, "let's find those chips embedded in you. Olivia, can you get Kraft and Kodiak up here."

She scrunched her nose.

I flicked my head. "Make the call."

Steven came out of the room as Olivia set down the laptop on the counter. I proceeded to down a container of blood, a welcome relief for my dry throat. Instantly, the room, my senses, and every noise in the lab sharpened to a knife's edge.

"Let's find out where Kate is," Steven ordered, not losing his pissed-off look.

Before I set to work finding my sister, I had one thing to do. I walked over to Steven and threw a left hook that landed on his jaw. I didn't throw one hard enough to send him flying, though.

Steven rubbed his jaw. "What the fuck was that for?"

"That is for sleeping with my sister." Sometimes I wondered if Steven had a compassionate bone in his body.

Olivia and Dr. Vieira gasped.

Steven narrowed his green eyes. "Don't believe everything she tells you."

"Then enlighten me." I wanted to know more. I was beginning to understand Kate's reasons for wanting to kill me, and that reason was the most powerful of vampires. "Because from where I stand, we could've averted a lot of trouble and maybe have killed Edmund already. More than that, I could still have my sister at my side. She's family, damn it. She shouldn't be with Edmund."

He laughed. He fucking *laughed*. "She made her bed." He powered up the laptop. "Focus on the task." He pointed to the screen.

"Do you think this is funny? What if your daughter or son ran willingly to the enemy? What then?"

Olivia stepped in between us. "Jo's and Sam's lives are at stake. Finish this shit another time."

Oh, he and I weren't through with our conversation. That was for sure.

My fingers flew over keys as I punched in my passcode to the tracking program attached to the device. Once in, I waited for the satellite view of the city to emerge. Houses, buildings, and the bay filled the screen, but no green dot. I zoomed out to a wider area. Nothing.

"Are you sure you planted one?" Steven asked through gritted teeth.

My heart rate was dropping fast. The aftertaste of the blood I'd drunk soured. I kept searching, zooming in then out, anxiety sinking its sharp claws into me.

Steven growled, low and lethal.

A quick glance at the Wi-Fi signal showed I only had one bar. Grabbing the computer, I moved into the room I'd been in earlier and went over to the window. The signal picked up. When it did, a flashing green dot brightened the screen.

With the laptop in my hands, I stalked out of the room. Standing in a line of sorts were Kraft, Kodiak, Tripp, and Ben. Wait. Ben? My gaze lingered on the boy. He was beefier and taller than I remembered. His scent was human, and at the same time, it wasn't. Jo had said she thought he was half human and half vampire.

Tripp broke out of the line and trudged up to me. His sandy-blond hair was tied at his nape, and his features were drawn as though he carried the entire universe on his shoulders. He probably did since he was working under the commander. I knew the feeling all too well. Tripp dipped his head at me but didn't smile. "Good to see you, Lieutenant."

What the fuck? He and I were best friends. I'd expected a warmer welcome.

He drilled his bronze gaze into me before his voice was blaring in my head. *I want you to stay calm. Let me handle what's about to happen.*

I glanced past Tripp. Kodiak and Kraft looked away. Something was about to go down.

"Did you get a location?" Steven asked.

I returned a telepathic message to Tripp. *Care to tell me what the commander's next move is?*

Do as you're told. I promise I'll take care of everything, Tripp responded.

I trusted Tripp with my life. So I said, "Yes, Commander." I had a feeling I knew what was coming.

Olivia shook her head at me.

"So is Ben a sentinel now?" I asked.

Ben smirked, and all I wanted to do was punch his lights out.

"Well? Kate's location," Steven barked.

"She's on the Indian reservation just outside of town," I said. "Address is on the screen."

Whatever was about to go down, I still acted as though I was part of the team. I walked over to the door. "I'll get my gear."

"You're not going," Steven said. "Kraft and Kodiak, escort Lieutenant London to the brig. If he tries anything, kill him. Ben, I want you to stand guard."

I laughed so hard, I could barely contain myself at the notion that Ben would guard me. "You've got to be kidding. Ben doesn't stand a chance," I said through laughter.

"He's not human anymore," Dr. Vieira said. "If I were you, I wouldn't test him, either. He's quite strong."

The thought of landing a punch to his face crossed my mind until Kraft and Kodiak secured my arms behind my back before locking me in handcuffs.

"You can't do this. You need me." I pinned a deathly look on Steven, who returned his own death stare.

If Steven wouldn't budge, maybe my team would. I opened a telepathic connection to Kraft. *You have to let me go.*

You're too close to this mission. Let us handle it, Kraft said.

We promise we'll get you out, Olivia said.

"And if any of you do anything to aid and abet Lieutenant London, then you'll find yourself in the brig. Is that clear?" Silver banished the green in the commander's eyes as he pinned a look on each of the sentinels.

"Don't worry, Commander," Ben said. "I'll make sure."

I laughed. "You're not a SEAL. And you're not on the team."

"That's for me to decide," Steven said. "Tripp, you're in charge. So get London to the brig then meet me in the control room."

I clenched my jaw as I was escorted out of the infirmary. I thought about pleading with Kraft, Kodiak, and Tripp, but I couldn't risk their military careers. *You also need to save Jo.* Somehow, I had to find a way out.

20

JO

Something hard hit my head, and I jolted awake. It took me a second to realize I was in a van, speeding around a curve so fast that we were sure to tip over. Another second ticked by, when I homed in on Bruno, who had his gnarly fingers wrapped around the steering wheel, driving as though he was on his way to a fire. Oh, wait. He was. He'd kidnapped me from Edmund.

"You stole me from my enemy? I don't understand." I moved my jaw back and forth. "And you punched me. Ass." I went to touch my bruised jaw, but my hands were cuffed with those stupid cobalt cuffs.

"That jerk owes me money, and until I get it, he doesn't get you."

"Go back. I have to get Sam. We're worth more together."

He banked around another sharp curve, and again, my head hit the window.

"It's too risky. Besides, I'll demand the full amount. They want you just as badly as your brother."

As crazy as he was driving, I had an even crazier idea. I was a vampire, which meant I would heal from my injuries. I tried for the door handle as best I could, considering my hands were locked together in my lap, but there was no handle.

He let out a maniacal laugh. "Do you like my van? You can get in but never get out."

Complete darkness wrapped around us as he turned off the headlights.

"Are you mad?" My nails bit into my legs. "Turn on the lights."

"It's too risky." He banked around another curve at Mach speed.

My vampire vision could only see so far. The road behind us was also shrouded in black, which meant no cars were chasing us and neither was Edmund's crew unless they were as nutso as Bruno and turned off their headlights. I almost wanted Edmund's men to capture us. I had to get back to Sam. Or I could find help then go back. The problem was I didn't know where we were. I only knew that the passing trees and brush indicated we were deep in the middle of nowhere.

"Where are we?" I asked.

"Somewhere on the Indian reservation," he said. The road straightened out, and Bruno kept his foot on the gas.

I shuddered. Bad things happened on the Indian reservation, at least that was what the TV stations reported on occasion.

"Take me to my father." I knew his answer would be no, but maybe Bruno had a softer side. "Please. My dad will help you get your money." I couldn't go through seeing Sam tortured again by Edmund and Uncle Patrick. *Sam's a big boy and now a vampire. He can handle himself. Get help.*

Bruno laughed as he turned down another country road. Bright lights from an oncoming car blinded us, while the city lights twinkled in the distance. Finally, he flicked on the headlights as more cars littered the road. He slowed the van to the speed limit as he kept checking in the rearview mirror. Before long, we were passing rich homes in the Highlands section of Fall River. For a moment, I thought Bruno was taking us to Ben's house or maybe Darcy's. But when he made a final turn into a gated estate, my jaw dropped.

He pulled up to the intercom then pushed the button. "Bruno Almeida to see Victor Costner," he said into the speaker.

"How do you know Mr. Costner?" I asked, not knowing whether to be scared or excited. The first time I'd met Victor Costner, he was rather intimidating. Not only that, he was the father of my super nice teacher, Alia Costner. Surely, they couldn't be working with Bruno.

The gates opened.

He pressed on the gas. "We're in business together."

He navigated the mile-long road up to the circular drive of the Colonial mansion, while my mind tried to navigate a way out of there. Maybe being there was a blessing in disguise. Ms. Costner lived in a small cottage on the vast estate. I could seek out her help.

Bruno came to a stop in front of the beautiful home that twinkled with landscape lighting. He hurried out and rounded the van. When he opened the passenger door, Mr. Costner was strutting out of the mansion, his long legs eating up the space between us.

My stomach did one of those bungee-jumping drops. Yeah, Victor still intimidated me as he eyed me with a look of either horror or fear, I couldn't tell. I got the impression he wasn't expecting me or even Bruno. Maybe that was a good thing. Maybe he wasn't a monster like my brain kept telling me he was.

I raised my cuffed hands. "Take these off. My powers don't work here." Ms. Costner's magic spells prevented a lot of things from happening on the estate. She'd had several in play the night I attended the gala.

Bruno's almost white eyebrows drew down.

"Victor's daughter is my teacher," I said in a snippy tone.

Victor settled alongside Bruno. "What's this?"

Bruno motioned to me. "We have a problem."

I certainly wasn't the problem.

Victor strode the ten steps over to me and helped me out of the van. I wanted to say thank you, but my tongue was tied. The power peppering the air was thick. I shouldn't have been afraid since I was more powerful than him, or at least I thought I was.

"Edmund won't pay. So I took what was ours until he did," Bruno said to Victor.

Victor pushed up the sleeves on his striped button-up shirt. "Where's her brother?"

I swallowed, the fear pushing its way up into my throat. So Victor and Bruno were working together. Webb had told me that Victor was a prominent figure in the city and that he owned a design firm. I guessed Victor was into more than just designing.

"I couldn't get to him," Bruno said.

"If you let me go, I promise I won't say a word. I just want to rescue my brother." My brain kicked into gear. "Please, Mr. Costner. You have to help me." He couldn't be the bad man I was witnessing.

Bruno chuckled. Victor didn't. A muscle skipped along Victor's square jaw.

"Does your daughter know you kidnap people?" I couldn't imagine that she did.

"I don't kidnap people." Victor's voice boomed over the sound of an oncoming car.

Headlights beamed, lighting up the perfectly manicured shrubs along the circular drive. My pulse sped up as Victor walked away to meet the car.

Bruno grabbed me at vampire speed then rushed me down a path and around the house.

"I'll scream."

He pulled out a dagger from his cargo pants then held it to my heart. "No, you won't."

The blade glinted off the landscape lights. I should have been afraid, but I wasn't. Still, I couldn't fight back with my wrists cuffed, and I didn't exactly want to die tonight. At the moment, I settled for homing in on my vampire hearing to listen to Victor and Alia.

"Dad," Ms. Costner said.

"Alia, honey. I thought you were helping out at the hospital tonight. Isn't today your day to read to the children?"

"I wasn't feeling well," she said.

"Why don't you go lie down?" Victor said.

"Who's here?" she asked.

"A friend," Victor said.

I moved slightly, and Bruno pushed me against the house.

"Is Matthew home yet?" Ms. Costner asked.

"Not yet, honey. Go inside. I'll be in shortly. I was just getting something out of the van."

"Dad, are you entertaining a lady?" A lightness colored her tone.

"Go inside," Victor said.

Heels clicked along the pavement, and Victor appeared before us with a phone to his ear. His formidable presence made me shiver. I still couldn't figure out if he was a bad guy or good guy. I hoped beyond hope that he was a good man. I adored Ms. Costner, and if her father was into illegal activities, especially with Edmund, she couldn't be my tutor anymore.

He lowered the phone when two stocky men emerged from a door on the side of the house. Both of them were dressed in dark suits.

"What's going on?" Suddenly, adrenaline spiked through me. "Please, Mr. Costner. Don't hurt me."

Victor nodded to the secret service lookalikes. "Take Bruno to the basement."

Bruno bared his fangs. "What the fuck?"

Victor stalked up to Bruno. "You made the wrong move bringing Jo Mason here. I told you I didn't want any trouble. She wasn't part of the deal."

"But that asshole owes me a million dollars." Bruno puffed out his chest. "You said we could do business together. Well, this is my business. Are you going to help or not?"

I stood dumbfounded at the exchange.

Victor towered two inches over Bruno. "I'll take her back to Edmund."

My confusion quickly turned to fear until I thought of Sam. "Let's go before my brother dies."

"You're not going anywhere." Bruno lunged for me, but the two beefy guards grasped his arms. "She's worth twice what Edmund owes me," Bruno shouted at Victor.

Victor waved his hand at the guards. "Check him for a key to her cuffs and his phone. I need Edmund's number."

One of the guards obeyed, finding the key and phone, then handed the items to Victor.

"Now, take him," Victor ordered.

The men hauled Bruno away while Bruno squirmed and kicked.

Hope energized me once again, making me smile as though I'd won. Then I quickly frowned. We were headed back into the lion's den. I had to think of a plan.

Victor wasted no time in getting me into the van, where he unlocked the cuffs. I breathed a sigh of relief as I massaged both wrists. My burnt skin slowly healed. Then we were on the road, traveling through the gates and onto the streets of Fall River. Mr. Costner drove toward the bay as the lights to the base twinkled in the distance.

"The Indian reservation is the other way," I said.

He gave me a tentative smile. "I'm sure your father would like to see you first."

"With all due respect, I don't understand. You work for Bruno. He's one of the bad guys."

"That, he is, but I don't work for Bruno."

Within ten minutes, Victor rolled to a stop at the base gate as a guard I didn't recognize approached.

"I'm here to see Steven Mason," Victor said to the guard. "Tell him it's Victor Costner and I have his daughter."

The man in fatigues shined a flashlight on us then pressed a button on the radio strapped to his shoulder. He relayed the message to the control room. In an instant, the gates opened and the guard was waving us through.

My stomach filled with nausea as the van wound through the base. My dad was about to direct all his anger on me for disappearing. But I was ready for his wrath. I was ready to take my punishment, but first, we had to rescue Sam.

Victor had barely stopped, when my dad whipped open my door and tugged me into his arms. He hugged me tightly for the longest time before he let me go. "Are you okay?"

I expected my father to scream, yell, and make the world shake to its core. Instead, relief washed over his inhuman face. Tears slipped out as I nodded at my dad. It was great to see him.

Victor cleared his throat. "We need to talk."

I dashed away my tears. "Dad, Edmund has Sam."

"I know, pumpkin. We'll get him back." Dad sounded quite confident.

"You know? How?" As soon as I asked, I knew the answer. "Webb. Where is he? Is he here?"

Dad turned his attention to Victor.

"Dad? Are you going to answer me?" I didn't want to think the worst. After all, Webb had met with Kate—the one person who was trying to kill him.

"Not now." Dad pressed his lips into a thin line. "Why do you have my daughter?" Dad matched Victor in height.

The doors to the main building opened, and Tripp walked out. He would know where Webb was. Without another thought, I ran to him. "Where's Webb? Is he here? Is he... dead?"

Tripp touched my arm. Instantly, a warm feeling traveled through my body. "Calm down. He's fine. He's just locked up for now."

I jerked my head at Dad. I shouldn't have been surprised.

However, what had me scratching my head was that Dad wasn't reading me my Miranda rights and escorting me to jail.

A crease formed in between Dad's eyebrows. "Webb is off limits. Tripp, take Jo up to the apartment and stay with her until I get answers from Victor."

"Dad, please. I just want to talk to Webb."

"Sorry, Jo. I'll be up in a bit. Then we can talk."

"I would prefer if your daughter was part of our conversation," Victor said. "I believe she will be instrumental in helping you and me."

My dad chewed on the inside of his cheek as he considered Victor's request.

"Dad, Victor isn't the bad guy here." I didn't know that for sure. But the despair written on Victor's face told me he needed our help.

Dad started for the building. "Very well. Come with me."

Victor, Tripp, and I followed him into a conference room off the main lobby. We settled into leather chairs around a rather large conference table. A picture of the President of the United States hung on the wall behind where Victor sat. Tripp and I were across from him, while Dad got comfortable in a chair at the head of the table.

"I want to start by saying that I would appreciate you not saying anything to my daughter." Victor addressed all of us. "Do I have your word?" He took our silence as a yes and continued. "I've been working as a liaison to the council of elders. As you know, Bruno Almeida has been on their radar for quite some time. After you botched that mission in Argentina, they contacted me and asked if I would get involved in helping them bring in Bruno. I said no. But they've been persistent for the last year. As you know, human bodies are turning up in alleys and on streets all over the globe. Bruno's blood smuggling has gotten out of control."

"That's nothing new," Tripp said.

"What could you possibly do to help the council reel in Bruno?"

Dad asked. "You're a businessman and nothing more." Dad had a bite to his words.

My guess was he didn't like Victor's inference that Dad had not done his job properly in Argentina.

"The council is desperate. The human government is starting to realize that they may have a supernatural problem since human bodies have been piling up, drained of all their blood. Also, let's not forget that Travis Jackson is still pushing desperately within the local government here to get answers on his son, Ben. Or the fact that"—Victor nodded at me—"Jo's picture was in the newspaper the morning after my charity gala, where her fangs were on full display for the entire city and the national news."

"Again," Dad said through a clenched jaw, "what is your role?"

Victor swallowed hard. "Money. A business deal with Bruno. One that would seal his fate to spend the rest of his vampire life in prison. Only I didn't get the chance to broker a deal. When I contacted him, he said he wasn't interested. This was around the time you sent troops to Alaska. Then this morning, I got a call from Bruno, saying he wants to chat and talk about a partnership if I was still interested. I told him I had to think about it. Then out of the blue, Bruno shows up with Jo tonight. Now here I am."

"Where's Bruno?" Dad asked.

"He's locked up at my estate."

"You had no idea that Bruno was working with Edmund?" Tripp asked.

"I didn't."

Dad studied Victor. "You're certain about that?"

"I know you can read minds, Steven. So why would I lie? What I do know is what the vampire public knows, thanks in part to Jo's murder trial, and that is Edmund's plan is and has been to build an army of vampires out of humans who are not natural-born vampires. In order to do that, he needs Jo's DNA."

"There's one thing that has been bugging me. Why did you ask Bruno where my brother was?" That piece didn't fit. Victor had given me the impression that he was in bed with Edmund and Bruno.

He lifted his eyebrows. "Ah. My daughter told me over dinner a couple of days ago that you and Sam were missing. I just assumed that if Bruno had you, then he would have Sam."

His answer made sense.

Dad leaned back in his chair. "Why are you here and not running to the council?"

Victor briefly dropped his gaze to his lap. "Because I have a daughter too. I know that if the tables were turned, I'd want you to do the same. And…" He bit his lip. "I believe that Edmund has my grandson."

I gaped. I'd met Matthew, who wasn't a natural-born vampire. Ms. Costner had said her son didn't carry the gene. "Do you know this for sure?"

"I don't. He hasn't come home from school, and when I contacted one of his friends, I was told that Matthew had been seen talking to a pretty lady named Nicki and he'd gotten into the car with her."

The room blurred for a split second as my eyes changed from silver to violet. If that girl was the same Nicki as Webb's old girlfriend, then no doubt, Edmund had Matthew.

"Does Bruno know that you're here?" Tripp asked.

"He thinks I'm returning Jo to Edmund."

"So you know where they're holding my son?" Dad's voice hitched.

"I don't," Victor said. "I took Bruno's phone, leading him to believe that I would call Edmund. I'm assuming Jo knows since she was there."

All eyes landed on me.

"All I know is that Edmund is somewhere on the Indian reservation," I said. "Bruno knocked me out when he threw me in the van."

Dad uttered the word "fuck" a few times as he stood. "I appreciate you returning my daughter. We'll take it from here. I'll also have my men at your estate to take Bruno into custody. He knows where Edmund is located. I need to get that information out of him."

"No," Victor rushed out. "I'll take care of Bruno, and I'll get a location for you."

Dad's face reddened. "Do you know what he's done to my men? Not only did he kidnap them, but he tortured them and even killed three SEAL team members."

"Look, Steven." Victor's voice lowered. "Let's not forget you're in the limelight. The council is still investigating you for the death of the Secretary of the Navy. You want to operate by the book. I promise you, Bruno will get what's coming to him. You know as well as I that our government will seek death for all that Bruno has done."

My dad grunted.

"Mr. Costner, you said earlier that I could be instrumental in helping both sides," I said. "How?"

"You know what my grandson looks like. So you can get in there and help him. He knows you. I'm sure he's scared."

Dad pushed to his feet. "Jo is not going back if that's what you're implying. If your grandson is in there, we'll get him out."

"I didn't see anyone while I was there except my uncle Patrick, Edmund, and Bruno. I didn't even see my brother."

Tears clouded Victor's eyes. "If we don't get Matthew back, it will ruin Alia."

"Is that why she wasn't feeling well?" Her illness was making sense.

"She doesn't know. Please, Steven. I don't want my grandson subjected to anything like that Blake Turner boy."

"I'll do whatever I can," Dad said. "But I'm not sending in Jo. She won't come out alive."

I sat up straighter. "Dad, hear me out." A plan was forming.

"Send me in while you get your team in place. He won't hurt me. I'm certain of this. I wasn't the one who escaped. Bruno shot Uncle Patrick and then took me. Edmund would believe I was back because of Sam. Look, Dad, we can't just keep raiding places where Edmund is. He's always one step ahead of us. At least if I return, I can try to glean a lot of information from him and Uncle Patrick. I also have to get my brother back."

Dad rubbed his jaw.

"Please, Dad. I'm your best shot at getting intel. I can handle myself."

Dad shoved a large hand through his thick black hair. "My daughter wants to go back into enemy hands."

"Sir," Tripp piped in. "Jo makes a good case. Think about the intel we could get for the council. So far, all we've done is lose soldiers. Not only that, why not plant our own mole within Edmund's organization? He would never suspect Jo as a mole."

I kicked Tripp under the table. Well, it was sort of a thank-you tap for agreeing with me, although Webb wouldn't be pleased with our plan.

"How long am I supposed to let Jo stay undercover?" Dad asked. "And what if Edmund decides to kill Jo and Sam?"

All I kept thinking about was my dream and what the panther had said. I was the key to my loved ones' survival. I believed that with all my heart. I had to convince my dad to let me help. I refused to be locked away. "He won't, Dad. He wants my DNA. Uncle Patrick wants to combine mine with Sam's. He said something about how powerful it would be. So they won't kill Sam and me until their testing is complete. I say we have about twenty-four hours. In that time, I'll find out everything I can. That will give you time to strategize."

"Steven, I beg of you. Jo is powerful. She seems like she can handle herself. I can't let Matthew become a monster." Victor was almost in tears.

If Matthew was one of Edmund's victims, then I might be too late. Regardless, I had to help.

The room fell silent as tension whipped around Dad. "Twenty-four hours. Not one second longer."

I flew off my chair and hugged him. "I promise I'll do a good job."

21

WEBB

I banged on the prison door for the thousandth time. "Ben, let me out."

It had been hours since I was thrown into the cell, and I'd spent those hours pacing and pleading. Hours thinking of Jo and what Edmund was doing to her. Hours of seething at the commander for allowing his anger to drive his actions. Hours of planning Edmund and Bruno's deaths. That was if I ever got out of there.

"How many times do I have to tell you no?" Ben's voice grated on me as he stood guard outside my door.

The boy had no business standing guard. He didn't stand a chance if I got out. Granted, he wasn't human, but that didn't mean he was stronger than me. The problem I had was that the cell door was impenetrable.

I paced the room, careful not to go near the walls. Cobalt swords were embedded into the walls in the event that a vampire got out of control. I didn't care to die in a cell. I would rather die in battle. I would rather die fighting to save Jo.

On the stairs, footsteps began their descent. I stopped in my tracks. Please. Please, let it be good news that the team had found Jo and Sam.

"Ben, you're relieved of your duty. I'll take it from here." Olivia's voice was music to my ears.

"I only take my orders from the commander," he said. "He put me in charge."

I roared with laughter. Steven had truly lost his mind. Then again, he might have been the smart one. He knew full well that my team sided with me and that they would do anything for me. Regardless, I wanted to strangle Ben.

I hurried to the door. The locks clicked, and the heavy door slid open before a rush of air swept in. I stepped out and found Ben sprawled out on the floor while Olivia checked his vitals.

"You didn't kill him?" I asked, even though I could hear his heart pumping.

Olivia pocketed the needle. "I want to. The kid gets on my nerves. But he's better on our side than he is roaming the streets or working for Edmund."

"You shot him with a sedative?"

"It was the only way," she said. "The commander doesn't know I'm here."

"Did you guys rescue the twins?" As soon as I asked, I knew the answer. If they had Jo, she would be down there.

"The house we raided was empty," she said. "Someone had been there because there was a warm plate of food on the table. So they knew we were coming."

"Did you remove the tracking devices that Bruno planted in us?" I still had mine in me somewhere.

She removed her dagger. "Yeah. Turn around." She carved into the back of my shoulder.

I felt nothing. Within a minute, she held the tiny device in her hand. She dropped it on the floor then smashed it to pieces with her booted foot.

"I take it you're here to break me out?" I knew Tripp or Olivia would come through. "Look, I don't want you putting your career on the line."

"Fuck my career. Bruno and Edmund deserve to die, and we have to do everything we can to stop them. The commander's judgment is a little clouded right now."

Mine probably was too. "Who else knows what you're doing?"

"No one."

I hugged her. "Thank you."

"Don't thank me just yet. We need to get off base. But before we leave here, I need to tell you something."

"We probably should get out of here first." I wouldn't put it past the commander to check in with Ben.

"We're fine. I have someone manning the cameras in the control room."

"Then speak." My patience was wearing thin. The sooner I got out of there, the faster I could locate Jo.

She hurried to barricade the doorway. "Um. Jo is on base."

No way. If she were, she would have been down there. Yet Olivia's pitiful expression told me she wasn't lying. "Is she hurt? Please don't tell me she's dead." Closing my hands into fists, I trudged up to her. "Explain."

"Bruno kidnapped Jo from Edmund and took off. Only he brought her to Victor Costner, who in turn brought her here. But the kicker in all this is she's getting ready to return to Edmund's compound. Victor has some blind notion that Jo can help save his grandson, Matthew, and Steven agreed to send her undercover to get information about Edmund's operation. He's given her twenty-four hours before we raid the joint. We need to get to her before that. You know as well as I that Edmund is smart. He'll figure out what she's doing. Then she doesn't stand a chance."

The small hallway behind Olivia spun before me as though a tornado had picked me up. "Let me out of here."

"Webb, you're turning into Steven. Stop thinking with your heart and start using your military mind. Please."

My vision cleared at her suggestion that Steven and I were alike. Maybe we were. We both loved Jo, and I had a place in my heart for Sam. Regardless, Olivia was right. We couldn't go off half-cocked. If we did, then we would fail. I settled against a wall that wasn't laden with swords. "What's your plan?"

Olivia was a great strategist. I learned early on to always listen to her, which was what the commander should've done in Argentina. A pang of hurt gripped my stomach as the images of Quade's and Crowe's heads bombarded me.

"You and I are going to take down Edmund tonight," Olivia said.

"Tripp said he would help. Where is he in all this?"

She looked away. "Tripp thought it was a good idea to send Jo back in."

"What the fuck? No way." Tripp would never pull a bonehead move like that.

Olivia raised her hand. "I promise. I'm not lying. We need to get to the twins. Twenty-four hours is too long."

"Did Steven not see Quade's and Crowe's heads in the lab?" Even the commander was losing his mind. "Do you have the location?"

She smirked. "Of course."

"Where's Bruno in all this?" That fucker deserved to die tonight as well.

"Bruno is under guard at Victor's estate," she said. "Victor's turning Bruno over to the council of elders."

"Fuck that. Bruno is ours." There was no way Bruno would get away with the deaths of Quade, Crowe, and Sloan, let alone the torture he had put us through.

"Steven agreed. Tripp said that Victor threw the Secretary of the Navy's death into Steven's face. Something about operating by the book. Look, there's a good chance Edmund already jumped ship and won't be at his compound when Jo arrives. Even so, we'll stay off the grid until we find Edmund."

I hoped like hell that Edmund had left, which would mean that Jo would return to base and be safe. "So Jo is going undercover to get information. Why again?" My mind was trying to make sense of all this.

"Tripp and Jo convinced the commander that we could get evidence against Edmund that would help put him away."

Footsteps trudged above us.

Slip back into the cell for a minute, Olivia said in my head.

I darted into the cell. The last thing I wanted was for her to get into trouble. Then again, she would anyway since Ben was laid out on the floor, breathing deeply.

"Olivia?" Jo asked in a whisper.

"God, you made my heart race," Olivia said.

I wanted to run to Jo but hesitated just in case the commander was with her or close by.

"I don't have long," Jo said. "I told my dad I had to run up to the apartment to change. We're leaving within the hour. Can I see Webb?"

She waltzed through the door like an angel. Her black hair was unbound and free about her shoulders. Her cheeks had a pink hue to them, and when we locked eyes, my heart sputtered for a second then sprinted. She ran into my arms, and it was all I could do to brace my knees as I caught her then held onto her as though she was my lifeline. Hell, she was. She was the reason why my life had meaning now. Before her, I had been a robot going about my day, not caring if I lived or died. With her, I wanted to do more than live. I wanted to soar. I wanted to show her how much I loved her. I wanted to wake up every day with her next to me. I wanted to chase her along the ocean's shore then tackle her to the ground before we made love on the beach. I wanted so much with her that I was afraid I wouldn't get the chance to do all those things, and I knew I wouldn't with Edmund still alive.

"I'm sorry," she said into my ear. "Sam and I couldn't react fast enough when Edmund's men found us."

I set her down and framed her face with my hands. "Not your fault."

She turned her head. "Oh my God. What happened to Ben?"

"He's sleeping," I said.

"What are you planning?" she asked.

I guided her face toward mine. "Nothing. Olivia wanted to talk to me, and Ben wouldn't allow it. He's fine. You can hear his heart working." I leaned down and planted a kiss on her lips. She tasted like chocolate. "Yum."

"I had a candy bar."

I wanted to taste more of her, but time was of the essence. "Listen, angel. I know what you're doing. You can't go undercover." I knew no matter what I said or did, she was determined, although I could lock her up.

"You're not locking me up. I'm doing this. I have to. I'm going to kill Edmund."

I guessed my magical potion had worn off.

She raised her eyebrow at my thought.

Busted.

I exchanged a wary look with Olivia. "So you're not going in to get evidence?" I asked Jo.

"Yes and no. In the end, Edmund needs to die, and I can kill him." She lifted her chin, defiance and confidence oozing off her at the same time. "Whatever happens, I love you."

I growled a little too loudly. "I should lock you in this cell, but then I wouldn't be any better than your father. I trust you. I know you can fight. I just don't like this plan." I would lose her if I locked her up. I could also lose her at the hands of Edmund.

"Trust me, please," she said.

"You need to go, Jo," Olivia chimed in.

I had to trust that she would come back alive. "I have your back." Once I was free, I would do whatever it took to save her.

She pressed her hand to my chest. "Please don't flee. We can convince my father that your actions were to protect Sam and me."

I tapped lightly on her nose. "Stop reading my mind. Concentrate on what you're about to face. Just know that I have your back. I'll be right behind you. And—"

"Yeah, the sedative. Dr. Vieira already injected me with his experimental solution. He said it helped you, but that was after you'd been injected with it. He's not sure how it will work pre-sedative. It doesn't matter. Edmund won't harm me. You know, he was really nice to me earlier today." She looked at my boots. "But…"

I lifted her chin.

"I might've screwed up. I asked him a question about what he would do if his daughter was kidnapped."

My body tensed.

"Then I thought about Abbey. I think he can read minds." She shivered. "I never said anything out loud. I promise."

"Jo, Edmund can never know about Abbey." That little girl didn't need to be subjected to Edmund and his cruel ways. No one did, for that matter.

"I know that. Look, I've got to go before my dad calls out the dogs. I promise I'll be safe." She lifted up on her tiptoes and kissed me quickly.

I was having none of the kiss and dash. So I tugged her to me, slipped my tongue into her mouth, and explored, taking, tasting, and teasing.

She moaned softly as our tongues collided.

Man, I didn't want her to go. I just didn't know how to convince her otherwise without ruining our relationship, although a tiny part of me believed she could kill Edmund. She was strong physically and metaphysically.

She pulled away. "I know I can't stop you from escaping. But please don't hurt my father. He's trying."

"Angel, you worry about what's ahead of you. I love you. I'll see you very soon."

"I know." She backed away, tapping her heart twice. A gesture she did with Sam that said she loved him.

My chest hurt as I watched her walk away. I had to believe that we would see each other again.

22

JO

It was approaching midnight as I rolled into Edmund's compound in Bruno's van. Dad thought it would be better to show up in the same vehicle I left with. I'd also fabricated a story about Bruno because I was certain Edmund would ask about him. As soon as I threw the gear shift into park alongside a black SUV, two spotlights came on. Then a camera on top of the two-story building swept from side to side. Before I even hopped out of the van, two men in black rushed out with their guns pointed at me.

I raised my hands. "I'm here to see Edmund."

One of the guards lowered his gun then frisked me. "She's clean."

I almost wished they would shoot me just to see if Dr. Vieira's drug worked. Yet it was best if they didn't. Because if I didn't react accordingly, then they would suspect I had been with my father.

The guard who frisked me grasped my arm and ushered me inside. I wanted to say I wasn't nervous or that I didn't want to puke, but I was and did. Even the drive over there was nail-biting. My dad had followed me until we were five miles out, then I'd traveled the

175

rest of the way on my own. I still couldn't believe he had allowed me to return. I also couldn't get past how Webb had even let me go. I'd expected that either Dad would barricade me in the apartment or Webb would've locked me up with him. The latter sounded wonderful. But it was time I took matters into my own hands. If my father hadn't agreed, I would've found a way to return. Sam needed my help, and so did any humans who were there.

I was escorted into the same room I'd been in earlier. A sterile table, medical supplies, cabinets, and bright lights decorated the room.

While I waited for Uncle Patrick or Edmund, I chewed on a nail. I felt as though I was at a normal doctor's appointment, waiting for the doc to come in and examine me. But this wasn't anything remotely similar to a doctor's visit. My mission was to cooperate with Edmund and gather information to use against him, at least that was my dad's plan. My plan was a bit different—kill Edmund. The problem was if I killed Edmund, my uncle Patrick would no doubt continue to experiment. So he had to die too, unless Bruno had in fact already killed him.

Edmund's body graced the doorway. "Well, you returned. Odd." Lines fanned out from his light-brown eyes. "Get her ready for transport," he said to the guards.

"Wait. Where are you taking me?" I asked.

His eyes flared red as his fangs lowered. "I was nice to you earlier. Not anymore."

"I didn't run. Your associate kidnapped me."

He held his chin in between his fingers. "Where is my associate?"

"He's locked up at Victor Costner's estate." I was supposed to tell him that I'd killed Bruno, but my gut told me to tell the truth. "When Victor left me alone, I took off. I drove Bruno's van back here." That part was a lie.

Edmund smirked. "Idiot. Why would you return?"

I rolled my shoulders back. "My brother. If your plan is to kill him, then you'll have to kill me too."

"Brave girl. So you didn't run to your father?"

"I talked to him." Time for some truth. Time for him to believe me. "He begged me not to come back here."

Edmund tapped his forefinger against his lips. "Is he about to show up with his army of men?"

"If he can find the place, I'm sure he'll show up," I said, sure and strong.

"Liar."

"Does it matter? Look, you need me."

"Actually, I don't. That's why I didn't chase Bruno when he kidnapped you, although your uncle was quite disappointed. His scientific mind was excited to study your DNA." He slipped a hand into his jeans pocket. "I guess now he can."

My throat became dry. "What do you mean you don't need me?"

He drew closer to me before he tucked a strand of my hair behind my ear. "You're truly beautiful." His eyes searched my face. "And so brave and strong." His voice was melodic. "You would be much better off at my side when I lead the vampire nation and the vampire SEALs."

I willed my body not to shake. "I thought your goal was a fabricated vampire army. Isn't that what you want to fight my dad and his men?"

He dragged one finger down the side of my face. "My plans are bigger than your father's little team of soldiers. I want everything. I want to be the one that rules the universe, and I'll need my so-called fabricated army. I am in need of something, though. I need someone to train those newly formed vampires who are almost ready to awaken. What say you?"

"You have an army already?" I held my breath.

"I do. They can't go out in the sun, but that's okay. The next batch of humans will, thanks to your brother's DNA."

He continued to stand a breath away from me.

"But you shouldn't be killing innocent humans who have no business in our world."

He smiled, showing fangs. "Darling, I'm not killing them. They signed a contract and waiver. Each person I've recruited has given legal consent."

I backed away from him then let out a breath. "Even Matthew Costner?"

"Even him, Jo." Edmund's voice was calm, soothing. He was talking to me as though we were good friends. "He signed the documents. He wants to be a vampire like his grandfather. Since he doesn't have the gene, he actually begged Nicki to bring him here."

I went over to the counter with the medical supplies and leaned against it. "So is he a misfit vampire like Blake?" *Please say no.*

"We injected him about two hours ago with our new serum that Patrick made up with your brother's DNA. So the verdict is still out."

His mom would have a fit. I kept my fingers crossed that he would at least turn out like Ben. "Does the council agree with you? Do they know what you're doing? You did kidnap Sam and me. We never consented."

"The council will see that what I'm doing is necessary if we want to adapt in this new age of war and poverty and all the fighting going on. We as vampires can stop the destruction that humans inflict upon each other."

He was delusional. "Our world has had laws in place for centuries to keep humans from knowing about our kind. The council will never agree to what you're doing. Or your beliefs in why you think that what you're doing will help this world."

His Adam's apple bobbed as he studied me. "I made you an offer. Work for me. You'll be free to do as you please. I won't lock you up like your father has."

It was my turn to study him. In a million years, I would've never expected to have a deep conversation with Edmund Rain. But I had been told many times by the sentinels and my dad that Edmund was a very intelligent man. "So you want me to train your army?" My dad certainly didn't have the confidence in me that Edmund had.

"Tell you what," he said. "Think about it. I need to get things ready to move us out of here. I'm certain it won't be long before your father shows up." He sauntered over to the door.

"Wait. How's my brother? I want to see him."

"He's fine. Pissed. But fine."

I sighed.

"I've enjoyed our little conversation." He scratched his perfectly styled hair. "But I do have a question that has been weighing on my mind."

The hairs on my neck stood at attention.

He ambled back to me and took my hand. "Come with me."

As I traipsed through the building, tethered to him, I found I was able to read his mind.

He couldn't get past how beautiful he thought I was. He loved Kate. He hated my father. And he believed most everything I'd said. Then darkness hit me before I was diving into the deepest recesses of his mind, where the darkest thoughts lived. Usually, I read immediate thoughts, but the ones that were deeply buried weren't always easy for me to read. I swallowed hard as he thought about Rachel, a girl with whom he was so in love, so much so he'd killed an innocent human when she'd broken up with him. In fact, the innocent human was Rachel's best friend.

I tried to pull away my hand, but he kept a tight grip on it as we entered another room that looked like the one we'd just left. The only difference was my brother was tied down on a table.

I ran to Sam's side. "Are you okay?"

His fangs shot out as he thrashed around, growling like an animal.

"Sam, relax," I said.

Edmund took up a spot across from me. "Give me your hand,

Jo." He extended his over Sam as though we were about to do an exorcism.

Sam switched his attention from me to Edmund then back to me.

I reached over and grasped Edmund's cold hand.

"What the fuck is going on?" Sam asked.

I had no clue except I could read that Edmund had a question. All of a sudden, a shiver zinged down my spine. It wasn't unusual for Edmund to do weird things. He did enjoy playing games. For example, he thought leaving me out on a yacht to die was comical.

"My question, Jo, is this. Do I have a daughter?" Edmund's eyes held mine so tightly, I swore he was trying to squeeze the life out of me with his glare.

Edmund can never know about Abbey.

Deflecting was the best course of action. "Why did you kill Rachel's best friend?"

"You should never answer a question with a question." Edmund held my hand like a vise. "Answer my question."

"How would I know?" I asked.

He let go of me.

Sam tugged on his chains. "Sis, tell me what's happening."

I wished I knew.

Edmund pulled out a dagger from inside of his jacket. Then he positioned it over Sam's heart. "One more time. Do I have a daughter named Abbey?"

Holy mother of pearl.

I scrambled to find an answer. I couldn't tell him. Maybe Kate had. I knew she hadn't. Dad had said only he, Webb, and me knew.

I checked on my brother, whose fangs were dripping with saliva, and his heart was beating out of control.

Edmund lowered the tip of the blade to Sam's chest, directly over his heart.

I placed a shaky hand on Sam's arm while keeping my focus on Edmund. "Put that away. You're a lunatic one minute, a nice guy the next. I don't get you." I should have been running from Edmund. Yet I wasn't. Mainly because of my brother, but also in part because I wanted to kill Edmund. The sad part was I had been enjoying our conversation, at least up until now. "How would you know if I were telling you the truth?" Unless… No way. Edmund could not read minds.

He pushed the tip of the blade into Sam's chest.

Sam screamed bloody murder.

I reached over and grabbed Edmund's wrist. "Stop." Equipment in the room began to shake and rattle.

Edmund sneered. "Tell me the truth."

Forgive me, Webb, Dad, and Abbey. "Yes."

Edmund stumbled backward, the dagger clattering on the floor.

Sam threw his head back on the table.

I almost slumped against the table. "Can you read minds, Edmund?"

He lowered his shoulders, confusion plaguing his features. "I have a daughter." He suddenly looked like a zombie.

"Edmund, answer me," I said.

"It's spotty." His voice cracked. "I get half of what you're thinking."

Sam's voice entered my head. *He has a daughter? Since when?*

Edmund held onto the counter. "So her name is Abbey?"

"Yes," I said.

"That's why Rachel broke up with me," he muttered.

"So you knew?" I asked.

"Of course not. But it makes sense now. She didn't want our child growing up around a wild man. Where are Rachel and Abbey? My guess is if you know about them, then your father helped to hide them. True?"

I lifted a shoulder. "I don't know the whole story, Edmund. I'm sorry. Look, I've told you the truth. We had a nice conversation. You said you didn't need me anymore, which means you don't need my brother. So let us go. I'll think about your offer too."

"His offer?" Sam asked.

Edmund shook his head once then locked his eyes on me. "I'm afraid things have changed. I do need you, and you'll have no choice in the matter. You're going to help me get my daughter."

My heart stopped. My dad would never let that happen.

23

WEBB

A car door slammed outside my house on base. Olivia was strapping a dagger to her leg and froze with her hands in midair. I hurried to the window in my living room and peeked through the curtains, not that I really needed to. I knew my guest was either Tripp or Steven or both.

Fuck. I'd waited too long to get my ass out of the prison. I didn't want to get caught and thrown back into the cell, and I didn't want Olivia to either. She'd been staunch in her decision to help me, even though I'd argued with her that I could rescue Jo and Sam alone.

She checked her watch. "We waited too long."

I harrumphed as I watched the commander and Tripp stalk up the porch. Before they could knock, I opened the door. Steven had an angry but despondent look on his face. Tripp, on the other hand, had his hand on his sentinel sword as though he was ready to fight me.

I glanced at his sword then back up at him. "If you plan on using that, you better be prepared for the outcome."

Tripp brushed past me. "Save the bravado, Webb."

I wanted to punch out my best friend's lights. Since when

183

wasn't he on my side? Since when was he stupid enough to send Jo to the wolves? *Let's not forget you let her go too.* Part of me believed she could get close enough to kill Edmund. After all, she had killed Blake Turner, although Blake wasn't as powerful as Edmund.

The commander trudged in without a word, which gave me reason to pause. I would've bet that he would have launched himself at me or had several guards standing ready to throw me back in jail.

"You realize that your career is in jeopardy for breaking London out," Tripp said to Olivia as he settled near my desk, which was situated behind the couch.

Olivia gripped the sentinel sword she had housed on her belt. "So what? Are you here to throw me in a cell too? Try it."

Steven chewed on his cheek as he observed Olivia then me. "Soldier—"

"Arrest us or get out of our way." I continued to arm myself with daggers, grenades, and my sentinel sword. I had no right to be insubordinate, but my patience was nil. Jo and Sam needed to get the fuck away from Edmund.

Steven pinned me with a hard gaze. "What's your plan?"

"Come again?" I asked.

Tripp's bronze eyes glinted in the soft glow of the desk lamp. "We're here, Webb, to talk about a plan to get Jo and Sam back. We don't want to send in troops. I want you on this mission, and it's best if we send in two sentinels. This one will require stealth and not a big hoorah."

I swung my gaze to Steven, who was sitting on the arm of the sofa. "I'm scratching my head as to why you would even let your daughter go undercover."

"At first, I thought sending Jo in was fucked up. But with all the pushback I've had from the council on arresting Edmund for what he did to Blake Turner, we need evidence. We had none at Jo's trial. We suspect that one of the elders is in Edmund's pocket. So again, it's imperative that we get some hard evidence against Edmund."

He shrugged. "I believe Jo can get us what we need. But I don't want her in there too long."

"Edmund isn't going to spill his guts as soon as Jo goes in. Trust takes time, Commander," Olivia said. "Plus, Edmund is a hothead, which means anything could happen. It's too risky for the twins, and the longer they're with him, the stronger the chance that they will end up like Webb and me—drugged for months on end while Edmund siphons their blood and uses them as lab experiments."

I rubbed my neck. "Look, I should've stopped Jo when she came down to see me in my cell. I didn't. She has this unbelievable confidence in herself. I too believe she can get evidence. But she can't kill Edmund. Olivia's right. Edmund isn't going to trust her as soon as she walks in, although…" Something hit me. "We're forgetting that Jo can read minds. That's how she's going to get evidence quickly."

Steven's shoulders slumped. Tripp lost his hard look, and Olivia and I smiled at each other. But as soon as I grinned, I frowned.

"What is it?" Steven asked.

"We need to get Jo out of there now." I threw on my flak vest. "You're not going to believe this, but Jo told me earlier that she thinks Edmund can read minds. If that's true, he'll know she's playing him, and he'll kill her."

Steven came up to me. "Stop for one minute. How is that possible?"

"Olivia, pack the car. Make sure we have bags of blood too."

Olivia set to work gathering gear.

Tripp began helping her.

"Webb," Steven said, his face turning ashen. "That is not possible."

"Whether it is or isn't, I'm not taking any chances. Oh, and where's Abbey and Rachel?"

Steven's face blanched even whiter.

"If Edmund can read minds, then he knows about Abbey. Get them somewhere safe." I grabbed a bag then rushed out to the car.

Olivia slid into the passenger seat. Before I got behind the steering wheel, I said to Steven and Tripp, "Send the blueprints of the building and anything else we might need to Olivia's phone. Also, wait for our word before you send in any troops."

I peeled out of my driveway before Steven or Tripp could say anything else. Time was of the essence. I blew past the guard at the gate then let up on the gas as I navigated the city streets. I didn't want to call attention to myself with the local police. While I drove, Olivia studied the map on her phone. Within twenty minutes, we were on the Indian reservation.

"Coming up on the right, there should be a dirt road," Olivia said. "We can hide our car there then hike the rest of the way."

I veered off and onto the dirt road.

"Pull up under the tall brush ahead," she said. "No one will see the car from the main road."

Once we were parked and loaded up with the rest of our weapons, Olivia punched the coordinates of Jo's location into the GPS before we began our trek through the dense woods. Coyotes howled, leaves crumbled, no doubt from other night creatures, and the moon's rays filtered through the tall trees.

As I trekked behind Olivia, my pulse and mind were all over the place. I kept thinking about Jo and how angry I was with Steven. He and I still had unfinished business. Sure, I had to take my licks for going AWOL, but he had some explaining to do about my sister. Afterward, I would be submitting my discharge papers from the military. It was time to start a new life with Jo, where there were no battles, distractions, or anyone trying to kidnap her.

"When we get close, remember don't go blazing in," Olivia said. "We need to scope out the area and find out what we're up against first."

I laughed at how the tables had turned. She was in charge, which was fine by me. She would make a great lieutenant. In fact, I would highly recommend her for my position, although Tripp would be a great leader too.

I walked around a large tree trunk that had fallen. "I asked Jo to marry me."

"All the more reason not to go in like a hothead," she said.

I had no plans of botching up this mission. I hadn't fucked up a mission in my career. "I can assure you that my mind is on nothing but killing Edmund after Jo and Sam are safe."

"What about the evidence that the commander wants to put Edmund away?" Olivia asked.

"Fuck the evidence. You know as well as I do that Edmund needs to die."

"I know," she said. "I just want to make sure you and I are on the same page when we get there because no matter what, my mission is to kill."

I loved Olivia like a sister. It seemed as though she and I were always on the same wavelength.

We hiked through mud, thick leaves, and dense brush as the scent of pine and dirt sat heavy in the air. After fifteen minutes, we found a good spot that gave us a somewhat shielded view of Edmund's compound from in between a cluster of trees.

Olivia whipped out her phone and brought up the blueprints of the building.

"You really should go back," I said. "I can take it from here." I didn't want anything to happen to her. I'd already lost three SEAL team members. I didn't need to lose any more.

"Webb, with all due respect, shut the fuck up. I know what's at stake, and I'm not doing this just for you. Besides, are you forgetting the commander allowed us to do this?"

"We lost three SEAL team members. I can't lose you too."

"Ditto. But this is my job. Now concentrate." She whipped out a set of night-vision goggles. "There's a large bay door on the north side of the building. We're sitting on the south side at the moment. No main entrances, just a side entry that should be visible from our position, and a door on the top floor that leads to the roof."

I positioned my own night-vision goggles at our target. These babies were a godsend, enhancing our vampire vision tenfold. I could see the door she spoke of. I also spotted two black SUVs parked about ten feet from the building.

I lowered my goggles. "If we can get on the roof, then we can go in there."

Olivia pulled out a pair of glasses from her flak vest that we'd had made for our black ops missions. The glasses had a host of features, including the ability to detect body heat and distinguish between a human and a vampire. She set the glasses on her nose. "I count five humans and four vampires."

"That's it? Only four vampires?" One of the five humans had to be Patrick Mason. But I'd suspected that we would be up against more vampires. Kate, Edmund, Sam, and Jo would make four vampires. Where were Edmund's guards?

I didn't want to panic just yet. "Can I see?" I slipped on the glasses.

All five humans were on the first floor of the two-story building. A human's core temperature ran about ten degrees cooler than ours. Therefore, they showed up as a bright white figure on the glasses. Two vampires, whose heat signals showed dark gray, were near the humans. The remaining two vampires were in a room on the second floor.

"Edmund isn't there," Olivia said. "He's moved. I'm sure of it."

I didn't want to wait any longer. "Let's find out."

She nodded. "We'll try the side door first."

We rushed toward the building at vampire speed.

Boom. Boom Boom.

Suddenly, I was catapulted backward.

Motherfucker.

I landed in a fucking tree, while two more explosions rocked the night. I struggled for air as I jumped down. Then I started running toward the fire.

"Jo!" My life flashed before me. *She can't be in there. She can't be in there.*

My thoughts were shattered as a large man ran out of the burning building.

I tackled him to the ground then began rolling him in the gravel, trying to put out the flames.

Olivia limped over. She had a foot-long branch embedded in her thigh.

"We need to check if Jo and Sam are in there," I said.

The man showed us his fangs. "They're not."

I stopped rolling him and almost kissed his burnt flesh. "Where are they? Is Edmund inside?"

His hands went to his throat. "Blood. The car."

Olivia and I both glanced at the burning SUV. The second one that had been parked next to it was flipped over on its roof at the edge of the forest.

I jogged over to the one that wasn't on fire. "Bring him over here," I said to Olivia. "That other vehicle is going to blow."

The vampire screamed when Olivia dragged him as if she was pulling a wagon.

I searched the overturned SUV and found two bags of blood in the console. I gave one to the vampire, who wasted no time in sinking his fangs into the bag. Then without warning, I yanked the branch out of Olivia's leg. She didn't flinch. *Tough girl.*

I handed her the second bag. "Drink."

Then I turned my attention to the burnt vampire. His face and arms were severely damaged, and his clothes were charred to almost nothing. But as he drank an entire bag of blood, his skin started to grow back, albeit only the first layer. He threw the empty bag off to the side. "I need another."

Olivia tossed her empty bag. "We need to move. The cops will be here with fire trucks. And we can't be here when the humans show up."

"This is your lucky day," I said to the vampire. "What's your name?"

"Howell." His voice was barely audible.

That was the dude that Sam had wanted to punch into oblivion, the same name that George had said was the nephew of one of his friends. But just to be sure, I asked, "Are you the Howell that transported Sam and Jo Mason to Alaska?"

Sirens peppered the quiet area.

"Come on," Olivia urged. "We need to go. Either pick him up or kill him."

He gripped my arm, pleading with his eyes as he tapped his throat. "No. I don't want to die. I am that Howell. Please help me."

I needed answers, and since this vampire was working for Edmund, he was going to give me all the answers I wanted. And if he didn't, then he would be the first of my victims to die.

I carried Howell as we trudged through the woods as fast as we could back to the car. Once at the car, I dangled a bag of blood in front of him. "Answer my questions correctly, and you can have this bag. Who was in that building? Where did Edmund go? Are Jo and Sam hurt?"

"Three other vampire guards and me. Five humans. Three boys and two girls. They were dead before the explosion. Whatever Edmund is injecting into the humans, it works on some and not on others. I don't know where Edmund is. And Jo and Sam are alive and well. Can I have the blood?"

"Not yet. How many humans and vampires left that compound?" I asked.

"All I know for sure is that four sleeping humans were wheeled out on stretchers." He held out his hand.

"I find it hard to believe that you don't know much," Olivia chimed in. "Like where Edmund was headed. Not only that, but if the humans were dead, why were you guarding the place?"

A car's engine grew louder. We were hidden from the main road, so we couldn't be seen.

"Our orders were to pack up the rest of the equipment then torch the place. Only someone beat us to it," Howell fired back. "If you want to know more, ask Bruno Almeida. He was brokering a deal with Edmund and some other silent partner, at least that's what I overheard. He probably knows where all Edmund's hiding spots are."

I threw the bag of blood to him. "Well then, let's pay Bruno a visit."

Olivia shoved Howell in the backseat, while I started the engine. I was determined to get answers even at four in the morning. *Fuck.* Edmund could have been on his way to Alaska. I remembered Steven mentioning something about activity in a warehouse in Alaska.

Olivia slid into the passenger seat. "Do you want to fuck with Victor Costner? I mean, he has a direct line to the elders."

"You said Edmund has his grandson. He'll get his ass out of bed."

I drove, staying within the speed limit since more red and blue lights were passing us in the other direction. After several turns onto side streets, the sirens faded. I sped up, not bothering to obey the stop signs. When we arrived at Victor's gated estate, I pressed the intercom button and held my finger on it until his sleepy voice blared through it.

"Webb London. Let me in."

The gates immediately opened, and I gunned the engine until we were at the front door, where Victor was waiting in plaid pajama bottoms and a robe to match. I would have given anything to be curled up in bed with Jo at my side. I growled as I flew out of the car.

"Did you find my grandson?" Victor asked.

I stalked into his house. "I want to talk to Bruno. Where is he?"

Olivia rushed in with Howell in her grasp.

Victor casually slipped his hands into his robe pockets. "I asked you a question."

With a sneer, I grabbed the collar of his robe. "And I told you I want to speak with Bruno. We don't have time for chit chat. If you want your grandson back, then fucking talk." My patience was on thin ice.

Olivia shoved Howell down onto the steps of the circular staircase. Then she broke me away from Victor.

I paced the veined tile floor.

"No, sir," Olivia said to Victor. "We believe Bruno can shed some light on Edmund's whereabouts."

Footsteps padded down the staircase. "Dad? What's going on?" Alia asked. "Is it Matthew?"

Victor closed his eyes then turned. "Honey, you need to get some rest."

Her eyes were puffy as though she'd been crying for days. When she set her blue gaze on me, she ran down the stairs, her blond hair wild around her face. "Webb, please tell me you found my son."

My heart hurt for her. "We'll find Matthew. I promise. If I know Jo, she'll do what she can to make sure he's okay." I didn't know how much Victor had told Alia.

"Alia, can you take them into the study while I get Bruno?"

While Victor went to retrieve Bruno, Alia escorted us into the study off the foyer. "Make yourself comfortable. I'll get some blood for you."

The three of us looked as though we were born out of the ashes. We fanned out in the large room made up of a sitting area, fireplace, bookcases, a pool table, bar, and desk. I walked over to the French doors that overlooked the gardens. Focusing on the landscape lighting, I blew out my pent-up energy, getting ready for round two. I would probably have to go ten more rounds before Jo and I could be together. But I didn't care. I would take the explosions, the pain, the anger, the heart palpitations, and even Steven's wrath if it meant that I got Jo back.

Olivia came up beside me. "Webb, I sent Tripp an update through a coded text. I also told him to stay put for now until we speak with Bruno. We'll find the twins." Her tone held confidence.

I wished I had faith. Granted, Howell said Jo and Sam were

alive when they left that building. But was she still alive?

Voices drew close. Olivia and I turned to find Victor pushing Bruno into the room. Someone had had a field day with the white-haired vampire. His face was healing from several cuts and bruises. My guess was that Victor had just beaten him a few times before bringing him into the study.

Bruno didn't move from the door until Victor pushed him again. Howell stayed seated on the rich leather sofa, not giving Bruno the time of day.

My legs ate up the space between Bruno and me. I clenched my fists as I stopped a foot from him. He grinned as though he wasn't scared in the least.

Olivia joined me.

"Where is Edmund?" I asked.

"You two don't scare me," Bruno said. "Besides, I told you where he was."

Victor hit him on the back of the head. "Well, you gave us bogus info. Try again or my men will torture you until you die a slow death."

He smirked proudly. "No, they won't. I heard you talking," he said to Victor. "The elders don't want you to kill me. You know, laws and all that."

"So you would rather rot in prison?" I asked.

He shrugged. "Why not? I get three squares a day. I get to read. I also get to lounge all day."

Olivia let out a roar of laughter before she hauled off and punched him in the face. Bruno's head bobbed back then forward as blood spilled from his nose.

I swung out my arm to stop Olivia. "Enough. Again, where's Edmund? He's not where you said he would be. So I want to know his other hiding spots. Is he going back to Alaska?"

Olivia muttered something.

Bruno licked his own blood from his upper lip. "He does have an army brewing there at some warehouse in Anchorage."

I reached for the dagger on my leg then positioned the tip of the blade on his upper chin. "Think harder, because I don't give a shit about laws and the council."

Bruno didn't flinch. "I'm ready to die. So go ahead and plunge that blade in my heart."

I backed away, grinning, even though the need to kill him was strong.

"So you believe that Edmund is on his way to Alaska?" Victor asked.

Alia came in with three containers of blood. "Alaska?" She handed one bag of blood to Howell.

I dragged my hand over my unshaven jaw. "Bruno, this is your time to shine. I'm sure if you help us, Victor will put in a good word for you with the elders."

With his hands cuffed in front of him, he picked at a nail. "No, he won't."

"He will," Alia said with conviction. "I'll make sure of it. I just want my son back. Please."

"I want more than a good word. I want two million dollars. Then I'll tell you where I suspect he could be."

At preternatural speed, my hand was around his throat, and he was pinned against the paneled wall. "You will talk." I drove the tip of the dagger into his chest. "If not, then say hi to the devil for me."

He grinned. I drove the dagger farther in.

Complete silence filled every corner and crevice in the room.

I pushed on the pummel.

Bruno's eyes started to bug out. "Okay. Aside from the warehouse in Anchorage, Edmund purchased a funeral home somewhere in Fall River. He uses it to incinerate dead bodies to keep the evidence at a minimum."

Olivia and I exchanged a horrified look. A funeral home? We'd found Jo locked in a coffin at a funeral home at the same time Sam had gone missing when he'd been a human.

"This funeral home. Do you know where it is?" I asked.

"It's on the other side of the Indian reservation," Bruno said. "That's all I know."

I removed the dagger then walked away. Bruno sighed. But without hesitation, I turned and threw the dagger with accurate precision. The blade embedded in Bruno's heart. He slid down the wall, his mouth agape as blood filled his eyes. He reached for the handle, but Olivia stopped him by holding the dagger in place. The cobalt blade would burn his heart, but the process wasn't instant. It could take several minutes or longer before the heart burned to a crisp, which in my book was why it was always better to behead a vampire. That way, death was instant.

Alia cried.

Victor glared at me. "Do you think that was the right thing to do?"

I returned his death stare. "He killed three of my men and tortured the rest of my team. He's better off in hell."

"The council won't like this," Victor said.

I didn't give a flying fuck what the council liked or didn't like. "Do you want your grandson back or not?"

"Of course we do," Alia cried as she ran up to me. "Please, Webb. Find him. My father will tell the council that Bruno died in a fight. We won't breathe anything else to them. Will we, father?"

"Our world is better off without Bruno," Victor said, glancing at his daughter.

It truly didn't matter to me whether he ratted me out to the council or not.

Olivia tossed me my dagger. "Let's go check out the funeral home."

"I'm going with you," Victor announced. "I'll get my sword."

I wasn't about to argue. "You listen to me, then," I said to Victor.

He nodded.

I returned my dagger to its sheath on my leg. "Then let's kill more vampires."

24

___

JO

I laughed uncontrollably as I sat in a funeral home, and not just any funeral home. Sam and I had been visitors here not that long ago when we were humans. The place had belonged to one of Dad's men.

Sam leaned forward, resting his forearms on his thighs. "Ironic or eerie?"

Shrugging, I stopped giggling. "More like weird."

The room had been remodeled. Gone were the coffin Dr. Case had locked me in, the wallpaper, the carpet, the scent of death, and the stained-glass window. Instead, cobalt lined the four walls. At least I assumed the shiny metal was the same metal that could harm vampires and prevent us from using our powers, although I hadn't tried yet.

"So how do we get out of here?" I opened and closed my fists, trying to conjure up my powers to at least make the empty chair next to me move. Nothing. "Our powers don't work in here."

"No clue. But we have to think of something," Sam said. "I overheard Edmund telling one of his men to get the plane ready for Alaska. We can't go back there."

196

I agreed. We might not be lucky enough to escape the second time around.

"I have an idea." My voice sounded hollow.

Sam's head shot up, his black hair falling over his forehead.

"I'll persuade the guard to open the door, then you compel him."

Sam tapped a foot on the floor. "We don't know how many guards are out there. Besides, if I compel a group, then I'm of no use to fight."

I'd counted ten vampires when we left the lab. "We know this place, Sam. The hallway outside the door leads to the main entrance. We can also assume we have two vampires guarding us. Compel them, then we can make a run for the exit."

"The other guards are probably at the main entrance or scattered around the house. We'll be shot with those drug-filled bullets."

I went over to the door. "Dr. Vieira injected me with his experimental antidote before I returned to Edmund. He didn't know how long it would last. Once we get out of this room, I'll build an invisible wall. That way, I can protect you." I didn't want to tell Sam that Dr. Vieira wasn't exactly certain if the drug would even counteract the sedative. Then he definitely wouldn't agree to my weak plan.

"Wait, Sis." Sam rushed to my side. "I just thought of something. When that door opens, the fresh air will give us more strength to combine our powers."

"Not with all the cobalt in this room."

"We have to try," he said. "At least cut off their oxygen so we can make a run for it."

Anything was possible. I banged on the door. "I need to speak to Edmund."

"Are you mad?" Sam mashed his lips together. "We can't test our power theory on Edmund. He's too strong. He'll wipe out both of us."

"We take out the king. Otherwise, we're dead." I banged again. "Hello?"

Sam walked away as tension spilled off him.

I kept pounding on the door. The more I did, the angrier I got. I hadn't slept in twenty-four hours, and I was beginning to get cranky. "Edmund," I shouted at the top of my lungs, clenching my fists.

"Um… Sis?"

I whirled around, about to snap at Sam, only to find the chairs skittering across the floor as though there were a ghost in the room. "I guess our powers do work in here." A few minutes ago, they hadn't worked. *You weren't angry a few minutes ago.* My anger always made my powers stronger.

I inhaled deeply, ready to test more of my telekinesis, when the door slid open.

With a phone to his ear, Edmund smirked at me. "If I get my daughter, then you get your children, Steven," Edmund said as the guard locked us in.

So that was how we were helping Edmund get Abbey. I'd asked him several times how we fit into his plan to get Abbey. Sam had guessed we were bait. While we now knew that for sure, Dad would never give Abbey to Edmund.

Sam scooted to my side just as Edmund hung up the phone.

"What's all the commotion about?" Edmund asked.

"My dad isn't going to hand over Abbey just like that." I snapped my fingers.

"If he wants you two back with beating hearts, he will." Edmund sounded extremely confident.

"What would you do with your daughter?" I hoped he wouldn't use her as one of his lab experiments.

"What every parent would do. Be a father," he said without feeling.

I rolled my eyes. "Seriously? How can a monster be a good father?"

He snarled, his eyes turning red. "Watch it."

"Have you not learned anything about our father?" Sam asked, slipping his hand in mine. "You two were best friends. So you must've known that he let us go when we were kids. We lived in foster care for years. He doesn't care what happens to us."

Edmund glanced at our joined hands then up at us. "How sweet. Brother and sister love."

Adrenaline filled my veins. Edmund had no clue what was about to happen, and as long as he didn't touch me, he couldn't read my mind.

Sam sneered. "More like powerful brother and sister love."

As I stared at Edmund, I thought about all the rotten things he'd done to me. Slowly, my anger began to take over, rising to the surface, energizing my powers. A tingling feeling throbbed along my arm, down to the tips of my fingers before it traveled up Sam's arm. The feeling was reminiscent of when I was a little girl and I'd touched a plug on a radio with a wet hand. Only this time, the charge was five times more powerful. My arm stiffened.

Fear plagued Edmund's face as he slowly retreated to the door. "What's going on?"

Funny thing was I'd never seen Edmund scared. He'd always been confident and creepy. I took comfort in knowing that I could make the color drain from his face. Sam and I lifted our free hands and squeezed the air as though we had our fingers clamped around his neck.

Edmund grabbed his throat. "Impossible," he managed to say. He kicked the door hard.

No sooner had the guard stormed in, than our powers grew stronger. Sam was right. The outside air helped to kick-start our elemental powers. The guard and Edmund were turning ashen. Within seconds, the guard collapsed.

Sam and I pushed forward, pouring every ounce of preternatural powers we had into blocking Edmund's ability to breathe. His eyes rolled back in his head before he joined the guard on the floor.

I let go of Sam's hand. "Edmund probably sent a telepathic

message to the others. So let's hurry. I'll get Edmund's phone and call Dad. You check them for weapons."

Once I had Edmund's cell, I tapped on my dad's name. I wanted to laugh at the fact that Edmund had my dad's name programmed into his phone.

"What now?" Dad's voice roared through the speaker.

"It's me. Sam and I managed to take out Edmund and a guard. We're at the funeral home that used to be called Foster and Sons."

"Get out of there and find somewhere safe then call me. My team and I are on our way."

Sam found a dagger, but nothing else. I found it odd that the guard didn't have a gun and that Edmund wasn't carrying any weapons. I dragged him away from the door just as glass shattered somewhere in the building. Heavy footsteps padded above us.

Sam held out his hand. "Jo, we don't have much time."

I reached for Sam when fingernails bit into my ankle.

"You're not going anywhere." Edmund yanked on me.

As I kicked, I fell forward, the floor rising up quickly. Sam dove for me but didn't reach me in time. My forehead bounced off the floor with a loud thud. Adrenaline kept me from feeling any pain. Kicking, I became a mop along the shiny floor.

"Not so fast, little one." Edmund's voice was hoarse but icy.

"Go," I said to Sam.

My brother stomped his way up to me, his eyes flashing vampire as the chairs spun out of control. "Not a chance I'm leaving you here." With his size ten feet, he smashed Edmund's head into the floor.

Edmund laughed, keeping his claws in me. I twisted around and pounded my heels into his stomach over and over again until he finally released me. I scooted back then jumped to my feet.

Sam drove the dagger into Edmund's chest. Edmund's eyes seemed to smile at me as though he was saying *you can't kill me*. He arched his back then began to laugh.

I tugged on Sam. "Let's go." As much as I wanted to wait so I could see Edmund die a slow death, we had to get out of there.

We bolted out of the room with me in the lead. I banked left toward the exit and ran directly into the point of a sharp and shiny blade. Before I could sidestep Kate London, she plunged the dagger into me.

"No!" Sam shouted as he went to grab her.

I held up my hand. "She's mine." At least I hoped I could tango with her, considering the pain radiating through my chest. The good news was that the blade had missed my heart. Regardless, I swayed, reaching for the black pommel. Once the leather grip was in my hand, I yanked out the dagger.

Kate stood there, smirking as though she'd caught the biggest fish in the sea.

Red blinded my vision for a split second before I used her dagger to stab her.

She continued to laugh. "If you're going to kill me, you shouldn't miss."

I withdrew the blade from her stomach. "You should take your own advice."

Blood started to coat her pink blouse. In a flash, she pulled out another dagger from the sheath strapped to her leg. "I won't miss this time."

The blade glinted beneath the muted lights overhead.

"So, what's it going to be, Jo?" Kate mocked. "You or me? Because one of us isn't walking out of here."

I couldn't kill her. She was Kate London. She was my fiancé's sister. She had been a friend to me at one time. *Never hesitate with your enemy,* Webb had said. That was my problem. Kate was the enemy, but she wasn't.

The dagger in my hand became heavy as my chest rose and fell. If she were Edmund, I wouldn't hesitate. But as her blade came toward me, my fight or flight instinct waged a war.

"Sis, let's go," Sam said. "Let her cry over her dead boyfriend."

Kate froze, darting her shocked gaze to Sam. "Edmund? Dead?" Her blue eyes turned liquid black.

"He looks peaceful," Sam taunted.

Her face darkened to a deep shade of red, and before I could say or do anything, her blade was on a collision course with my heart. Sam went to pull me away, but Kate was quicker. For the second time in a matter of minutes, a burning sensation spread throughout my chest.

Sam shouted or said something, but all I could hear was the pumping of my heart against my rib cage. I started to choke as the metallic taste of blood filled my mouth. I spit, almost puking. Kate and Sam were moving around me. Bone hit bone. Grunts ensued. I shook my head as I spit blood on the floor. Then Sam fell at my feet. I blinked several times, trying to clear my head.

Kate snarled.

Sucking in a large amount of air, I examined the dagger in my hand. That war raging inside me ended as I catapulted into action. In one smooth motion, I launched my dagger at her, when a gust of cold air flooded the funeral home along with a bright light. Yep, I'd read stories of people seeing a bright white light just before they died. I listed to one side, when strong arms caught me. I wanted to look up at my savior, but I couldn't take my eyes off of Kate. She slid down the wall, her eyebrows pinching together.

Webb's voice filled the room, barking orders. "Olivia, check on my sister." Then large warm hands were guiding me to a cushioned bench. "I got you, angel." Webb's voice was soft, breathy, and slid along my arms like a balm on a humid night.

Oh my God. I'd killed Kate. But as I glanced down at the black-and-silver pommel sticking out of me, I prayed for my own survival. I hadn't had a chance to marry Webb. I hadn't really lived. My whole life had been nothing but chaos around every corner. I wanted at least a small window to enjoy what it felt like to love and be loved, to lose my virginity, to sleep naked in the arms of the man I love, and maybe I could do something good in this world.

A quiet voice inside my head told me to remove the blade. *If you don't, the metal will continue to burn your heart.* The room was spinning. I blew out breath after breath as I reached for the dagger. Darkness pressed into the funeral home, or maybe I was about to pass out.

My heart was on fire. "I'm not going to last."

"You're not dying today, angel." He yanked the dagger out of me.

I sucked in large amounts of air as I arched my back. Before I could do anything else, Webb's wrist was on my mouth.

"Bite," Webb ordered. "The faster you drink, the more likely your heart will heal."

As my fangs sank into his wrist, my heart felt as if it was being diced into a million tiny pieces. I drank like a starved animal. Webb's blood cooled the burn in my throat, chest, and everywhere else. It was as though I could feel every piece of me knitting back together. The more I drank, the room around me sharpened. When I zeroed in on Webb, I almost smiled until I met his teary eyes.

At that moment, I wanted to hide. I'd killed his sister. *You don't know that she's dead.* "Is Kate dead?"

He glanced at his sister. Olivia removed the blade and started feeding Kate her blood.

My fangs retracted. The need to run blazoned through me. I touched his face. "I'm so sorry."

"Webb, Kate moved," Olivia said.

Webb flew to his sister's side.

"Where's Edmund?" Olivia asked Sam.

Running two hands through his hair, he came over to me. "He's dead. Sis, are you okay?"

Another sigh came from me when I saw that Sam was breathing. I wouldn't know what to do if I lost my brother.

"Are you sure about that?" Olivia asked.

I should've been worried about Olivia's question. After all, I didn't die. Which was odd since I'd had a cobalt blade in my heart. Regardless, I couldn't take my eyes away from Kate. As much as we were enemies, I didn't want her to die. Webb would never look at me the same again.

"Kate," Webb said.

Her eyes opened for a split second before they closed. Webb checked her pulse. Then he dropped his head before he looked at me. Sadness, hurt, and pain flickered across his face. I propelled to my feet, wobbling as I stepped backward, away from Kate, Webb, Sam, and Olivia. I couldn't breathe and probably never would again. I tore away my gaze from them and looked at the broken window to my right then back to Webb. Cold air blew over me, cooling the sweat on my face. I was about to throw myself through the window when Webb shouted, "Watch out, Jo."

In the blink of an eye, someone was holding a sharp blade to my throat, while his other hand anchored me to his chest. "You will pay for hurting Kate," Edmund said in my ear.

Seriously? This vampire wouldn't die.

"You son of a bitch," Webb said through a clenched jaw as he stalked toward us. "I will behead you once and for all. But before that, I will slice each limb from your body while you watch."

Edmund let out a rip-roaring laugh. "All talk, London. But I like your spunk."

Web fisted his hands at his sides, and his blue eyes became molten black.

Edmund pressed the blade into me. "Come any closer, and I'll kill her."

I shook my head at Webb. "Don't. I can handle Edmund."

Edmund choked out a laugh. "So brave."

"If you wanted to kill me, then the dagger would be positioned at my heart and not my throat," I said evenly. "Unless you don't want to kill me."

He breathed in my ear.

Then a lightbulb came on. "You don't want to kill me, do you?"

"I need you," he whispered in my ear. "If I make it out of here alive, think about my offer."

I was speechless. My enemy was trying to recruit me when his life was on the line.

"There's no way out," I said.

"Of course there is." Edmund's breath tickled my ear.

He was right. The window.

Webb was two feet from us when he came to an abrupt halt. He diverted his gaze past Edmund and me.

"Let her go, you bastard," the voice behind Edmund said.

Edmund tensed.

"I said let her go." Victor Costner sounded as though he was possessed with a demon's voice.

"Seems to me that you're a dead man," I said to Edmund.

"Maybe so. But they'll have to catch me first."

A gust of wind blew in. Sam nodded at me. He raised his hand and opened and closed his fist. I would do the same, except my arms were locked under Edmund's strong hold.

Edmund coughed while keeping me tethered to him. Sam didn't seem to have the juice to take the oxygen from Edmund.

"Where's my grandson?" Victor asked. "You have one second to answer me before I cut off your head."

Dear Lord, Victor couldn't perform that act without cutting off mine. Then Webb's voice was in my head. *I want you to head-butt him. It will stymy him for a second, and you can get away. Then Victor can do what he does best.*

I obeyed. When my head hit Edmund's chin, he grunted before he loosened his arms.

I spun around and ran backward, keeping my eye on my enemy.

Edmund cocked an eyebrow. "I guess I'm in quite the quandary now."

Victor raised the sword like a left-handed batter. As he swung, Edmund dove through the broken window.

Victor tossed himself through after Edmund.

"Olivia," Webb said in a deep voice. "Help Victor."

"I will too," Sam said.

A car screeched to a halt along with a thud.

Webb and I ran to the window. The streetlights dulled as the sky lightened.

Men spilled out of the SUV, followed by my dad. Beyond them, Edmund ran through the park, vaulting over benches and around the playground equipment. Sam, Olivia, and Victor chased him, while Dad barked orders. His team split up. Some fanned out into the park; others disappeared around the side of the funeral home, while Dad trudged toward Webb and me. I'd never been happier to see my father.

As the adrenaline slowly left me, I wanted to throw myself at Webb and beg his forgiveness. But I was afraid he would shun me. So I wobbled over to Kate. Her brown hair was neatly pulled off her face. Her long lashes swept her snow-white skin, and her red-painted lips were turned slightly upward at the corners as though she was having a really good dream. I hoped that she was. Tears sprang forth. "I'm so sorry," I said to her. I truly was.

"It was self-defense," Webb whispered as he took my hand.

I launched myself at him, tears flowing down my cheeks like a raging river. "She was your sister."

He wrapped strong arms around me. "She was also the enemy."

"Why did she die from a dagger to the heart, when I didn't and neither did Edmund?"

"More than likely because you're powerful," Webb said into my hair.

"And Edmund?" As soon as I asked, I knew the answer. "Never mind." I peered up at Webb. "He's powerful too. Is that even possible?" For so long, the Mason family had been the most powerful among our kind.

"Anything is possible," Webb muttered. "What did Edmund whisper to you? The only word I caught was the word need."

I planted my hands on his chest and peered up at him. "He wants me to work for him."

Webb chuckled, a sound that made me smile.

Dad gave more orders to someone on the porch.

"Let's disappear before my dad reads us our rights."

Again, Webb laughed. "As much as I would love to do that, I have to take my punishment."

I did too, which was one of the reasons I wanted to run.

WEBB

With Kate dead at my feet, I shook slightly as I held onto Jo. My heart hurt for my sister even though she had been my enemy. When I'd stormed in and saw the dagger in Jo and one in my sister, the scene had been surreal. Both were on a collision course with death. Both women tugged at my heart. They were both family, but only one was my future. I couldn't let Jo die. Kate had made her decision to throw away our brother-and-sister relationship. Still, my stomach was all in knots at seeing Kate's lifeless body.

I knew Jo had acted in self-defense. I knew she would never do anything to hurt me. I also could feel Jo's pain over what she'd done. I'd always thought I would be the one to battle my sister. At least then I would have harbored the guilt and not anyone else, especially the woman I was about to marry.

"Jo?" The commander ran up and cocooned her in his arms. "Are you okay?"

"I didn't mean to tell Edmund about Abbey," she said in tears. "I'm sorry."

"Did you get them to a safe place like we discussed?" I asked Steven.

Steven let go of his daughter. "Abbey and her mom are safe and in a place only I know where they are."

Thank God. Abbey was turning out to be more powerful at the age of four than any natural-born vampire in existence, including the Mason family. It was unheard of to have a natural-born vampire who hadn't reached puberty yet to be able to read the future or make objects move. Her abilities only confirmed what Jo had said about Edmund. He was powerful, probably more so than Steven, and that thought alone made me cringe.

"The place is secure," Steven said. "We've found four humans in the embalming room in the basement. Jo, why don't you go and see if Matthew is one of them? Webb and I have some unfinished business."

"You're not locking Webb in a cell," she said.

"Pumpkin, what I do with Webb is none of your business," he said in his commander tone.

"He's right, Jo," I said. "We have laws and rules to abide by." As much as I wanted to flee with Jo, I couldn't. I was a soldier, a good one, and I wanted my team to see that I was the leader they believed in. More importantly, if I wanted an honorable discharge, I had to follow the rules.

She didn't argue. Instead, she kissed her father on the cheek. "Please don't kill each other. Oh, and Dad, Webb has asked me to marry him. So if you kill my fiancé, then you can kiss me good-bye." She gave me a sad but sexy look. "Well, that is if he still wants me."

Warmth slid down to my stomach as she batted her beautiful violet eyes. Yeah, she changed her eye color as she spoke. In part, because of her emotions, but she also knew that I loved her violet eyes—smart woman. She knew how to get inside my heart, not to mention other body parts. Then she bounced away.

Steven hadn't even blinked at Jo's admission of our future nuptials. I couldn't say I was surprised. He hardly displayed any emotions unless it was anger.

"I'll take whatever you deem is necessary for going AWOL, leaving my team in Alaska, and for putting Jo's and Sam's lives in jeopardy. After that, I'm submitting my papers for discharge."

He tucked his hands into his fatigues, studying Kate's body. Then he squatted down and took her hand. "I loved her. But I couldn't give her what she wanted. I couldn't marry her. You know as vampires, we love someone so fucking hard that sometimes it's impossible to let go. But I had to. When I finally found Jo and Sam, I couldn't be with your sister anymore. I couldn't let my kids see that I was in a happy relationship. I was afraid that they would think I didn't love their mother." He kissed my sister's hand. "I'm truly sorry, Kate. My heart was and will always be yours." A tear dropped, splashing on Kate's wrist, before he pushed to his feet. "It killed me when I found out that she betrayed me. I wanted to throw myself off a cliff. Not only because she was with Edmund, but because she decided the enemy was better than her own family, than you."

I was at a loss for words. I'd been so worried about what Steven would think of me falling for his daughter, when he had done the same with my sister.

He wiped a lone tear away then squeezed my shoulder. "You can't leave the military. I need you, and not because of Jo. I need to take some time off. I'm not making clear decisions. My head is not in the game. I know that's the last thing the council will agree to if we don't catch Edmund. But if they don't, I will recommend you take my position. I have to spend time being a father to Jo and Sam."

Again, I was at a loss for words. He was baring his soul, something Steven Mason never did.

Sam and Olivia ran in with sweat running down their red faces.

"Edmund got away," Olivia said. "He jumped into a stopped car at a light."

Sam eyed his father wearily. "Pops, are you crying?"

Olivia darted her dark gaze to me.

I flicked my head at the door. "Tripp needs help."

Olivia grabbed Sam's arm. "Come on, big guy."

With a blank expression, Sam kept his eyes on his father.

"Go, Son," Steven said. "We'll talk later."

Once Olivia and Sam left, I dropped down on the bench, heaving a sigh, and not at the fact that Edmund had gotten away. Frankly, I wasn't surprised. If Edmund was as powerful as Steven, Jo, and Sam, then killing him would be a monumental task, which meant we would be fighting forever. In turn, that meant Jo and I would never be able to live a quiet life.

Steven sat beside me. "You've been awfully quiet. I know you loved Kate."

"Kate told me when I met with her that she still wanted me dead, and I shouldn't feel remorseful or sad, but as I look at her dead body, I do. She was my family, regardless of her actions." I shoved both hands through my hair. "Jo killed her, and I hate that she'll carry around guilt for defending herself. More importantly, I blame myself for Kate's actions and death. I wasn't there for my sister."

Silence stretched between us. We were both distraught over the choices we'd made. But there was one choice I wanted to make sure I did right.

I slid a sidelong glance at Steven. "Can I have your daughter's hand in marriage?"

He chuckled. "I wouldn't want any other man to marry her." He slapped me on the back. "You have my blessing."

I covered my face with my hands when I should've been running to Jo and kissing her as though she was heaven and earth and every-thing in between. She was, but my body was shutting down... well, until I heard her voice. Then my blood fired on all cylinders, espe-cially when she came around the corner with a smile that rendered me speechless. I knew then that nothing on this planet could stop me from marrying the one woman who could split open my heart and sew it back together at the same time.

JO

Dad, Sam, Webb, and I sat in the front pew of the base chapel, listening to a sermon about how the dead were free from their demons. I prayed that Sloan, Quade, Crowe, and Kate were somewhere having the time of their lives. I certainly wasn't. A week had passed, and I couldn't get past Kate's dead body or how I was the one to kill her. I also didn't understand why she died and I didn't. I knew one thing. I was far from free of anything. Edmund was on the loose. I was no longer the prime prospect in his plan to build his army, although he'd said he needed me. But my guess was that he needed me for an entirely different reason other than my DNA. He wanted me to work for him. I suspected he wanted me to help him get his daughter, Abbey. But I would die before I put that little girl through hell. I was thankful that Dad had found a safe place for Abbey and her mom. I was also relieved that Dad didn't and wouldn't tell anyone their whereabouts. I didn't want to be responsible for leaking to Edmund that I knew where Abbey was.

Webb slid his hand over mine. My stomach did one of those flips whenever I was around him, although I'd hardly been with Webb since I killed his sister. It wasn't that he was avoiding me or I was avoiding him. He had work to do with my father. Dad was making arrangements to take some time off, and he was leaving Webb in charge. I was surprised since Webb had mentioned he had submitted his discharge papers. Dad had argued with him, telling Webb he was positioned to receive a promotion and was slotted to fill my dad's position one day, but Webb had declined. I stayed silent on the issue. I didn't want to sway Webb's decision. He had served in the military for way more than the allotted twenty years. He'd told my dad that he was better off as a contractor for the military. That way, he could go undercover on missions like the one to catch Edmund.

"Amen," the priest said.

Sniffles echoed around. Fabric rustled together, and people sighed as they began to leave the chapel. The families of Sloan, Quade, and Crowe were set to give them a proper burial. As for Kate, Webb hadn't mentioned anything about where she would be buried, and neither had my father. I couldn't bring myself to ask, at least not right now.

Dad went over to talk to the priest. Sam and the sentinels who had been sitting in the pew behind us started for the exit.

Out of nowhere, Ben stalked up to us, all six feet of him. "I'll meet you in the training room," he said to Webb.

Webb nodded. "I'll be there in ten."

Then Ben bowed his head to me before he disappeared. I was happy that Ben had found a place to call home. He was training to become a sentinel along with my brother.

"Has Ben reached out to his father?" I asked. I hadn't talked to Ben since he'd shown up on base, and the last time I'd seen him, he was knocked out on the floor in the prison building.

"He has," Webb said. "He's told his father that he joined the military and he would be in contact with him soon."

I smiled for the first time in a week. I was happy that at least Ben was able to finally talk with his dad.

Webb pushed to his feet before he extended his hand. "Let's go somewhere quiet. We haven't seen each other in a while, and I'm dying to kiss you."

My heart soared. "It will have to be my bedroom since my dad hasn't lifted my punishment."

A devious grin broke out on his rugged face. My cheeks flushed as I grabbed his warm, massive hand.

Then Dad returned. "Jo, I need to talk to Webb."

I eyed my father's drawn features. He needed to take a long vacation.

"I'll be up in a little while," Webb said as he kissed me quickly on the lips.

I wanted to protest, but the last thing on my agenda was getting on my dad's bad side. He'd been through hell as much as the rest of us. He was mourning Kate's death more than anyone else. My heart hurt for him. I had no idea he was in love with Kate. I kissed my dad on the cheek then headed for the exit. When I walked into the chapel's entryway, Ms. Costner and her dad waltzed in.

She immediately threw her arms around me. "I'm so glad you're okay."

I eased away to find tears streaming out of her pretty blue eyes. "How's Matthew?" The last time I'd seen him was in our infirmary. He was in and out of consciousness as were the other humans who'd survived the change.

"He's good," Victor said, towering over me. "We have to wait and see how the change affects him."

I craned my neck to look up at Victor. "Let's hope he's like Ben."

Ms. Costner patted her nose with a tissue. "We just wanted to pay our respects, but I see we're too late."

Victor glanced through the doorway into the chapel. "I need to speak with your dad."

My father locked eyes with Victor then strode up with Webb beside him.

Ms. Costner opened her mouth to speak when the doors opened

once again. Gregory Hollings, one of the newly appointed elders, breezed in with four guardians in black suits. The elders always had bodyguards with them. In my world, the elders were like the human president, only we had more than one elder who ruled the vampire nation.

Hollings unbuttoned his expensive suit jacket as he set his dark-colored gaze on my dad. "It pains me, Steven, to have to do this. But the council has strong evidence to charge you with the murder of the Secretary of the Navy."

I rushed to Dad's side only to be blocked by two of the guardians who were the equivalent of the police in the human world. Webb gently grasped my shoulders and guided me to him. Ms. Costner paled, and pity washed over Victor's face. Suddenly, I remembered the conversation with Victor when we'd been in the conference room. *Let's not forget you're in the limelight. The council is still investigating you for the death of the Secretary of the Navy. You want to operate by the book.* But Dad had operated by the book, at least I thought he had.

"You're under arrest, Steven Mason," Hollings said, not too proudly. He had respect for my father and had been lenient with me at my trial. "Until we can convene a trial by a jury of your peers, you will be remanded into custody at headquarters in Boston."

"You can't do this," I blurted out. "My dad operated by the book. Victor, tell them. We did everything to save Matthew."

Victor's pitiful expression only deepened. "My words don't carry any weight in this instance."

Webb's arms encircled me. "We'll figure this out," he said in my ear.

Hollings gave me a weak smile. "I'm sorry, Jo. But the evidence is pretty strong."

One guardian cuffed my dad.

"Webb, give Mr. Rose a call," Dad said. "Have him meet me at headquarters."

Webb nodded. "Yes, sir."

Hollings then turned his attention to Webb. "Lieutenant London, your discharge papers have been denied. You are now in charge of this base until further notice."

Webb tightened his hold on me. He'd been banking on the council approving his discharge. Now, everything was changing, even the vacation Dad, Sam, and I had planned to a secluded place somewhere in Michigan.

"Gregory," Victor said. "What about Edmund Rain? I want him captured and sentenced to death for what he's done to my grandson."

Hollings raised his chin, and some type of look I couldn't quite decipher washed over his angular features. "We have our guardians searching for him. Once we catch him, he'll be prosecuted to the fullest."

I almost laughed. Not if I got to Edmund first. "My dad didn't kill the Secretary of the Navy. Edmund did."

Everyone glanced at me.

"That's not what the evidence says," Hollings said.

Dad shuffled over to me then kissed me on the forehead. "Mr. Rose is a good lawyer. We'll get through this."

I remembered Edmund telling me he was the one who'd killed the Secretary of the Navy. But that was just hearsay. I had to have hard evidence. Dad couldn't take the fall for something Edmund had done. It was time to take Edmund up on his job offer.

***

On the Edge of Infinity is now available in Ebook and paperback formats.
Turn the page to read a sample.

War is coming.

I've dreamed of it. I feel it deep down in my bones. It's pulsing with a sinister strength deadlier than anything I've faced before.

My father is in prison for murder. My enemy has teamed up with the CIA to build super soldiers with vampire DNA. And ghosts from Webb's past have a target on my head.

It's time to take a stand. To rise up against my adversaries who want me dead or enslaved.

I want a family, an ordinary life, and that fable happy ending with my one true love, Webb.

Now, I can only pray we both make it out alive.

Chapter 1
Webb

I paced the carpeted floor of Hollings's chamber. Jo and I had traveled to Boston to visit with her father. I didn't know what I was supposed to do with the state of our affairs. I couldn't get out of the military. My discharge papers had been denied. Steven Mason was in jail for murdering the Secretary of the Navy, and I was now in charge of a bag of shit. Yet, all I could think about was marrying Jo. I'd asked her to marry me, and she had said yes. But we couldn't tie the knot until we were free and clear of the hornets' nest we were in.

Jo was convinced that Edmund had killed the Secretary of the Navy and pinned the blame on Steven. It wasn't that I didn't believe her, because what she said was probably one hundred percent true. The pile of crap we were stuck in was figuring out how to prove Steven's innocence when the evidence the elders had against him seemed to prove his guilt without a question. They had the murder weapon—the dagger that slit the secretary's throat—with Steven's DNA on the blade. Why the dagger suddenly showed up months after the murder was also a burning question.

I shoved a hand through my hair, the back of which fell out of the leather strap.

Jo glided in, all five feet six inches of her. Her black hair was unbound and flowing like a smooth wave on a subtle breeze.

After two weeks of not being able to visit or talk with her father and working hard to help Dr. Vieira in the lab, Jo appeared tired and dazed. She hadn't been sleeping. I knew firsthand since I'd insisted on staying with her in the apartment that Steven called home on base. She hadn't protested, but I didn't think she would. I was the one having a hard time controlling my libido. I was the one who wanted to wait until we were married to make love. I wasn't sure I would be able to keep the promise that I'd made more for me than for her. Actually, I'd made the promise mostly to show her father that I was a gentleman. Still, with her long, silky legs and lavender scent, I could barely keep my hands off her, let alone sleep. But I would torture myself if it meant that she was happy and safe.

"How did they find the murder weapon? And where?" she asked for the millionth time.

I grabbed her by the shoulders. "The where doesn't matter. Your father's DNA is all over that dagger along with the secretary's."

Her nostrils flared. "The where *does* matter. It could lead us to the real murderer. I would bet the trail leads to Edmund. If you recall, around the time of the secretary's murder, Edmund and your sister, Kate, stole my dad's blood."

I flinched when she said Kate's name. Part of me had come to terms with her death. I flinched more when Jo looked away as she said my sister's name. She'd killed Kate in self-defense. I got that. I didn't blame Jo at all, but if the tables had been turned, I probably would have felt the same remorse if I'd killed her brother, Sam.

Jo waved a hand in front of my face. "Webb?" Then her nails grazed my unshaven jaw. "I'm sorry to bring up Kate. I'm also sorry that I was the one to end her life."

I met her silver gaze. Immediately, I relaxed. Jo had a way of calming me with her soft look and equally soft touch. She was my family now, and the earth could crumble, but we would get our happily ever after.

I sighed as I dragged my fingers down her cheek. "Please stop apologizing. Kate made her choice. You were protecting yourself."

She wrapped her arms around me. "I can't help but think that one day you'll hate me for what I've done."

I grasped her arms gently then eased back as I peered down at her. "Never, angel. I love you. You're my life now. Forever."

Her eyes bled from silver to violet, water pooling in them.

"We'll get through this," I whispered since I was getting choked up too.

She angled her head as the color of her eyes turned a dark violet. "My dad is innocent."

"I know he is. I recall that day vividly." I started pacing again in front of the large cherry credenza while Jo watched me. "Your dad met with the Secretary of the Navy that morning after we dropped you and Sam off at school. If you recall, that's the same day you killed Blake Turner. So your dad had to rush out of his meeting when I called him. When he left a room full of government officials, the secretary included, no one was dead. But the evidence is damning. Maybe we'll have luck with the coroner's report. That should show the time of death, which could prove your father's innocence."

She pursed her lips. "Not if Edmund bribed the coroner or threatened him. Or if he's bribing one of the elders. Maybe one of the elders is in on Edmund's plan to take out my father. Remember, Edmund wants to run the military. Again, he told me so two weeks ago when I was having a decent conversation with him." She ran her tongue across the tip of one of her fangs.

"Jo, please. You have to calm down." I had to calm down. I was as worked up as she was, not only because of her father's circumstances but because Edmund knew about his daughter, Abbey, and Steven had yet to divulge the whereabouts of Abbey and her mom, Rachel.

I couldn't protect them if I didn't know where they were. Edmund wanted his daughter, and if I knew him—and I did—he wouldn't stop until he got Abbey. I couldn't blame him. After all, she was his daughter. The problem was that Rachel didn't want Abbey anywhere near Edmund. Steven and I didn't, either. Edmund would use his daughter as a lab rat, especially when he found out the little girl had supernatural powers at the age of four, which was unheard of in our world.

Jo darted over to Hollings's desk that sat in front of the window. "What I need is to get to Edmund. I need to find him and—"

"And what? He's not going to confess. He's not coming in to get locked up or put to his death if Victor has any say in this." Victor Costner was a ticking time bomb who wanted Edmund's head on a platter for injecting a new form of vampire serum into Victor's grandson, Matthew. "And let's not forget that Edmund wants Abbey."

She sifted through files on the desk. "I would stake my life on the fact that Edmund mailed the murder weapon to Hollings with a letter."

I hurried over to her as she threw one folder aside and dove into another. I caught her wrist. "Stop. Are you insane? If Hollings walks in, he'll throw you in a cell."

She shrugged out of my hold. "So?" She started opening drawers.

I grasped her arm and pulled her to me. She pushed me, but I was stronger.

She let out a soft growl. "I can't sit around and do nothing. I'm tired of Edmund screwing up our lives. I want him dead."

I glanced around, hoping the walls weren't thin. "Keep your voice down. If Edmund did show up dead somewhere, you would be the first one they'd implicate. Besides, if Edmund is responsible for the secretary's murder, then we need him alive."

She huffed as she relaxed in my arms.

I rested my chin on her head. "You know what you need?"

"You," she blurted out as she peered up at me. "I want you. I don't want to wait for our wedding night to consummate our love for each other. I'm dying here, Webb. I sleep with you every night, and the more we're together, the more I can't contain myself. I know you want me. I feel you every damn waking minute. I'm literally going to explode."

I grinned like an ass. She was so incredibly beautiful with her flushed cheeks and her eyes flashing from silver to violet.

She pouted. "Are you mocking me?"

I ushered her over to the window. The city skyline of Boston twinkled against the backdrop of the setting sun. The days were getting shorter as we entered November.

"I would never mock you. You're my angel. You do things to me that I've never experienced in my life. I want you so badly that it's hard with you rubbing against me night after night. But I want all the time in the world to show you how much I love you. And tonight, we'll start with a romantic night in Boston. No phones, no fights, and no biting on nails." I winked. "Just necks." I'd been wanting to do something I hadn't had the chance to do since I proposed, and tonight I was going to do it.

"Time is precious, Webb." Her voice was breathy. "Who knows if we'll be here tomorrow or an hour from now? If we wait for Edmund to come clean or die, we could be waiting a lifetime to get married."

I twisted her to face me, and I wasted no time capturing her lips in mine. "You're right. But I want to be the perfect gentleman."

She arched into me. "Screw being a gentleman." She wiggled her sweet hips into my groin. "See, you want me. It doesn't take much for you to react to my body. Please, just one night, then we can wait until we're married."

I chuckled as my fangs grazed her jaw down to her neck, where her pulse beat rapidly. The best thing about our relationship was the explosion of feelings that erupted when I bit her. Jo's blood did things to me, and the more blood I took, the stronger those things got. At first, I would get dizzy, high, and I would feel anything she felt. Anything she thought about, I got a glimpse of. But the more we drank from each other, the more we were connected, and the more my body craved her. She was right. Time was precious, and I didn't want to waste another minute without showing her how beautiful she was.

I was about to sink my fangs into her when I heard footsteps outside the door. An elder's chambers wasn't the place to show Jo how I felt, and I certainly needed to be the commander in charge in front of Hollings, not some horny vampire only after my boss's daughter.

In vampire speed, I had us both settled into the chairs in front of the desk.

Jo giggled as her rosy cheeks darkened. "It's not a crime to kiss me."

"It might be if I got out of control," I teased as the door opened.

Hollings strutted in, smoothing a hand over his thick dark hair. His wide black eyes were trained on me. "Doing something you're not supposed to?" He circled his desk as his gaze lingered too long on me.

Jo slowly slid her foot over to mine and kicked me. It took me a minute to realize the folders on Hollings's desk were scattered and not in a neat pile like they had been before Jo tackled the contents.

"Just spending time with my girl," I said. "Can we see Commander Mason now?"

He collected the out-of-place folders. "He's meeting with his attorney. They should be done momentarily. Before you head down, I wanted to talk to both of you." He folded his bulk into his chair. "Let's start with you, Jo. Tell me about Edmund. I understand you've had quality time with him. Has he opened up to you about anything?"

Jo sat back in the wooden armchair as she chewed on her bottom lip. "What exactly do you want to know?"

I opened up a telepathic connection to her. *Until we know who the mole is, don't tell him much.*

Hollings leaned forward with his elbows on his desk. "Other than building an army of vampires out of humans who don't carry the vampire gene, what else is he after?"

"Power. He wants my dad's job. Hence, why he's framing my dad."

"I don't disagree. Someone definitely wants your father out of the picture. But Edmund knows he could never command a SEAL team or step foot on a military base again."

She pinched her eyebrows together. "Why would he want something he can't have?"

"Maybe he thinks he can have it," Hollings said. "Maybe his plan is to kill you, your family, the elders, the SEAL team—"

"Or maybe Edmund has someone working on the inside," I said. "So he knows he'll get what he wants."

"You mean someone on the council of elders?" Hollings asked.

I rubbed the stubble on my chin. "Someone who can make the decision or at least be Edmund's cheerleader. Edmund can't commandeer an entire vampire community without help. And he can't rule the military without someone on the inside. Which is probably why he killed the Secretary of the Navy. He knew the secretary would never appoint him to any position."

The puzzle pieces were coming together. Edmund had to have someone on the council in his court or on the team of humans within the government. He needed someone who knew about vampires and who could make those high-level decisions. But as I studied Hollings, I didn't get the sense he was that person, at least not with the curious expression on his face. If I had hit a nerve, then I would've gotten a different reaction.

Hollings tapped his forefinger on his lips. "Interesting observation, Lieutenant."

"Is Webb right?" Jo blurted out.

Hollings shook his head. "I don't know."

"The mole could be you," Jo said.

Hollings narrowed his eyes. "Jo, be careful."

Jo slid her butt to the edge of her seat. "With all due respect, I trust no one. Plus, it's odd that you were appointed to the elder position not that long ago, and now the murder weapon shows up."

"Jo," I warned. Elders had free rein to punish someone as they saw fit.

She jumped up. "No, Webb. I'm tired of always looking over my shoulder, of worrying if Edmund is going to kidnap me, or what surprise he's going to dish out next. We know he's working with someone within the vampire government. Or maybe he's working with more than one person. But we have to attack this like everyone is a suspect."

I chuckled when I should have been agreeing with her. But she was acting as though she was a seasoned detective, and I was dumbfounded at her strategic thinking.

Hollings grinned too.

She stomped her foot, her eyes flashing vampire. "Stop mocking me. Both of you."

"Jo," Hollings said. "You raise all good points. And while you might not believe me, I'm not the mole. I do, however, agree that a mole within our organization, whether in my circle or the SEAL's circle, does exist. But we have to work together to bring Edmund down once and for all."

Her eyes went wide. "Really?" She sat back down.

Hollings interlocked his fingers. "Yes. Edmund has wreaked havoc since his departure from the military. The elders are tired and quite frustrated with covering up his dirty work. Those within the human government who don't know about vampires are starting to question things. Their superiors are not going to be able to keep the lid on our world much longer. We thought with Bruno dead, we could breathe a little. But with dead human bodies showing up in alleys and dumpsters in the last two weeks, it's just a matter of time before humans find out about our existence. With the lab explosion on the Indian reservation, the same place Edmund was holding you, the media and government are wondering why the dead bodies found at the scene have canines that rival wolves. We can't let the public know about us. We have to put a stop to all this, which is why you're here. I need your help, Jo."

My gut told me I wasn't about to like his next statement.

Hollings sat back. "The elders have agreed that we need someone on the inside of Edmund's operation. Someone who can gain Edmund's trust. I feel that person is you, Jo."

Jo choked then laughed. "Me?"

"No way," I blurted out. "She almost got killed the last time she was with Edmund. And what if one of the other elders is the mole? They'll tell Edmund immediately. Sir, let me do my job. You want Edmund's operation shut down? Then let me handle this. My team and I will do everything we can to bring him in."

Hollings rose. "Steven believes the only match to take out Edmund is Jo."

"What?" Jo and I asked at the same time.

Hollings tucked a hand into his pants pocket. "Go down and chat with your father. I need to rethink my strategy. Then we can talk again when I get back from my business trip in a couple of days."

His strategy wasn't worth shit. My team and I had come up with the strategy to take out an enemy, not an elder.

"What about my dad?" Jo bounced her knee. "He's innocent."

"Until we can put all the pieces of the puzzle together on the secretary's murder, we can't let your father out of jail," Hollings said. "Besides, right now, the top echelons within the human government are content, knowing we have a suspect."

I stood and held out my hand to Jo, cursing under my breath that Hollings thought he could run the show. Maybe he could with Steven in command, but not with me. Maybe the blessing in disguise was that Steven was out of the picture for now. That way, I could get shit done.

On the Edge of Infinity is available in Ebook and paperback formats.

GLOSSARY OF TERMS

Natural-born vampire: A human born with the vampire gene that, when activated, will turn them into a vampire.

Activation process: Those who carry the vampire gene can only turn by drinking the blood of their vampire father at the age of sixteen years or older.

Council of Elders – A group of five vampires who set the laws.

Genetic engineering: Turning humans into vampires through a process of restructuring their DNA.

Cobalt – A vampire's kryptonite. The metal will kill a vampire if staked through the heart. It will also burn a vampire's skin if they come in contact with it.

Reproduction: A natural-born vampire is born by a male vampire and a human female with a rare blood type of Vel negative.

Council of Eternal Affairs: The legal department of the vampire government.

Vampire characteristics: Sunlight doesn't burn them. Their hearts beat at <5 bpm. Skin temperature is ten degrees cooler than a human. Eye color changes to black except for a few chosen ones.

Steven Mason: Vampire and father to twins Jo and Sam Mason. He's dubbed the most powerful of all vampires because of his many powers, including his mind-reading abilities. He can only read minds when touching someone except when it comes to his children. His normal eye color is green. His vampire eye color is silver.

Jo Mason: Turned at sixteen. Powers include seeing the future through her dreams, mind-reading without touching a person, telekinesis, and she's an elemental with the ability to manipulate water, air, earth, and fire. Her normal eye color is silver. Her vampire eye color is violet.

Sam Mason: Turned at sixteen. Powers include feeling what others feel (Empath), telekinesis, and he can compel a person using a series of numbers woven into a magical spell. He's also an elemental with the ability to manipulate water, air, earth, and fire. His normal eye color is green. His vampire eye color is silver.

Jupiter Sentinels: A secret and elite Navy SEAL Team within the military. Their role is to help the human military and guard the supernatural world.

Plutariums: A rogue team of vampires who want power and to engineer an army that would change humans into vampires.

Guardians: Vampires who are equivalent to the human police.

ABOUT THE AUTHOR

Bestselling author **S.B. Alexander** is an independent author with over 20 titles to date. She writes paranormal, new adult, and sweet romances that feature hot heroes stealing hearts.

S.B. or Susan as she likes to be called is a navy veteran, former high school teacher, and former corporate sales executive. She's a lover of sports, especially baseball, although nowadays you can find her glued to the TV during football season.

When she's not writing, she's a full-time caregiver to her soul mate of twenty-two years who got a bad deal in life when he was diagnosed with ALS. Her motto: "Life is too short to waste. So live every moment like it's your last."

You can connect with S.B. Alexander in the following ways:
Reader Group: https://sbalexander.com/beastsandbitches
TikTok: https://www.tiktok.com/@susanbalexander
Author Website: https://sbalexander.com
Newsletter: https://sbalexander.com/newsletter
Email: susan@sbalexander.com

NEVER MISS A NEW RELEASE:
Sign up for her Author App
iTunes: https://bit.ly/sbalexanderitunes

Android: https://bit.ly/sbalexanderandroid

facebook.com/sbalexander.authorpage
twitter.com/sbalex_author
instagram.com/sbalexanderauthor
bookbub.com/authors/s-b-alexander
goodreads.com/sbalexander
amazon.com/author/sbalexander

ALSO BY S.B. ALEXANDER

MAXWELL SERIES

Upper Young Adult/New Adult Contemporary Romance

Dare to Kiss

Dare to Dream

Dare to Love

Dare to Dance

Dare to Live

Dare to Breathe

Dare to Embrace

THE MAXWELL FAMILY SAGA SERIES

Young Adult Sweet Romance

My Heart to Touch

My Heart to Hold

My Heart to Give

My Heart to Keep

THE VAMPIRE NAVY SEAL SERIES

Paranormal Romance

On the Edge of Humanity

On the Edge of Eternity

On the Edge of Destiny

On the Edge of Misery

On the Edge of Infinity

STAND-ALONES

New Adult Contemporary Romance

Crazy For You

Unforgettable

Holding Onto Forever

Breaking Rules

Rescuing Riley

THE HART SERIES

New Adult Contemporary Romance

Hart of Darkness

Hart of Vengeance

Visit https://sbalexander.com/all-books/ to learn more about S.B. Alexander books and future releases. Please note release dates are subject to change based on reader demand and the author's schedule. Subscribing to the author's newsletter or following her on Facebook is the best way to stay updated with planned new releases.